HAUNTED OHIO

Ghostly Tales From the Buckeye State

CHRIS WOODYARD

Kestrel
Publications

1811 Stonewood Drive
Beavercreek, OH 45432

ALSO BY CHRIS WOODYARD

The Wright Stuff: A Guide to Life in the Dayton Area
Haunted Ohio II: More Ghostly Tales from the Buckeye State
Haunted Ohio III: Still More Ghostly Tales from the Buckeye State
Haunted Ohio IV: Restless Spirits
Spooky Ohio: 13 Traditional Tales

Seventh Printing 1997
Printed in the United States of America
Typesetting by Copy Plus, Dayton, OH
Cover Art by Larry Hensel, Hensel Graphics, Xenia, OH
Author photo by Rosi Mackey, Xenia, OH
Library of Congress Catalog Card Number: 91-75343

Woodyard, Chris
Haunted Ohio: Ghostly Tales from the Buckeye State / Chris
Woodyard.
SUMMARY: A collection of Ohio ghost stories and ghostlore from
Native American tales to contemporary haunted houses.

ISBN 0-962847208
1. Ghost Stories — United States — Ohio
2. Ghosts — United States — Ohio
3. Haunted Houses — United States — Ohio
I. Woodyard, Chris II. Title
PS648.G48 H3 1991   070.593 Wo
Z1033.L73

For My Little Green Ghost,
with love and apologies for giving her the "cweeps."

ACKNOWLEDGMENTS

Many people have contributed their stories to *Haunted Ohio*. In particular I want to thank the following: John B. Briley, Manager, Campus Martius/Ohio River Museum Complex, Marietta; Billie Broaddus, Director, Cincinnati Medical Heritage Center; Julie Carrier, Kelton House, Columbus; Kathy Cook; Patty Donahey, The Thurber House, Columbus; Galen Finley, McConnelsville Opera House; Jan Fields, Public Information Specialist, Ohio Dept. of Natural Resources; Professor Geoffrey D. Fishburn, Miami University, Oxford; Scott Fletcher, Park Naturalist, Malabar Farm State Park, Lucas County; Susan Gawron; Matt Goeller; Chris G. Grupenhof, Lake Alma State Park, Wellston; Steve Hale, Greene County Prosecutor's Office, Xenia; Marsha Hamilton; Bob Hankey; David Hastings, Victoria Theatre, Dayton; Jim Hertenstein; Rebecca Hill, Co-Head Librarian, Rutherford B. Hayes Presidential Center, Fremont; Joann G. King, Curator, Medina County Historical Society, Medina; Karyol Kirkpatrick; Mary Klei, Librarian, Warren County Historical Society; Alfred Kleine-Kreutzmann, Curator of Rare Books & Special Collections, Public Library of Cincinnati; Barbara A.H. LaPierre; Kerrie A. Moore, University Archivist, The University of Dayton; Robert J. Moore, Jr., Chief of Interpretation, William Howard Taft National Historic Site, Cincinnati; Anne Oscard, Montgomery County Historical Society, Dayton; Lloyd Ostendorf, Lincoln Picture Studio, Dayton; Jami Peelle, Special Collections Librarian, Kenyon College; Ted Peters; Kathy J. Petras, Library Associate, Medina County District Library, Medina; Betty Plank, The Ashland County Historical Society; Jim Regan, Associate Curator, James A. Garfield National Historical Site, Mentor; Larry Russell, Curator, Edison Birthplace Museum, Milan; Miriam Sayre and all the other guides at Brownella Cottage, Galion; Mary Sherman; Phillip R. Shriver, President Emeritus, Miami University, Oxford; Richard Strong, Psychic Science International Inc.; Kirby Turner, Director, Montgomery County Historical Society, Dayton; Robert Van Der Velde, Mentor-on-the-Lake; Sister Rita Walker, O.P.; Phil Walker; Ruth Webb; Mollie Williams, Manager, Patterson Homestead, Dayton; and Karen Young.

Special thanks to Jo Ellen Fannin, Susan Griffin, and Mary Ann Reese, Reference Librarians, Beavercreek Public Library, who first suggested this book. Their endless assistance, ungrudging supply of ILL books, and good humor whenever I tried to do their job were invaluable. Thanks also to Rosi Mackey, Laura Rea, Linda Marcas, Marsha Hamilton, and Susan Durtschi—proofreaders and critics deluxe. Stars in their crowns go to Tanya Albert, Diane Davis, and Anne Oscard for listening.

Lastly, I ought to thank the good spirits who brought me and my husband together in a haunted house in Columbus's Victorian Village. This book couldn't have materialized without him.

TABLE OF CONTENTS

Introduction

Prelude: All Flesh Is Grass

INTRODUCTION

I don't believe in ghosts, but I've been
afraid of them all my life.
-Charles A. Dana-

When I was a child, I was terrified of ghosts. It seemed to me that I spent my whole childhood cringing from invisible horrors. But now that I'm older, presumably wiser, and have had a chance to study the habits of ghosts, to learn more about why they do the things they do—I'm still terrified of them.

I suppose that's why I've collected these ghost stories from around Ohio—to exorcise the ghosts who have haunted me for so long: the little girl in the dress of a bygone age who crouched, weeping, on the hearth of my great-grandmother's house; the dead man who walked the hall of my apartment; the Things that lurked in attic and basement: invisibly, but terribly, hauntingly present.

The sensing of spirits seems to run in the family. My grandfather and his father before him saw spirits. My grandfather used to tell us about the friendly ghost near his grandmother's Galion home. As he walked by the second lamp post on Kroft Ave., he said, there would be the ghost, just standing there, plain as day. And the ghost would talk to him, nice and friendly like, for it was always as pleasant as could be. Grandpa would stop and pass the time of day and then he'd say he'd have to be getting on, and the ghost would smile and nod goodbye and lean up against the second light post on Kroft Ave.

What is a ghost? There are many answers and no answers to that question. We usually think of a ghost as a lovely, if transparent woman in filmy white robes. Ohio has its share of ghostly women in white. But its ghostly wonders go far beyond that: There are ghostly scents, music, animals, and machines, even apparitions of cities, which have been identified as the Heavenly Jerusalem, or perhaps Sandusky.

Some say that ghosts are the spirits of the dead. If this is so, many of them do not seem to realize that they are dead. They look like they did in life, solid and corporeal. Some even wear their favorite clothes although fabric is not commonly believed to have a soul. Ghosts ascend staircases that are no longer there. They walk through walls where once there was a door. Some are playful, some are threatening, some just seem to want to be noticed. Others come to warn, admonish, or frighten wrongdoers into repentance. Many perform what seem to us, the living, to be pointless rituals. What is the meaning of an apparition that walks down a staircase every night at 10 P.M. only to vanish?

Some spirits seem doomed to repeat an action, perhaps the last action of their life, like the motorcyclist who is seen riding repeatedly to his death. Is this evidence of survival after death? Or is it a sort of spectral video tape, played over and over *ad infinitum*?

I have talked to dozens of people who have experienced ghosts. None of them struck me as a crank or a person with an ax to grind. None of them gained financially by telling me their story. They seemed to be ordinary people in ordinary jobs, with one thing in common: a puzzling experience they couldn't explain away by ordinary means. Many seemed anxious to tell me their stories, relieved to have found someone who would understand. Some were afraid that I would think they were crazy. They themselves were not sure if they were. Astericked names indicate that a name has been changed to protect these people from unwanted publicity.

Of course, when I state that "the ghost walks at midnight," I mean that the ghost is *alleged* to walk at that time. I have personally witnessed or experienced very few of these manifestations; the line between folklore and actuality may be very finely drawn.

And not all ghosts are quite what they seem. I was told a remarkable story by an employee of an advertising agency that occupies the first school building in Kettering. The building is rumored to be haunted by a former schoolteacher who has been seen to float through the premises. Lately, it seemed, the schoolteacher had been manifesting herself in a most schoolteacherly way: by printing a happy face on the office's computers, which had no graphic software.

I told a friend about the happy faces, sure I had a ghost cornered.

"Oh, *that*," she said crushingly, "that's a virus."

But it was such a good story.... And, as told in good faith, apparently irrefutable evidence of spirit mischief. Ghost-hunting is like that: just when you think you've got one captured, it melts away. No, not all ghosts are real. But can they be brought to some hideous life of their own?

Alan Miller told the *Columbus Dispatch* about a ghost he "created." "Eddie" was a clothing store dummy that Miller propped in the window of his rather spooky 113-year-old home in Newark. He did it for a joke, but people began whispering that the house was haunted, going so far as to invent a story to account for the ghost:

"They said an old lady and her brother lived there and the old lady killed the brother, and from certain angles on certain nights you can see his ghost in the upstairs window."

Merely a new urban legend? Miller found out that an old lady *had* lived in the house. "And she had a brother, sort of a character, who died there. Now, each time our 2-year old daughter goes into the room where the brother stayed, she says hello to an empty chair."

If you've ever felt alone—yet not alone. If you've ever felt a breath, a stirring, a chill in an empty house. Then you know what it is to be haunted. And this collection is for you.

Come with me now to Haunted Ohio. There you'll meet the angry spirit of an Indian who wanted his skull back; visit a haunted costume museum, where, for the owner of a certain party dress, the party still goes on. You'll read of famous men and women from Ohio—including United States presidents—who had encounters with the unseen world. You'll see a ghostly motorcyclist repeat his fatal ride in the Great Black Swamp. You'll applaud as an actress who disappeared from her dressing room now takes endless curtain calls.

None of these ghosts turn out to be swamp gas or rats in the wainscoting or a goat observed by a comically terrified drunkard (with many a pun on the word "spirits"). None of these ghost stories end, "And then I woke up." For some there can be no awakening.

Are these stories true?
Perhaps. In spirit.

If you fear what you can't see, can't explain. If you are haunted by that which—logically—should not exist, visit that altered state of consciousness—Haunted Ohio.

ALL FLESH IS GRASS

*Man that is born of a woman hath but a short time
to live...he cometh up, and is cut down like a flower.*
-Job 14: 2-

One summer's afternoon a young Cincinnati housewife
was washing up the lunch dishes, looking out the window over
the sink at the beautiful day. Suddenly a figure dashed madly
across the lawn. She grew cold as she recognized the unbeliev-
able: It was the Grim Reaper, the sleeves of his dark robe
flapping like the wings of some hideous moth. She saw the
creature's skeletal feet—sandal straps surrounding the bones—
and in a daze, she wondered if the joints would shake themselves loose, scattering the bones like jacks.

The Reaper was gone in a flash, before it could turn the
hood back from its grinning face. The woman sank to her
knees, sick and shaken. She somehow knew that something
terrible had happened to her husband.

She expected her husband back at 3 P.M., but he did not
come. As she paced the floor, at 7 P.M. the phone rang. It was
the hospital calling to say that her husband had been in an
accident and was unconscious. At the very time she saw the
Grim Reaper, her husband's car was struck by a speeding truck
which crushed him against the windshield. He was badly hurt,
but he lived.

Now when the woman does the dishes, she looks out over
the lawn and is chilled as she ponders the dark vision. The
Reaper was in a hurry, she thinks. *When will he return to finish
the job?*

THE HAUNTED GARDEN-PARTY DRESS
Clothes to die for

Wearing...like a white dress, her death.
-Stephen Spender-

The Haunted Garden-Party Dress

It was August, with the stiflingly humid weather that made Alexis* want to crawl to a pool of water and stay in it until first frost. She was on her way to the Historical Society's costume collection to begin another day of photographing and cleaning antique garments. In the front hall she passed the Egyptian mummy, which had always given her the creeps as a child. She rode up to the attic workrooms in the tiny elevator. Its walls seemed to close in on her like the walls of a coffin.

Alexis tried to shake free of such morbid thoughts, but all her life she had been unusually sensitive to atmosphere and what she called "vibrations" from objects and people. She walked down the hall past what had been the servants' quarters in the former mansion and unlocked the door of the workroom.

In spite of the heat outside, the air conditioners were doing their job and Alexis began to relax as she put away her purse and got out the materials she needed: fine needles and cotton thread to stitch catalogue numbers on garments, acid-free tissue paper to stuff into sleeves and bodices, the Polaroid camera and extra film.

Alexis had a passion for antique clothes. She loved the beautiful materials, the tiny stitches and exquisite workmanship, the laces, beads, and sequins. In exchange for volunteering to remove rusted pins and staples from the old labeling system and to stuff tissue into sleeves, she'd gotten permission to photograph and study items in the collection.

She sighed as she handled an 1880s champagne velvet evening cloak, slit in the back to accommodate a bustle. Cascading over the shoulders and bodice was a encrustation of corded ivory embroidery and around the neck and sleeves, a froth of swansdown to keep the wearer from the cold. It transported Alexis to a faraway world, a world of late suppers at Maxim's, of the *Merry Widow Waltz*, of top-hatted admirers calling out, "Cheri, where *have* you been?"

Her favorite dress was a luminous scarlet velvet sprinkled with garnets. The fabric glowed from within, while the garnets winked at the slightest motion. There were two bodices, one cut low, with heavy lace sleeves, for evening wear, the other molded to the body, with those same glittering garnets, like drops of blood on the bosom.

Alexis loved antique textiles, but she also had a problem with "vibing out" whenever she was around a lot of old clothes in one place. There were over 7,000 items in this collection, Alexis realized. She also realized that it was the costume curator's day off. She would be alone in the attic. She started with a rack of clothes from the 1880s up to the First World War, not by any means the oldest items in the collection. The garments were grouped by type. There was a collection of slipper satin evening skirts with trains—a whole row of pale ivory, sky blue, a vivid gold. There were racks of fine chiffons, looking as though they had been spun by spiders and a section of velvet evening gowns—soft and black as a raven's wing.

Alexis pulled out a dull green velvet dress that looked like it could have been worn by one of Oscar Wilde's "aesthetic dress" disciples. She hung it on the wall and took a Polaroid shot. As she put the dress back on the rack, her hand brushed the velvet and she shivered.

Alexis hung another dress on the end of the rack and stepped back to frame the picture. The dress was a garden-party muslin, white with great garlands of heavy, heavenly blue embroidery looping around the bottom of the wide skirt. She squinted through the viewfinder of the camera. The bosom of the dress stirred. Slowly she lowered the camera. Inside the dress, tissue paper crackled as it uncrumpled itself. She smiled and raised the camera once more. Her hands began to shake. If I press the button, she thought, driven by an overpowering certainty, I will see the woman in the dress.

She began to panic in slow motion. She realized that it wasn't a matter of: "wouldn't it be funny *if* the woman showed up on the photo?" but an emphatic, "I *will* see the woman when the photo comes out."

At that moment, as though a radio had been switched on, came a chaos of voices. Women: shrieking, imploring, summoning, commanding—all demanding to be heard, desperate to make her understand. Some imperious, some furious, some insane with frustration. All struggling like birds against a glass to get through, to make her hear.

Look at me Listen to me Hear what I'm saying **Listen**

The noise swept over her like a wave. She couldn't breathe; her heart was bursting. I will die, she thought, calmly as a drowning person, and then I will scream too.

The frothiest pieces seemed the noisiest, Alexis thought incongruously. The lawn dress, c. 1918...a lot of the young women in lawn dresses didn't make it through the influenza epidemic.

Later, in a haze, Alexis remembered hanging all the dresses back on their racks. Remembered putting away the tags and supplies and locking the door. Remembered forcing herself to take a photo of the dress, even though a woman from another time would appear on the film.

But when she returned the next day the door stood open. Cautiously she entered, careful not to brush against the racks of clothes. The dresses were where she had left them: the red velvet dress lying on the table, the white dress with blue embroidery at the end of the rack. She held her breath, listened. Nothing but her own heartbeat in her ears. Quickly she hung the dresses in their places, put away the supplies, picked up bits of lint. Slowly she sorted the photos on the work table. There was none of a white dress.

Alexis picked up her portfolio, placed the photos in it, her muscles tensed as if for flight. In the doorway, she looked back at the racks and racks of gleaming silks and velvets. A jet dangle on a beaded cape winked at her.

She shut the door and locked it, feeling as if time were running out. She quietly pushed on the knob to make sure the door was latched and turned away. Something, a breath of air from under the door, made her turn back. Made her stand listening, pressed against the door, to the taffetas whispering among themselves.

The Ghost of Unicorn Vintage Clothing

I used to live above a haunted store in Columbus. After college I opened a vintage clothing store in an old apartment house on a corner of High Street across from Ohio State University. "Unicorn Vintage Clothing," read the black and white sign painted with a leaping unicorn in a circle of stars. Unicorns were big the year we opened; so was vintage clothing. We soon expanded into the apartment next door, unboarding the doors between the two sections and building dressing rooms and display racks. Conveniently, the new section had an upstairs apartment which I claimed for my home.   At night the store was an eerie place, with its mannequins that never failed to startle me, with its racks of clothes where madmen—or ghosts—could lurk. Although the shop was quaint and pleasant during the day, after dark I always hurried upstairs as quickly as I could and locked the door behind me. The west side of the store, where I lived, was sunny and comfortable. But when I stepped into the east side, there was a chill about the air—a touch of the damp, like a room that rarely sees the sun.

My apartment had a few idiosyncrasies. Many nights I would wake to footsteps creaking slowly up and down the hall or plodding up the stairs. The first time it happened, I called the police. When they arrived, the doors and windows were all locked, just I had left them. The officers exchanged glances as I explained. The next time I lay in bed, clutching the covers, telling myself it was only my neighbors three apartments away. I also found things missing—crazy things, like a pair of wool tights, books, a kitchen knife. And I had the only key.

Customers used to joke about bringing in the dead owners with the clothing. I smiled, but I had seen what looked like an attempt by a dead owner to reclaim her earthly garment. A customer had tried on an Edwardian blouse. When she came out of the dressing room to show it to us, her face became a blank, her eyes unfocused.

"I've been here before," she said, "We're at a lake, on a picnic." and went on to describe a old-fashioned outing. She went back into the dressing room and came out wondering vaguely about her odd experience. She bought the blouse but I wasn't sure if I should sell it to her; my liability insurance didn't cover repossession.

Ellen*, the Unicorn's manager, was a tall redhead with a soulful, high-cheekboned face beneath a cloud of Pre-Raphaelite hair. With her model's figure, she could wear clothing from all periods. Often she looked like she had just stepped out of an antique photo.

Ellen herself was haunted. She had parents who saw ghosts; she had a brother with a crystal ball and a house that positively seethed with spirits. And, recently, poltergeist activity had begun to break out at her own house where she had two rebellious adolescent daughters. She took supernatural phenomena for granted. So when she told me that she had been pushed down the stairs by "the old man," I gulped but I listened.

"You just tripped on your skirt or something. Yeah, that's it." I suggested nervously.

"I felt a definite shove on my back," she insisted. "Almost like, 'hey there, notice me!'"

And it didn't really seem to bother her.

It bothered me, though, having to look nervously over my shoulder as I clung to the handrail. It bothered me that things disappeared from my locked apartment. It bothered me, as I realized that no trick of acoustics could transmit footsteps from

three apartments away. I began to get a mental picture of the
old man: a stooped, grey-haired, rather untidy person in a
cardigan, his shirt sleeves rolled up, shuffling about in his
slippers. On the stairs, Ellen repeatedly felt a hand nudge her
back. She began to talk to the old man, teasing the spirit about
his "ratty greenish-brown cardigan."

One day I mentioned something—very tentatively—about
the upstairs to our maintenance man. He looked thoughtful.

"Hmm," he said. "I'm interested in this kind of thing. Let
me do a little research."

A few days later he came by again. "I asked Karl* [our
landlord] and I'll tell you what he told me. You know, this
used to be an optometrist's office. Well, the old doctor, he
lived upstairs, in the side opposite your apartment. And," he
paused triumphantly "he died in that back room!"

It explained a lot. In fact it was a classic ghostly phenomena—the dead person who doesn't know he's dead. As Ellen
said, he just wanted some attention. I should have felt sorry for
the pathetic old man, with nothing better to do than wander
around my halls and push people down the stairs, but he still
frightened me.

Or was there another, more malevolent ghost at the
Unicorn? One day Alexis, who I had only just met, came to the
store. On a whim I asked her to go upstairs and get something
out of the back room, the sewing room. When she came down,
I nonchalantly asked her if she had noticed anything about the
room. She started to speak, but when I was distracted by a
customer, she made some excuse and left quickly. I let it drop
until I was researching this book, when she told me the whole
story:

Alexis felt a crawling in her stomach as she went up the
stairs and was enveloped by the chill of the upper hall. At each
step and all the way down the hall, she fought her fear, wanting
only to run back downstairs. She forced herself to turn into the
door of the back room. In the closet was a man—a tall man in
black clothes with a gaunt face, black greasy hair and beard. He
grinned at her—a devilish grin. Terrified and shaken, she
rushed back downstairs, only to have me casually ask her if
she'd noticed anything!

"I could have strangled you for sending me up there! I was *totally* afraid, like I'd come face to face with someone deranged."

She told me then that her mother considers herself psychic and that she herself is unusually sensitive to "vibrations" from anything old. Alexis has a theory that the sweat in old clothes contains pheromones that can be sensed by certain people and trigger a "psychic" experience. Researchers have shown that the sweat of aggressive rats can provoke other rats to violence. Similar studies with similar results have been done with humans.

"It makes a certain amount of sense." said Alexis. "People sweat when they're having an intense emotional experience. Why couldn't particles of these emotions—in the phero-mones—be left behind to be picked up by people who are sensitive to them?" She could be right. Customers had accused me of bringing in spooks with the clothes. Perhaps the man in black was one of them.

Alexis isn't sure. He could have been a real spirit—"the old man" when younger?, a pheromonic memory, or a hole in the fabric of time. Whatever he was, she doesn't want to experience anything like him again. As a result of her psychic uneasiness from the things hanging in her closets, she decided to give away her cherished collection of vintage fashions. These days, she still wears vintage styles: modern copies made from modern fabrics. These days, Alexis feels much less haunted.

I made a similar decision, to sell the store. I moved away from the old man and the terrors in the night, away from the clothes and any former owners who happened to be hanging around. I moved into a nice, sun-filled Victorian house, which, if it was haunted, was haunted only by mice. Only then could I relax and realize just how much the atmosphere at the Unicorn had haunted me.

I drive by my old store occasionally. It's been a drug crisis center, a swim-wear store, and a number of other things. No tenant ever stays very long. And I wonder, Does the old man know he's dead yet?

DEARLY DEPARTED
Ghostly Lovers

For love is strong as death.
-Song of Solomon 8:6-

"Until death do us part..." We've all wept over the stories of lovers tragically parted by death: Tristam and Isolda, Romeo and Juliet... But there is a more sinister side to deathless romance—the demon lover: "If I can't have you, nobody will." "I can't live without you." And love may create ghosts of a different sort as the next story tells.

A Trace of Poisoner

Ceely Rose, by all accounts, was painfully plain: a heavy, lumpish girl whose mind was "never quite right." Yet like any young girl she fell in love—a love that her family died for.

In 1896, on the farm next to the Richland County property where the Roses operated a grist mill, lived a young man named Jim Brunner*. He seems to have been one of those gentle men who would rather die than hurt anyone's feelings, particularly someone as unattractive as Ceely. She made no secret of her passion for Jim and was ridiculed by the other girls. He seems to have felt sorry for her, with her graceless figure and slow wits. At any rate, he spoke kindly to Ceely when they met. And Ceely, somewhere in the depths of her dull mind took it for something more: the hope of a husband and home. When the other girls laughed at her, she proudly told them that she and Jim were going to be married.

Jim was shocked when he heard the story, but he still couldn't bear to cause Ceely pain. To let her down gently, he told her that her parents didn't approve of him, that they had better not meet again. We can only guess at Ceely's reaction, but soon after Jim told his harmless white lie, the Rose family paid for it.

Rebecca Rose was the first to be taken sick—writhing with cramps like fire in her vitals. Her husband David went for the doctor in Newville, and fell sick at the doctor's office. Walter, Ceely's older brother had gone out on business after breakfast and was taken very ill while away from home. Ceely's father lingered many agonizing days, while Mrs. Rose and Walter were not expected to recover.

There was some debate over who fixed breakfast in the ill-fated household—Ceely or her mother. Ceely originally told a neighbor woman that she got breakfast that morning. Said the paper, "This she now denies. Up to Sunday Mrs. Rose who is still a very sick woman, knew nothing of the deaths in the family nor the attending circumstances and suspicions. A friend told her and since that time she declared that she cooked the breakfast the morning all fell sick. It has also been ascertained that on that Wednesday morning, David Rose, the father, drank two cups of coffee, the son Walter drank one, and Mrs. Rose, who was not feeling well, drank a half cup of the beverage. The father died first; the son who drank the next largest amount, died next and Mrs. Rose, who got the smallest amount is still very sick."[1]

When Mrs. Rose miraculously showed signs of recovering, Ceely tenderly administered another reviving cup of coffee. The patient suffered an immediate relapse and expired in agony. The coroner reported in his analysis of Mrs. Rose's internal organs, "I am lead [Sic] to believe that Mrs. Rose was given an additional dose of arsenic on the day of her sudden death."[2]

As in the case of Lizzie Borden, authorities either lacked conclusive evidence or were reluctant to accuse a daughter of so heinous a crime. But when it was learned that Ceely wanted to get married and her father had opposed the marriage—and when it came out that Ceely had remarked darkly that her father wouldn't live forever, suspicion was thrown on the daughter who had escaped illness. At this, Jim Brunner disappeared from the scene.

Testimony further revealed that Ceely's brother Walter had unwittingly furnished the poison for his own death. In May, Mrs. Rose asked him to purchase rat poison on one of his trips to the city. He brought her an arsenic-based poison in a bottle from Barton's Drug Store. Mrs. Rose used a little and set the rest in a cupboard. A short time before the poisonings, Mrs. Rose went to the cupboard and found that it was bare.

Court testimony brought out that "while [Ceely] may not be deemed exactly insane [she] has the mind of a child although fully developed physically." A schoolmate of Ceely's stated that the Rose girl "was not regarded as altogether right and did not act as other children when she attended school."[3]

The engraved portrait in the newspaper shows a sullen, depressed young woman, her hair carelessly pulled back, a lock hanging limply over her protruding forehead. She slumps as if she had been hanging her head when they told her, sharply, to look at the camera. Her eyes turn down at the corners—blank, despairing eyes—and one eyelid droops. Her thin mouth, pursed tightly at the corners, is clamped over her secret with the dogged determination of the simple. It is a bitter face, a hopeless face, the face of one driven beyond despair by the loss of the only person she ever cared for.

That stubborn mouth had no intention of revealing its secret. Ceely continued to live on alone in the family home. She had nowhere else to go and she wanted to make sure Jim could find her when he came back. It must have been a lonely, haunted life, with the ghosts of her parents whispering in the kitchen where she fixed herself coffee for breakfast. Did she ever have nightmares where their greenish, sweating faces materialized, vomiting ectoplasm in the dark?

Ceely had one friend—a young woman named Teresa Davis, known as Tracey. One day Tracey invited Ceely over to her farm for a visit. It was a hot day, and they went up into the hay loft for a nap. Gossiping drowsily, Tracey confided to Ceely that she was in love. Ceely's dull eyes must have brightened then, as she thought of her Jim.

Tracey told Ceely that her lover's family was feuding with her own and her parents refused permission for them to marry. She declared that there was only one thing to do: she would poison her parents and be free to marry her love.

"What would you do, Ceely?" she asked.

And Ceely said, "I'd kill 'em. That's what I'd do. That's just what I did." And she told Tracey of how easy it had been to doctor the coffee with rat poison.

She finished her story; a breeze sighed through the barn, like spirits who have seen justice done.

"Celia Rose, in the name of the law I arrest you for the murder..." The sheriff and the prosecuting attorney stepped into the hay.[4]

Some people said it was a mean trick to get a confession in such a way, but others said there was no doubt she was as crazy as a bedbug to do such a thing. The newspaper called her "A Modern Borgia" and commented, "The young woman, whether or not mentally defective, certainly has a moral nature thoroughly perverted, as at no time has she evinced any remorse over her terrible crime."[5]

They condemned her to life in a hospital for the criminally insane. We know what life was like in asylums at the turn of the century—women shrouded in sheets drenched in icy water; inmates chained, beaten, and tortured. Ceely Rose lived on and on to the age of 83.

We know nothing of her own death. Perhaps her parents came for her—smiling with blackened lips, holding out their clawed, convulsed hands. Perhaps the God of Love sent his angels to bring home this simple-minded child of His, who had so conspicuously failed to honor her father and mother.

But if she is at rest, why has her ghost been seen at the small white farmhouse on what is now Malabar Farm? It is only a plain two-story frame house, with no sign that it was the scene of a family tragedy more suited to the Greek stage than to a Midwest farm. But Ceely's ghost walks the halls and stares vacant-eyed out the window on the creek side, her stupid, stubborn mouth set for eternity.

What does Ceely Rose look for? The sheriff and his men riding up to arrest her? The dark wagon with barred windows to fetch her to the living death of the asylum? Or, pathetically, the lover who never was?

Sex and Death

Psychic investigators agree that sexual energy is a major source of psychic disturbance. Children poised on the brink of puberty can cause poltergeist activity. It has been suggested by researchers that many mediums are sexually abnormal. There is also evidence that some ghosts are obsessed beyond the grave by their former sexual partners. Sexual harrassment does not necessarily cease when the victimizer no longer has a body. Such was the case in Freyburg, where the ghost of a rapist and his victim still played out a brutal drama.

It began with a little girl's complaint about a man who would not leave her alone and the child's—quite literal—wet dreams. Three-year old Jessica* would wake up in the morning with her sheets soaked with so much water her mother could barely lift them off the bed. The odd thing was, her pajamas were always dry.

The building where Jessica lived was originally built as a farm house, but had served as a grocery store and dance hall. Later it was remodeled into apartments. Many apartment residents had sensed "an old man" hanging around and had experienced phenomena such as phantom knockings and objects, like a bulky saddle, being inexplicably moved.

After a few days of wet sheets, the apartment's owners called in two investigators: Rich Strong, retired Air Force Major and president of Psychic Science International Inc. and Kathleen Cook, psychic and medium, and, in real life, one of the only two female waste water treatment plant managers in the State of Ohio. Cook invited Dave Hill along as an observer.

Cook said, "The old man is here because he wants to be here. He lost the building when he died. He owned the building and he doesn't like it being broken up into apartments." But the old man was also there because he was tied to the spirit of his victim.

Strong sensed a young woman with long, straight black hair—an Indian girl, whose old, ragged clothing was covered with blood. Cook saw the girl too: "She was emaciated and not very pretty," said Cook, also stating that the girl had been the old man's sexual slave. "He was mean to her."

A gross understatement—the old man, who was a respectable married member of the community, had beaten and repeatedly raped the girl, sometimes keeping her chained to the wall in an attic room where she slept on a mat on the floor. The girl became pregnant and bled to death in childbirth. As Cook and Strong sensed the story, the Indian girl materialized, clinging to Cook's knees.

"He took my baby, he took my baby," sobbed the girl. Tears began to roll down Cook's face as the spirit's emotions flowed through her. Cook felt heat where the ghost clasped her legs. Then, with Cook's permission, the Indian girl took over Cook's body and spoke through her:

"Where's my baby? He took my baby. I hunted and hunted and it's not here. Did he kill my baby? I wasn't around to see. Where's my baby?" The sobs rose to a scream.

"Everybody was frightened," Cook says later, "because they didn't know I was in control. I allowed her to do it, while I was kind of up in a corner of the room. I was there, but I wasn't really there." Usually Cook does not allow a spirit to take over her body, but she explains, "The girl had been mourning so long and she was frantic. To make her realize that she was dead, she had to come into the body and 'awaken,' to hear with physical ears that she was dead."

Cook sensed that the old man had killed the baby, stuffing it down a drain pipe or a chimney to save himself the embarrassment of a half-breed child.

Pathetically the Indian girl asked over and over for help in finding her child. Strong tried to explain that the baby's soul had gone on. The girl would not listen.

"She will not leave, she wants to know where her baby is," said Cook. Trying to break the hold the girl had on her legs, she stood up, but the girl would not let go, and clung to Cook's ankles, sobbing.

At this Dave Hill who had only watched skeptically, began to feel the Indian girl reaching out to him, pleading with him for help in finding her child.

"Do you know you are dead?" he asked the girl gently. Like so many ghosts, she did not realize that she was no longer living. She had spent the long, lonely years tied to the house, vainly searching for her child.

"You've been looking for a living baby," Hill said, trying to explain that she must go on.

For the first time the girl seemed to understand. She spoke through Cook: "If I go, will I find my baby?"

The mediums assured her that her baby had gone on before her into Heaven, that she should follow and everything would be all right. The mediums prayed that she would be led to find her baby.

"A white lady in a gray dress came to get her," Cook said, feeling the pressure ease off her legs. "She came from somewhere out of the light, took the Indian girl by the hand and said, 'come with me' and they both left. The girl had been earthbound because she was unconscious when she died and didn't realize what had happened. We were able to release her."

This left the old man and a whole host of spirits to be dealt with if the house was to be cleared. After the Indian girl moved on, Cook sensed a lightening of the atmosphere. Strong saw the other spirits finally able to move along freely, "leaving in large groups, in boatloads," as he put it, to the other side.

The old man would not speak to them. In fact, he fled into the other part of the house.

"Mean old thing!" says Cook "You couldn't reason or talk with him. We upset him because we were taking everything away."

Strong contacted a spirit named Pendleton who told him that the old man was tied to the house because he had died horribly, had perhaps hanged himself. With his brutalization of the Indian girl, the baby's murder and his suicide, the old man had much to account for. With so many terrible emotions tying him to the house, it was no wonder he went mad.

"The curious thing was," says Strong, "that these horrific events started a whole chain of spirits hanging about the building. The old man's suicide somehow 'caught' other earthbound spirits. One thing led to another to another—like a soap opera, until there was a group of ghosts tied to the house."

The residents of the other part of the house would not allow Strong or Cook to enter it, so as far as they know, the old man still haunts the house. But somewhere the Indian girl is happily reunited with her child.

In fact, says Cook, "She came back a couple of years later to say, 'Thank you. Everything's fine now and I have my baby.'"[6]

The Haunting Husband

A large percentage of bereaved spouses believe that their loved one has not abandoned them completely. They report seeing, feeling, or sensing a beloved presence. My grand-mother said she would feel my grandfather's hand in hers, linking them between their two chairs in front of the television. Such manifestations can bring feelings of joy and protection to the survivor.

From Columbus comes the story of a husband who continued to watch over his wife after his death.

The house is a two-story brick, built in 1903. Hidden behind two tall pine trees, it boasts the original dark woodwork, carved art nouveau brass door knobs, and a stained glass window picturing cascades of luminous purple grapes worthy of Tiffany himself. Mr. and Mrs. Harmon* lived there for over 40 years until Mr. Harmon died in the 1970s. Devastated, his widow put the house on the market at below its real value. Construction worker Fred Albert* snapped it up, assuring her that he would take good care of it. Mrs. Harmon moved to Florida and Fred didn't hear anything more from her. But he did hear from Mr. Harmon.

Fred, bearded, burly, and down-to-earth, lived by himself and was not in the habit of imagining things. But one evening, as he was sitting in the living room, he felt somebody standing in the room with him. He turned around and saw a dark area— darker than the surrounding air. The more he looked at it, the stranger it got. The hair on the back of his neck stood up. If he looked very hard, he could make out the form of a man.

After that the apparitions appeared fairly often. They appeared upstairs in the hall or sometimes downstairs in the living room. Gradually Fred got used to sharing the house with "Sarge," as he called the ghost. Fred loved the house and didn't want to get rid of it, although he did wonder if a ghost was a real estate defect that needed to be disclosed by the seller.

Fred sometimes rented out rooms to students from Ohio State University. Naturally reticent, he never mentioned the "ghost" to any of them. He didn't have to. Most of them came to him, timidly querying whether he'd "felt" or "noticed" anything. Steve*, asked him point blank: "Is there a ghost in the house?" He had seen the darkening air repeatedly. When Fred got married, he didn't even tell his wife about the apparition. But she saw it—and was terrified. Caitlin*, a guest who spent a few nights there, had only heard some vague rumor about the ghost. She couldn't sleep for strange dreams and for being wakened by the door to her room bursting violently open. Unperturbed, Fred said it was due to unequal air pressure.

One day, Fred suddenly realized that his ghostly companion hadn't been around for quite a while. The house felt a little lonely without "Sarge." Shortly after this, Fred was puttering around the back yard. A neighbor woman who had kept in touch with Mrs. Harmon, called to him over the fence.

"Mrs. Harmon just died in Florida," she said.

Fred realized why "Sarge" didn't need to keep an eye on the house any more. His sweetheart had finally joined him in the other world.

The Lonely Ghost

Unrequited love can kill—and it can bind a lonely spirit to earth.

The Reynolds* family in the Salem Mall area of Dayton knew they had a ghost. Things had been going on for some time—a strange figure seen out of the corner of one eye or mysteriously moving objects. The Reynolds children in the house could actually see the spirit.

"Who's that person standing there?" they would ask, to the bewilderment of their parents.

The last straw came when Mrs. Reynolds was cooking chili for dinner. As she stood stirring the spicy-smelling stew, she felt someone pinch her bottom. Then psychic investigator Rich Strong was called in. He says that the family was quite surprised by how low-key he was.

"The family was expecting something sensational: a seance with ghosts materializing—and who knows what else..."

Strong picked up information about how the room used to be. He kept getting a startling picture of animals in the kitchen area. He couldn't figure it out. The Reynolds laughed and told Strong that when the house had stood empty for a while, deer had strayed into the kitchen. A ghost had strayed into the house as well.

"It turned out that the previous occupant was a lonely lady who had been disappointed in love. She was a very sensitive soul, which is why she didn't like the strong smell of the chili! She was a very well-mannered person, very ladylike. She was a poetess. Her lover marched off to war, but never returned to her. Because he never came back, she lost all faith in her religion."

Bereft of God and lover, the woman sat at her window, watching people go by on Salem Avenue. She watched until she was a shadow.

This sad, love-lorn ghost knew that there was no record of her existence. She had written poetry, but no one read it or remembered that she had written. She just wanted to be recognized, to have it said that she once existed. She liked the children and they liked her, she said wistfully, which is why they could see her.

"Fine," said Strong, "but you're scaring Mrs. Reynolds. Would you please go?"

Strong performed what is called a "soul rescue," where spirit guides are called in to lead a lost one to the Light. Strong stresses that this is not an exorcism.

"The main message I'd like to get across is that [ghosts are] not scary. They're just regular people who are all dressed up with no place to go. Their mind is more on what's here [on earth] than *there*." As the poetess bound herself to earth by her intense longing for her lover, when with a little faith she could have easily joined him.

Since Strong's visit, the Reynolds haven't heard from their ghostly poetess. Perhaps that lonely spirit has been reunited with her lost lover beyond the veil. There is no marriage or giving in marriage in Heaven. But there is Love.

IT IS VERY BEAUTIFUL
OVER THERE
Mr. Edison calls up the dead

> *The communication*
> *Of the dead is tongued with fire beyond the language*
> *of the living.*
> -T.S. Eliot-

Mr. Edison's Apparatus

He said, "Let there be light!" and there was light. He
created the modern world with his inventions: phonograph,
incandescent light, moving pictures—the list extends to over
1,300 patents. He was Thomas Alva Edison, born at Milan in
1847. But he was not God, and he could not return from the
grave. Or could he?

First and foremost a scientist, Edison had little interest in
matters taken on faith. He belonged to no church and was
scornful of his wife's religious interests. What he wanted was
proof.

> I have never seen the slightest scientific proof of
> the religious theories of heaven and hell, of future life

for individuals, or of a personal God....I work on
certain lines that might be called, perhaps,
mechanical....If there is really any soul I have found
no evidence of it in my investigations....But I have
found repeatedly evidence of mind....I do not believe
in the God of the theologians; but that there is a
Supreme Intelligence, I do not doubt....[1]

Edison had a unique theory about survival after death. He
suggested that our bodies are composed of "myriads and
myriads of infinitesimally small individuals, each in itself a
unit of life, and that these units work in squads—or swarms, as
I prefer to call them—and that these infinitesimally small units
live forever." These units are so small that they can pass
through solid matter, yet they still contain individual memories
and skills—all that makes a living personality. Edison believed
that these "swarms" survived, rather than a "soul."[2]

If the units of life which compose an individual's
memory hold together after that individual's "death,"
[perhaps]...these memory swarms could retain the
powers they formerly possessed, and thus retain what
we call the individual's personality after "dissolution"
of the body....If so, then that individual's memory, or
personality, ought to be able to function as before.[3]

Edison corresponded with the English physicist Sir
William Crooke who developed the vacuum tube which Edison
transformed into the light bulb. Crooke was deeply involved in
spiritualism and had even photographed spirits. Edison figured
that if spirit entities could be recorded on a photographic plate
with emulsions, then possibly they could communicate through
a highly sensitive "instrument" or "apparatus" (even his choice
of words is clinical rather than mystical).

Edison thought he could build such an apparatus. He told
author and psychic researcher Hamlin Garland, "All along my
way I've come upon hints of these mysterious forces—and
sometime I am going to stop commercial inventing and follow
out these leadings."[4]

In 1920 he announced, "I have been at work for some time building an apparatus to see if it is possible for personalities which have left this earth to communicate with us....I am engaged in the construction of one such apparatus now, and I hope to be able to finish it before very many months pass.[5]

Always blunt, he displayed considerable impatience with "the tilting tables and raps and ouija boards and mediums and...other crude methods now purported to be the only means of communication" and declared:

> the methods and apparatus commonly used...are just a lot of unscientific nonsense. I don't say that all these so-called 'mediums' are simply fakers scheming to fool the public and line their own pockets. Some of them may be sincere enough. They may really have got themselves into such a state of mind that they imagine they are in communication with spirits.[6]
>
> In truth, it is the crudeness of the present methods that makes me doubt the authenticity of purported communications with deceased persons. Why should personalities in another existence...waste their time working a little triangular piece of wood over a board with certain lettering on it? Why should such person- alities play pranks with a table? The whole business seems so childish to me that I frankly cannot give it my serious consideration.[7]

What Edison had in mind was an apparatus which operated like a valve. He likened it to a modern powerhouse, where a man with one-eighth horsepower could turn a valve which started a 50,000-horsepower steam turbine. The device would be so sensitive "that the slightest effort which it intercepts will be magnified many times" making it as valuable to the psychic researcher, he believed, as the microscope is to the scientist.

Edison thought that his "apparatus" would best be under- stood by those who, in this life, had been engineers or electri- cians. Edison's partner on this project had recently died and Edison said of him,

In that he knew exactly what I am after in this work, I believe he ought to be the first to use it if he is able to do so. Of course, don't forget that I am making no claims for the survival of personality; I am not promising communication with those who have passed out of this life. I merely state that I am giving the psychic investigators an apparatus which may help them in their work, just as optical experts have given the microscope to the medical world. And if this apparatus fails to reveal anything of exceptional interest, I am afraid that I shall have lost all faith in the survival of personality....[8]

Inevitably, Edison's research was parodied by the media. French journalists wrote stories about Edison's "telegraph office to the world beyond" where the bereaved waited in line to have their messages rapped out to the dead. A cartoon showed St. Peter at a switchboard saying, "Sorry, that number's busy."

But Edison saw his work as a search for truth. In a 1920 interview he told the journalist, "If the apparatus I am now constructing should provide a channel for the inflow of knowledge from the unknown world—a form of existence different from that of this life—we may be brought an important step nearer the fountainhead of all knowledge, nearer the intelligence which directs all."[9]

Edison died in 1931. Norman Vincent Peale and many others believe that Edison saw the land beyond on his deathbed:

"Mrs. Thomas A. Edison told me that when her husband was dying it was evident that he wanted very much to speak. Bending low, the physician distinctly heard the great scientist say, 'It is very beautiful over there.' Comments Peale, "Edison never reported as fact something he did not believe or see. He was not a dreamer or a poet but an exact scientist."[10]

Several of Edison's workers found that their clocks had stopped exactly at 3:24 A.M.—the time of Edison's death.

After his death the plans for his "apparatus" could not be located. Ten years later, it was rumored that the great inventor had "come through" at a seance in New York. Irascible as ever, "Edison" told the sitters that the plans for his machine were with three of his assistants and that the machine should be built. His instructions were followed and the plans duly located. The apparatus was constructed—but it remained silent. Edison's spirit materialized at another seance and suggested some technical changes. J. Gilbert Wright, the discoverer of putty and a member of the seance circle, made the changes and claimed to have contacted the spirit of genius inventor Charles Steinmetz who suggested other improvements to the machine. Wright kept tinkering with the apparatus until his death in 1959 when the machine, like many ghostly phenomena, disappeared.[11]

Was Edison's energy indestructible? Have his "swarms," in fact, survived? If the Wizard of Menlo Park has truly discovered a method of communicating with the living, over there in that very beautiful place, he's keeping it to himself.

Invisible Visitors to the Edison Museum

On the other hand, something invisible seems to be communicating with visitors to the Edison Birthplace Museum in Milan.

The curator writes:

"This winter I took a family of four on tour, and at the end the four year old boy turned to his mother and said, 'Mother, do you hear the angel voices here?' Rather a strange comment from a boy that young."

Angel voices? Or, if Edison has got his apparatus work-ing, some spirit communication coming through the ether.

"Several summers ago a young man on tour with me said angrily to me, 'What's going on here?' The hair was erect on his arms and he was sure that there was a presence in the home....

"One lady with another guide said that she too sensed a presence in the house, but when she saw a picture of Edison's cousin, Miss Marietta Wadsworth, she decided that *she* was residing there. Miss Wadsworth was caretaker of the

Birthplace for Thomas Alva Edison for about 30 years starting in 1914."[12]

The Last Trump

Direct voice communication with the dead was a common phenomenon of the seance room. Mediums who produced voices were often known as "trumpet mediums" because the "spirit voices" manifested themselves through a tin trumpet.

In 1913 the American Society for Psychical Research reported on a trumpet medium named Elizabeth Blake from Bradrick in Lawrence County. Mrs. Blake could produce voices, which apparently came from the spirit world, by placing the wide ends of two aluminum cones together and listening at the narrow end.

David Abbott, an expert magician and exposer of fraudulent mediums became interested in the case and persuaded James Hyslop of the American Society for Psychical Research (who was born in Ohio) to investigate.

They visited Mrs. Blake, giving false names. She was crippled, elderly and lived in a small rural town so the investigators thought it unlikely that she would know who her visitors really were. After holding the trumpets, the medium told another investigator, George Clawson, to listen at the opening. Faint whisperings began to be heard from the opening. The medium put one end of the trumpet to her ear and told Clawson to put the other to his. The whisperings went on. Clawson only caught a few of the words; most were indistinct, a kind of hissing.

The voice claimed to be Eddie, Clawson's dead brother. Clawson was puzzled by the messages, which were difficult to understand and passed the trumpet to David Abbott.

The voice said in a loud whisper, "I am your brother and I want to talk to Mother. Tell her..." The voice failed. Abbott encouraged it to go on. "Tell her that I love her."

Impatiently Abbott handed the trumpet back to Clawson, but the voice repeated, "I want to talk to my brother. I want to talk to my brother Davie—brother Davie Abbott."

The investigators went away baffled, convinced that Mrs. Blake had actually produced the voices of the dead.[13]

Voices From Beyond

Electronic Voice Phenomena (EVP) has long been a dream of many psychic researchers. In the 1960s, Konstantin Raudive, a psychologist interested in paranormal phenomena, tried to tape record the voices of the dead. Raudive designed something he called a "goniometer," which he believed received voices from beyond. The voices spoke in a mixture of foreign languages and static and listeners had to be trained to analyze the highly amplified voices. Other researchers think that the voices were a mixture of radio transmissions and wishful thinking, with a few "messages" transmitted telekinetically from or through Raudive.[14]

Ohio scientist and inventor George Meek, born in Springfield, is also intrigued by radio communication with the dead. Working with an eccentric electronics wizard, Bill O'Neil, Meek believed that he had succeeded in establishing two-way radio communication with voices from beyond the grave.

As told in *The Ghost of 29 Megacycles*, Bill O'Neil first noticed ghostly body parts materializing in a small aquarium he kept in his workshop. (Some ghost-hunters feel that water is an excellent transmitter of psychic vibrations.) Then a former rocket scientist named Doctor Mueller materialized. He coached O'Neil, telling him what frequencies to try. (Shades of Edison's idea that dead scientists would help with his "apparatus"!) The brusque Dr. Mueller was impatient when O'Neil wanted proof that he was who he said he was. When he finally gave O'Neil details of his life, all of them checked out. O'Neil and Meek held a press conference in Washington to announce that two-way radio communication with the dead had been achieved. That was over a decade ago. The rest is silence.[15]

Phone Call From the Dead

Diane*, a woman from Akron lost her favorite aunt in a car crash. She was devastated because she and her aunt were very close: "We were like sisters." Six months later Diane received a phone call from the dead woman, but somehow it didn't seem any different than an ordinary conversation—until afterwards.

They chatted as they had always done: "We talked about different things we had done in the past, places we had been together, just sort of reminiscing. I was home alone. This went on for about half an hour. When I hung up, I thought, 'It was Lorraine! But she's dead. She was killed instantly in an automobile accident six or seven months ago!' I even get chills now, talking about it. In fact I was so upset I dialed her number, but nobody answered."[16] And what if they had?

Long Distance

Susan Gawron of Middletown had an unearthly phone call the night her father was buried:

"For some reason when a relative dies, I seem to be in tune with it. The night we buried my father, the phone rang and rang and rang. It was very late and it woke me, but finally I got up and answered the phone and I heard my father's very distinctive voice."

"Jujee," said her father's voice, using his pet name for her. "What am I doing here? What has happened?" In shock, she hung up. She was home alone, and the call scared her "to death!" She turned every light in the house on and immediately called a friend to come over and stay with her. Shaking, she thought about the conversation over and over. Had it been a hallucination? Was she going crazy? She had been certain it was her father's voice. And most chilling of all, where was her father calling from?

Says Susan, "It was a very bad connection. Like long, *long* distance."

THE GHOSTLY GRANDPA
Children and the supernatural

...from the cradle to the grave....
-Percy Bysshe Shelley-

It is said that all children have psychic gifts that they lose as they grow older. Did you have an imaginary playmate that was very real to you? Perhaps it was a ghost...

A Ghost of Christmas Past

In Springfield on Christmas Eve, 1904, young Frederica Coblentz was putting the finishing touches on the Christmas tree decorations. Her mother, who had been ill, called downstairs, asking her for a glass of water. Like some older houses, the house had a front and back staircase that met at a landing. As Frederica climbed up the back staircase that led from the kitchen, she saw her mother going down the front stairs.

"Mother, here is your water," she called, but her mother didn't seem to hear. Frederica turned and followed her.

"Mother, here is your glass of water," she said again.

Her mother walked on. Frederica followed her down into the front hall. She said again, "Mother, here is your glass of water." When her mother didn't answer, Frederica said, a little impatiently, "Why on earth don't you take it? Where are you going?"

Her mother had turned into the dark front parlor. Frederica watched as her mother walked haltingly around the parlor, sometimes stopping as if she was searching for matches to light the gaslights.

"Are you looking for the matches?" Frederica asked.

Suddenly, Frederica saw the outline of her mother's body blurring as if the room was getting darker. Her mother's form grew fainter and fainter and then vanished. The glass of water slipped from her numb hand and broke on the hall floor. Frederica started to shake, thinking that her mother had died upstairs and she had seen her mother's ghost. Racing upstairs, she found her mother safely in bed. Neither of them could ever account for this strange apparition.[1]

And Death Shall Be No More

Only rarely are children's visions of the dead shared by adults as in this episode which happened in Columbus in 1921.

Becky* lived with her parents in her grandparents' house. Next door lived their minister, Mr. Crowell*, his wife, and their four teen-age daughters. The church Mr. Crowell led was very conservative: its members tried to follow the Bible to the very letter. The Crowells did not even prepare food on the Sabbath, but made it the night before.

Despite this rigid code, their God was Love. Becky thought that the gentle, saintly minister was a very nice man, but she believed that Mrs. Crowell was an angel straight from Heaven. She smiled when Becky hung over the fence, chattering gaily as Mrs. Crowell picked apples from the backyard tree. She gave the little girl milk in mugs and plates of doll-size apple tarts for picnic tea parties.

But one day Mrs. Crowell died of heart trouble very suddenly—so suddenly that young Becky could not—or refused to grasp the fact. She overheard the adults whispering that Mrs. Crowell's body had been packed on ice in the funeral home until the day of the funeral. Embalming would have violated the Biblical "Ashes to ashes, dust to dust." She shivered as she thought of how cold Mrs. Crowell must be feeling packed in all that ice like a fish.

This was Becky's first experience with death. The night before the funeral, she could not sleep. She heard her father get up and walk past her door to the bathroom without turning on any lights. She listened to his footsteps creak on the landing. Suddenly he stopped and Becky heard her father give a smothered exclamation. It was just the excuse she had been waiting for. She was out of bed and by his side in a flash.

He was standing by the hall window at the head of the stairs, staring down into the Crowell's dining room. Becky followed his gaze and saw a small light in the room, like a newly-lit candle just beginning to shine. In this light walked Mrs. Crowell.

The dumbfounded father and daughter could see her plainly. It looked as though she was walking in a halo of light, not walking in and out of a pool of candle or lamp light. Mrs. Crowell looked as well and happy as they had ever seen her. It looked to Becky like she was just going about her housework.

"Why doesn't she switch on the electric light?" she asked her father, but when she looked at him, he seemed dazed, like someone in a trance.

Becky turned back to watch Mrs. Crowell. They watched her for some time, probably for 10 or 12 minutes. Becky asked again, "Why doesn't she turn on the light?" Again, she got no answer.

Shortly after this, Mrs. Crowell and the light both walked out of their range of sight and the glow faded—as though she had walked into another room.

Becky went back to bed, her question still unanswered. But now she went easily to sleep. The next morning at breakfast Becky's grandmother spoke about Mrs. Crowell's funeral and burial.

"She isn't dead," Becky said, eating her oatmeal. "Daddy and I saw her."

Conversation stopped dead. Everyone looked at Becky, then at her father. He squirmed. With his eyes fixed on his plate, he said, "Yes...we saw her. Walking in the dining room last night."

Becky's grandmother said, "Oh, Edward*, you couldn't have! You must have seen one of the girls."

"She isn't dead," Becky cried, "I *know* Mrs. Crowell when I see her."

Becky's grandmother left the table, gesturing imperiously at her son to follow her. Becky never knew what her grandmother said to her father, but the incident was not mentioned again by either of them.

Their silence did not change Becky's mind. *She* knew that she had seen her friend—alive. And a short time after the funeral Becky got confirmation of that fact. One morning Becky went into her backyard and there, next door in the bright sunlight, picking apples, was Mrs. Crowell.

"Mrs. Crowell!" screamed Becky. The woman turned and smiled and waved at the little girl in the most everyday manner. Becky tore around the house, through their gate, the Crowell's gate and back around their house to get to her. But when Becky got to the backyard the woman was gone.

Becky knocked on the kitchen door, supposing that Mrs. Crowell was inside. One of her daughters answered her knock and when the girl asked for Mrs. Crowell, the daughter picked up the child and hugged her. Then she sat her on her knee, gave her a sugar cookie and made her laugh with a puppet made out of a knotted handkerchief until Becky forgot why she had come.

But the next day, Becky saw Mr. Crowell in the yard and remembered. She came close to the fence, called to him in excitement and began to tell him about seeing his wife. The man took a large white handkerchief from his pocket, put it over his face and walked into the house overcome with his sorrow, brought on by the cruel innocence of a child.

News of this reached Becky's grandmother. She sat Becky down and gave her a stern talking-to. She said that Becky was never to go around anymore telling people that she saw Mrs. Crowell.

Years passed. Becky went to school and the Crowell girls married. The minister too married again. Many experiences had jostled the memory of the first Mrs. Crowell into a corner of her mind. To the growing Becky, she was an enigma, a puzzling incident that troubled her vaguely, although she had come to accept that Mrs. Crowell was dead.

Many more years passed. Becky's mother died and her father was devastated. Desperate for consolation, he consulted mediums, receiving some small comfort in the messages purporting to come from his dead wife.

Fourteen years after Becky's mother died, her father fell ill. As he approached death, he was sad and anxious and afraid. Despite his contacts with the afterlife, he harbored lingering doubts, he still did not *know* for certain.   One day he said to Becky from his bed, "How do I know that I'll see your mother again? The messages could have been mind reading. So many have died but none have come back. Not one ever came back to me—I never saw any of them."

Suddenly the old memory blazed up in Becky's mind.

"You saw Mrs. Crowell," she said to him.

"What?" he said, staring at his daughter.

"You saw Mrs. Crowell, that night in the dark in the hall. We both saw her down there in her dining room."

As he remembered, it was like a light had been turned on behind his eyes; his features seemed almost luminous.

"I did," he said slowly, wonderingly. "How could I have forgotten it?

We did see her, didn't we? And these 40 years we never spoke of it...."

Becky left her father musing on the past. He died later that week, easily, as a man who looks forward to a reunion with his loved ones. Becky was certain it was because of their shared memory of Mrs. Crowell.

Says Becky, "We saw her, we saw her, we saw her. And we kept silent too long."[2]

The Ghostly Grandpa

The house was just an ordinary, cute two-bedroom ranch house in an ordinary suburban neighborhood. in East Dayton. The night in 1982 the Brill* family moved in, Karen Brill* fell into bed, exhausted from shifting boxes and furniture. Something woke her about 2:30 A.M.

Standing by her bed was a little old man. There was nothing at all alarming about him. She certainly didn't think he was a burglar. He had white hair and was dressed in blue pajamas with a navy and burgundy robe over it and he wore navy slippers.

"When I saw him, I felt so peaceful that I couldn't make myself move. I immediately drifted into peaceful sleep. I never felt fear at all—that's what makes this sighting so unique. I felt pulled into sleep."

In the morning she told her husband about her very vivid dream. Then she put it out of her mind as she spent a busy day unpacking.

Their neighbors, the Wilsons* invited them over for a cookout that evening. Making small talk, Brill mentioned the dream. Mrs. Wilson gave a scream and ran into their house. Mr. Wilson looked uneasy.

"Do you know," he said "that you just described Mr. Schultz*? He lived in your house until his death six months ago."

Strange as it was, Karen had too much else to think about—a new house, a young child, and another one on the way—to dwell on a dream. But a month before the birth of their second child, another mysterious incident occurred.

Karen was trying to steer belly, laundry basket, and son Peter* down the basement stairs to the washing machine. Peter jerked away and flew, head-first, down the steps. Horrified, then stunned, Karen watched as he seemed to float above the open wood steps. He gently bounced once, then swerved to avoid a pillar. Finally he touched down lightly on the basement floor. Karen scrambled down the stairs to the child and snatched him up. She stripped him completely, but there was not a mark on him.

There was also a closet door that would never stay closed. Says Karen, "When family or friends stopped by, we would tell them about our ghost and how the ghost would open the closet door. A few minutes after I hung up the guests' coats, it never failed—the closet always popped open when everyone was least expecting it."

After new baby Alison* arrived, a second crib was added to the nursery. Karen and her husband often heard their babies jabbering and giggling. If either parent went into the room, the babies would point to the center of the room as if wishing to introduce someone whom they alone could see. Sometimes their pantomime was so realistic Karen almost believed she could see a shape gesturing and making faces at the babies.

Karen's husband worked third shift so she was often alone at night. One night both children had colds and Karen decided to let them sleep in her bedroom. Alison snored in her bassinet; Peter had a bad earache and shared his mother's bed, tossing in pain. He finally fell asleep curled up against her. Karen dozed off too.

She awoke in the middle of the night to a terrifying noise coming from the babies' bedroom. The sound was unmistakable. "Someone was in there shaking both those old cribs....They were shaking and rattling so bad I thought surely the neighbors would hear. Finally the noise stopped. I was scared but I suddenly knew I had to check it out. Someone might have broken in and could possibly harm my children. I got up and looked into the other bedroom, then the rest of the house—there was no one there."

But *someone* had been shaking those bars furiously. That someone, Karen believes, was the old man, lost somewhere beyond death, desperately afraid that he had lost his little friends.

The Ghost Ate Nuts

Lonzo Green, author of *Tales from the Buckeye Land* recalls his mother telling the following story.

"If anyone else had told it," says Green, "I could not have believed it."

When Mrs. Green was a child, she and her brothers and sisters were cracking and eating hickory nuts in the hall by the stairs of her old family home. Suddenly, as in Biblical accounts, an old man appeared in their midst. He spoke to them kindly and they offered him some of their hickory nuts. He shook his head when they tried to put the nuts in his hands. (Did he think that the nuts would fall through?) Instead, he gestured that they should place the nuts on one of the stairs. The children did so and the old man picked up the nuts and ate them with relish, smiling and talking to the children. After a while he walked out into the sunlit yard and, in full sight of all the children, and their mother who had joined them, he vanished.[3]

A Small Medium

Child mediums were popular during the heyday of Spiritualism. One of the youngest was "Miss Lovejoy" of Cincinnati:

Mrs. Lovejoy, of Cincinnati...brought with her a baby of four months old, who is a remarkable medium. We have been accustomed to sit around the cradle whilst the little one lies asleep, ever since she has been here, and always receive satisfactory responses from our spirit friends, either by raps or rockings of the cradle. If the baby wakes during our circle she never cries, but seems, by the happy smile over her sweet face, and the delight with which she crows along with the raps, to receive some pleasant influence from the power which is operating.

Last evening [April 3], as we were holding a circle round the cradle, I asked the spirits why the Christians did not give the signs which are promised to the believers in the last chapter of St. Mark? When the spirits rapped out, by the alphabet—'Because the Christians of this century were believers with their lips, but too many of their hearts were far from God.' They added, 'They would show what belief in the truth of Scripture meant, through that baby, to-morrow, and prove that it was something more than lip service.'

The next day [this morning], as I returned to dinner, I found my wife and Mrs. Lovejoy sitting on the verandah outside the house. They rose up and went into the parlor with me, also accompanied by Mr. Newman, my overseer, from Mississippi, who was along with me.

On entering the parlor, we were all four horrified to behold the baby's cradle literally a mass of flames;

a spark from the pine fire probably had flown out, and
the cradle being incautiously left near the open
fireplace, had taken fire, and was now wrapped in
flames. I shall never forget the shrieks of the women,
or my own feelings of horror at the sight; but Mr.
Newman gallantly rushed towards the blazing mass,
and plunging his hands in, snatched the infant from the
cradle, and rolled it in its blazing night dress on the
matting of the floor, until the fire was extinguished. I
seized a bucket of water at the door, brought by Sam
for our horses, and hurled it at the cradle, by which the
flames were soon put out; but the strange part of the
story is that the little one never cried, nor even
whimpered, and that, though its night dress was
burned to a cinder, not a single scorch can be found on
its body, nor the least token of injury; even the bit of
hair on its little poll is not singed.

Mrs. Lovejoy is now in bed, attended by my wife,
in a painful condition of hysterical emotion; but the
little angel—guarded sign of true Christianity—is
merrily crowing in the arms of her nurse, Cherry, on
the floor at my feet as I write.[4]

The Spectral Sibling

In a small town in Ohio, the Potter* sisters shared a
bedroom. One night, ten-year-old Ruth* wandered into her
parent's neighboring bedroom, and complained to her mother
that her older sister Shirley* was standing by her bed and
wouldn't go away. Groggily Mrs. Potter went with Ruth, saw
that Shirley was asleep in her own bed, and decided that Ruth
had imagined the whole thing.

Before long Ruth was back again, complaining that not
only was Shirley standing by her bed, she wouldn't say a word,
she just stood and looked at her. Once again, Mrs. Potter found
Shirley sound asleep and scolded Ruth, warning her not to
bother her again or she'd get a spanking.

All through an endless night, Ruth asked the silent Shirley
to please, please go back to her own bed. Shirley just looked
down at her with a cold stillness that terrified her sister.

The next morning Ruth left Shirley sleeping, for she was not very strong and needed extra sleep. Later, when it came time to make the beds, her mother called Shirley. There was no response. Mrs. Potter looked closer and, to her horror, found that her daughter was dead. The doctor who examined her believed that she died soon after going to bed.[5]

OLD SOLDIERS NEVER DIE
Custer's last march,
John Brown's soul

The last enemy to be destroyed is Death.
-1 Corinthians 15:26-

Old soldiers never die, they just fade away. Ghostly
soldiers rise to refight Civil War battles. Spectral pilots return
to the planes they loved in life. Whether they rise to rattle
sabers or rattle their bones, Ohio's phantom forces continue to
soldier on.

Death on a Pale Horse

In horse and buggy days a young woman and her beau
were driving home from a church social. The moon was out,
and as they approached Bouquet's Watering Trough in
Coshocton County they saw a beautiful white horse, luminous
as a ghost, approaching on Millcreek Road.

The horse's rider wore a uniform of the Revolutionary War
period. In the bright light of the moon they could see the
polished buttons on his coat and vest, the milky white ruffles of

his sleeves, the shiny riding boots—every detail except his face, which was hidden in the shadow of his three-cornered hat.

As the mysterious rider drew abreast, the couple's horse began to plunge and shy. The driver fought to keep the horse from bolting, then tried to get past the horse and rider. As he did so, the pale horse cut in front of them, and went straight up the hill, pacing as evenly as if he were on level ground.

The shocked couple watched horse and rider climb the impossibly steep hill, growing fainter and fainter, and finally fading away like a glimmer of moonlight.[1]

A Revolutionary War Ghost

One of the spooks at Patrick's* parents' home in Dayton was "a Revolutionary War soldier" who would appear for a few seconds in the backyard and then disappear. He wore a double-breasted blue uniform coat, tight-fitting breeches, and high black boots and from the uniform, Patrick theorizes that the soldier died when the American army of 1812 was making its way to Lake Erie. Some units bivouacked in the Dayton area; many soldiers were felled by sickness or by wolves. One lone soldier, who missed the roll call up yonder, still stands his post.

The Ghost of Simon Girty

Simon Girty was a renegade. Adopted as a young man by the Seneca, he sided with the British to unsettle the Ohio Territory. He laughed as his comrades tortured and burned his stepfather. He led an Indian war party against Col. Crawford's troops and watched Crawford burned at the stake.

For his crimes, Girty is condemned to guard the cannons of Mad Anthony Wayne, which are buried at the eastern point of Girty's Island, seven miles west of Napoleon. Three boys who went searching for the cannons saw a lantern bobbing towards them through the underbrush. As the lonely light approached, they saw that it was carried by a man in fringed shirt and moccasins with a tomahawk tucked in his belt—the ghost of Simon Girty. They fled in terror when they saw that it was the man, and not the lantern, that gave off light.

The cannon were removed long ago, but Girty is condemned to a unique hell: every midnight, in the cold, stinking
sweat of fear he rises to claw the earth away from the ghostly
guns, to clean and swab them, to prime them and load them
with shot. As he works, his blood-rimmed eyes dart back and
forth frantically, seeing ghostly enemies arising about him.
Then he suffers the terrors he delighted in inflicting during his
life. Such fear could kill a living man, but Girty cannot die.[2]

Ghost Riders in the Sky

General George Armstrong Custer was born at New
Rumley in 1839. At age 23, he was the youngest general in the
Union army. He was dashing and flamboyant and his men
worshiped him, as did his wife, Elizabeth, who wrote several
books about their life together. She saw an eerie vision of
ghost riders in the sky as Custer and his men departed for their
fatal rendezvous at Little Big Horn:

From the hour of breaking camp, before the sun
was up, a mist had enveloped everything. Soon the
bright sun began to penetrate its veil and dispel the
haze, and a scene of wonder and beauty appeared. The
cavalry and infantry in the order named, the scouts,
pack-mules, and artillery, and behind all the long line
of white-covered wagons, made a column altogether
some two miles in length. As the sun broke through
the mist a mirage appeared, which took up about half
of the line of cavalry, and therefore for a little distance
it marched equally plain to the sight on the earth and
in the sky.
    The future of the heroic band, whose days were
even then numbered, seemed to be revealed, and
already there seemed a premonition in the supernatural
translation as their forms were reflected from the
opaque mist of the early dawn....
    With my husband's departure my last happy days
in garrison were ended, as a premonition of disaster
that I had never known before weighed me down. I
could not shake off the baleful influence of depressing

thoughts. This presentiment and suspense, such as I
had never known, made me selfish, and I shut into my
heart the most uncontrollable anxiety, and could
lighten no one else's burden.[3]

John Brown's Soul

While John Brown's body lies a'moulderin' in the grave,
his soul—and possibly his ghost—goes marching on.

Abolitionist John Brown was born in Connecticut, but his
family moved to Ohio when he was five years old. His father
bought a farm in Hudson, 25 miles south of Cleveland and
established a tannery. Brown grew up to believe in the
brotherhood of man and did all he could to aid runaway slaves.
Gradually he was possessed by the idea that he had a divine
mission to provoke an uprising of the slaves, who would then
fight alongside the white man for his freedom. His disastrous
1859 raid at Harper's Ferry, Virginia, led to his capture and
hanging.

A curious little book, *Interviews with Spirits* (1885),
contains a post-mortem interview with John Brown obtained
through medium Carrie E. S. Twing. Brown interrupted a talk
between author Samuel Bowles and the late Wendell Phillips,
anti-slavery orator:

"Mr. Bowles," said Mr. Phillips, "here comes our
veteran hero, John Brown, to join our conversation.
Welcome brother, be seated. You know the old adage,
'Birds of a feather &c.' Well at least I am not ashamed
of my company."

John Brown was not as attractive in appearance as
Mr. Phillips, but there was an earnestness about him
that bespoke candor and truth.

"We were talking up this slavery question," said
Mr. Phillips," and I wish you would tell Mr. Bowles
your sentiments at present."

"I will not withhold from you, Mr. Bowles," said
he, "that I have regretted many of my actions while on
earth. I placed upon my family the stigma of an
ignominious death. I anticipated that which would

have finally come. My insurrection was an eye-opener
to the colored race held in slavery, and unduly incited
the slaveholders to excessive reaction. I know many
of my plans were ill-advised. In my intense sympathy
for the slaves, I did not stop to think that they were a
class, swayed by the impulses of the moment, revel-
ling in variable moods and wholly uneducated.
Therefore my teachings were for a time, like throwing
bomb-shells. I could not understand why, having
waited all their lives, they might best wait a little
longer. Though I lost my earth-life by my rash
expedition, I have no spirit of revenge. I shudder
when I think of my own execution at the scaffold. I do
not wish my executioners to meet the same fate, for it
is a terrible experience to pass out of earth-life that
way. I have striven many times to put the most
rigorous curb on my will, to remember that the signs
of the times were then so different, but I cannot yet. I
shall grow out of it but it will be a slow process, sir.
Still I can now see where before all was dark.[4]

John Brown Jr., Brown's eldest son, was a practicing
phrenologist, one who read a person's character by examining
the bumps on the head. He also practiced hypnotism, believed
in clairvoyance, and attended seances. In an interview with
John Brown Jr. in a Cleveland newspaper, he told of how his
father had been comforted and encouraged by the spirit of
Dianthe, his first wife, as she came to him in a dream shortly
before the Harper's Ferry incident. John Brown Sr. may have
favored rifle shots over spirit rappings, but he did not totally
reject the idea that the dead return.[5]

Some say they have seen John Brown on his way to his
last battle, his white hair and white beard shining like beacons
in the moonlight. The old man is unnaturally tall and he strides
forward, soundlessly urging on his phantom host. His beard
blows like smoke from a torch destined to set the country on
fire. "A stray ghost-walker with a ghostly gun,"[6] John Brown's
soul goes marching on....

Commands from Beyond

In Cincinnati a ghost gave a young soldier his marching orders:

In Cincinnati...the author [Emma Hardinge] met a brave young soldier, Lieutenant Emmett, who had been compelled to retire from a career of honorable distinction in the army on account of the loss of an arm.

He was a strong Spiritualist, and an excellent writing medium. On one occasion, being at a circle where the author was present, he drew from his pocket-book a communication from his spirit father, which read to the following effect: that if he [Frank] would go to the war no bullet which was yet forged, should harm him; no sword could maim him, or fire scorch him for he [his father, in the spirit-world] could and would protect him through all the perils of war; and that he, Frank Emmett, would be safer far on the battle-field than in the peaceful scenes of home.

"How then is it," asked one of the circle, "that we see you thus maimed, but still in the uniform of the army?"

Lieutenant Emmett replied; "My spirit father kept his word. I enlisted with the First New York Volunteers as a private. I won my present rank step by step, serving in six battles and always finding myself forward,—sometimes in defiance of orders,—in the thickest of every fray. I have been the target at which a hundred muskets were aimed; I have been the centre of a forest of swords, and have had no less than five bayonets pointed at my very throat; yet, somehow, and in a variety of ways too numerous to relate, I escaped them all, without a single scratch.

My play-going comrades used to call me "Der Frieschutz," ["the free-shooter," a character in German folklore who sells his soul to the Devil in exchange for magic bullets] and say I "bore a charmed life." But, forgetful that my blessed father's promise of protection extended only to the battle-field, and that he had again and again answered to my poor wife, who was always remonstrating against my continuance in the army, "Frank will always be safer on the battle-field than at home, whilst the war lasts," I at last yielded to Mary's earnest solicitations, obtained a leave of absence, and went down to New Orleans to spend my furlough with her. The second day of my visit, whilst out riding with my wife, her horse took fright, and I, in my endeavor to arrest him, was thrown down and broke my arm, The poor stump which I now carry, is the testimony to the truth of my spirit father's warning."[7]

The Unknown Soldier

On Old Route 40, somewhere near Zanesville, there is a little brick one-room schoolhouse, now used as a residence. In the fall of 1973, Inez* drove from Toledo to visit her parents at their schoolhouse home. They had a pleasant, uneventful visit and Inez climbed up to her second-story bedroom Saturday night between midnight and 1 A.M.

"I went up to go to bed and had just lain down. All of a sudden, at the foot of the bed I saw a wounded soldier. He was wearing what looked like a Civil War uniform. The colors were not vivid, but I know it was not a navy or dark blue suit. It was more of a greyish blue.

"The minute I saw it, my heart raced! I sat right up, I was so frightened. Immediately it vanished. It was totally unexpected! My heart pounded for quite a while. It looked like a person, but you could see through it to the beams in the ceiling; it was not solid flesh.

"He had a bandage on his head, on his arm and on his leg. There was blood leaking through the bandage on his head. The bandaging was mostly on his right side, like he'd gotten hit on that side and he had what I think was a crutch, although it was more like a stick—not like our modern crutches.

"Afterwards my heart was still pounding and I thought, 'Well, maybe I'm either overtired and hallucinating, or there was some kind of a—ghost.'" Inez seems extremely reluctant to use the word.

Did the house have a reputation for being haunted? Was it built on a cemetery or had it been used as a hospital during the Civil War?

"Around Zanesville there was the Underground Railroad, that's all I know," says Inez. "There were times my younger brother thought he and his friends saw people walking by the front windows of the house. They'd go out to look and there'd be nobody there. *They* talked about the house being haunted, but that was years ago. Nobody had mentioned it the day I saw it. For a long time I didn't tell anybody because I thought, 'Am I losing my peanuts?'

"I don't quite understand—as far as the person's soul is concerned—where the soul goes, whether ghosts are the soul or just some kind of physical energy. I've often wondered. I would think that the promises of Christ mean that He would allow a soul to go on unless this is a form of purgatory. I don't understand ghosts in a Christian sense unless they're just energy."

I mention the theory that ghosts are a kind of spectral video tape playing over and over after being "recorded" by some extreme stress or emotion. Inez is thoughtful. "That's kind of what it was like. It wasn't a solid mass, there was a flickering movement, like an old-time movie. And it didn't stand still. I saw it and then it got slightly bigger as it moved towards me." She shudders. "I can actually see it today. I could draw you a picture of it, it made such an impression."

Apparently the sufferings of an unknown soldier also made a vivid impression on the atmosphere of the house. One can only hope that the soldier has gone on to the place where there is no more weeping or pain and where death shall be no more.

The Grey Lady of the Confederate Cemetery

For years fresh flowers have appeared mysteriously on the grave of Benjamin E. Allen, Company D, 50th Tennessee Regiment at the Confederate cemetery along Sullivant Avenue in Columbus. Flowers have also been found on the grave of the Unknown Soldier. Are they placed there by a sentimental Southern sympathizer? Or are they a token from the ghostly Lady in Grey?

The Lady in Grey is a young woman, dressed in a grey traveling suit trimmed with black in the style of the 1860s. Her light brown hair is done up in a bun under a grey hat. She always looks down and seems to weep. She floats right through trees and the very solid cemetery gates.

In the summer of 1988, during a Civil War re-enactment, many participants heard an invisible person crying. The weather was perfectly quiet until a violent gust of wind suddenly blew over tents and tables. Then all was calm again. Was it the Lady in Grey passing by? And why has she not found and followed her loved one instead of haunting his grave? The War is over, but the grieving—and the flowers—still go on. Perhaps they will, until the South rises again.[8]

War and Ouija Boards

Wars traditionally stimulate an interest in the possibility of life after death. When Life's questions are unspeakable, grief-stricken people turn to the supernatural for answers. During the Great War, manufacturers of ouija boards were over-whelmed with orders and had to expand their operations.[9]

The Ghost Cast a 'Yes' Vote

Prior to the United States involvement in World War II, Mrs. Frances Bolton, Republican congresswoman from Cleveland, was undecided on how to vote on the 1941 Lend-Lease Act. Most fellow-Republicans were voting against this measure which Roosevelt hoped would help send much-needed military equipment to besieged Britain.

Bolton was close friends with the highly respected English medium, Eileen Garrett, who had come to America to have her gifts investigated by researchers at Duke University. Troubled over the vote, Bolton consulted Garrett. At the session, Garrett's spirit guide, Uvani, came through, advising her to vote for the measure. Mrs. Bolton did and her vote was decisive in passing this life-saving bill.[10]

Security-minded Spirits

During the Second World War, in 1942, a spiritualist convention in Cleveland resolved that "for the duration no medium should ask the spirit of a departed service man any questions whose answer might furnish military information to enemy agents lurking in the audience." [11]

Ghosts of the Air

Dayton is the home of the United States Air Force Museum. Each year this popular museum draws millions of visitors from all over the world to view exhibits on the history of flight, the Wright brothers, and military aircraft of all kinds. Anne*, who lives in Beavercreek, has visited the Museum several times. She says she will not go back.

"The place is full of death," she says uneasily. "There are dead guys looking over my shoulder whenever I stop to look at something. I have to tell them, 'Go away, you're dead.'"

Anne was relieved to hear that other people have experienced the same thing at the Museum. "I personally believe that it's haunted!"

Patrick R.*, (see above) has the gift of seeing spirits. He too believes that strange things go on at the Museum.

Says Patrick, "My buddy worked there; he's retired now. They had a Waco airplane on display with a dummy pilot sitting in the cockpit. One morning they found the pilot thrown out of the airplane onto the floor. Of course, they thought it was a prank, but the airplane was dusted for prints and they found nothing."

Patrick notes that the Museum is located on a working Air Force base and contains many valuable exhibits. Security is tight and it would be difficult if not impossible for a prankster to gain access.

"My buddy told me he often heard noises and weird things like people talking in places where nobody should have been. Tools would get moved mysteriously. A lot of people won't work in there nights." Including security guards, Patrick has heard: "There are some guards who'll do anything to get out of working there after dark."

Anne wonders why any ghosts would hang around airplanes that, for the most part, never crashed and never killed anybody. But Patrick has an idea. He believes that many of the planes contain parts cannibalized from other aircraft: "Ghosts latch on to whatever they are familiar with—and fliers get very attached to their aircraft."

Could these phantom fliers have identified parts from planes they once flew? Patrick thinks that it's likely: "Those dead guys—they're still trying to hold on to what they once had."

6

THE PHANTOMS OF THE OPERA
Theatrical ghosts

Ghosts do fear no laws
Nor do they care for popular applause.
-Anonymous-

"A poor player who frets and struts his hour upon the stage..." If life can be represented by the image of the ephemeral actor, the theatre becomes the world in microcosm. All of life's passions cross the boards of the stage, echoing to the farthest balconies in a ghostly whisper. If intense emotions can create a ghost, perhaps even those simulated on the stage can leave a remnant. Or perhaps the play still goes on long after the curtain is rung down.

Alice, the Ghostly Actress

Joe E. Brown and Eva Marie Saint: two unlikely theatrical bedfellows, but linked at Bowling Green State University as the names of of two University theatres haunted by a ghostly actress named Alice. Despite differing stories about the origins of the theatrical apparition, Alice's appearances are real enough—at least as real as the magic of the stage.

In one tale, Alice was an actress playing Desdemona who was killed by a falling object during a performance of *Othello*. In the second story, she was a former theatre student killed in a car crash while returning to the University to collect her award as Actress of the Year. Superstition holds that Alice must be officially invited to all performances by the stage manager, alone on the stage after the final dress rehearsal.

"You have to thank her for letting you use the theatre, invite her to the performance, and thank her for letting the play get that far," said Senior theatre major, Wes*, who did the honors one year. "As soon as I was done inviting her, I heard this rumbling that sounded like 'I'll be there.' I ran out of the theatre." If she feels snubbed, says Wes, Alice shows her resentment. "She's in control. If she doesn't want you there, she'll make sure you know it. You have to be nice to her," he says, citing the minor disasters that have happened when Alice's favorite "ghost light" (which is always left burning on stage as a safety precaution) is inadvertently turned off: "Nails come out of sets, things get tipped over, lights burn out...things that could happen anyway but they only tend to happen when you don't leave her light on."

Another theatre major, Mark*, was setting up the stage one Friday, when he thought he saw something out of the corner of his eye. Turning around, he realized that there was a figure standing next to him.

"The part about it that bothered me was that I kept looking and she didn't fade." The figure had long hair and wore a skirt. "She was pale white, but I could see through her. She was more like a shadow and she held out her arm to me." Mark ran out of the theatre in terror. Later he regretted not staying and getting to know Alice a little better.

Alice seems to enjoy her role of spirit stage manager, but she still harbors ambitions to go back on the stage. During a 1986 performance of *Othello*, Craig* was waiting in the wings to go on when he was startled by a figure in Elizabethan costume standing in the stairwell. Thinking that the actress playing Desdemona was not on stage as she should have been, he screamed, "Where's Mary*?" The figure vanished; then Craig saw Mary on stage.

If it is true that the actress who was Alice died as
Desdemona, what could be more natural than Alice's making
her comeback in that role, returning for one final curtain call?[1]

The Ghost of Fisher Hall

Fisher Hall on the campus of Miami University, Oxford,
had been a beautiful building. Originally built as a dormitory
for a women's college, it possessed a sweepingly elegant
staircase, an upper-floor ballroom ornamented with carved
plaster work—and a resident ghost.

By the time Professor Geoffrey Fishburn of the Miami
University Theatre Department came to Miami in September of
1967, the upper stories of the building had been condemned as
unsafe for public use. The beautiful staircases were blocked
with walls of drywall and barbed wire. The upper floors,
divided into small rooms, were used only for storage.

"It was a strange place to work," says Fishburn who taught
at Fisher from 1967 to 1969. Some of the first stories Fishburn
heard were about the alleged haunting of the Hall. One told
how a large and heavy portrait bust of Judge Elam Fisher, (who
gave the money to build the hall) moved each night to a
different room. After a few rounds of hide-and-seek with the
bust, someone had the idea of graphing its movements. When
plotted on graph paper they spelled out "E.F.": for "Elam
Fisher." What was more puzzling was a square or diamond-
shaped figure formed by the last four movements of the bust.
Until someone remembered that Fisher had been known as "the
Diamond Judge" for the diamond stickpin he sported in his
cravat.

Several weeks after its disappearance, the bust was
discovered on the top floor of the building. Security was
baffled: the bust was too large and too unwieldy to have been
carried up the only flight of stairs left open to the top floor.
While they were trying to figure out what to do with it, the bust
disappeared again, this time for good.

Three months after his arrival, Fishburn got his own taste
of Fisher's mysteries. He taught in the old dining hall that had
been converted into a theatre by risers and some folding chairs.
A small platform had been built over the door to hold the light

and sound boards. In order to hoist heavy equipment onto the platform, a winch was improvised from a steel drum and about fifteen feet of heavy rope. The winch was placed in a storage room directly over the platform, a hole was drilled through the ceiling and the rope let down through the hole. When not in use, the rope hung by the platform, knotted into a ball so it wouldn't slip through the hole.

As Fishburn began his lecture that day, he saw the rope quivering. Joking, he said to the class, "You have an unparalleled opportunity to see the ghost of Judge Fisher shaking that rope. He just wants to let you know that he's here." The whole class turned to stare at the rope, which was still moving. Some students laughed, then Fishburn resumed the lecture and the rope stopped.

"We didn't really think too much about it. We were used to hearing noises overhead—footsteps and dragging sounds— from workmen moving things in and out of the storage areas. I just assumed that somebody working up there had moved the rope."

A few minutes later, Fishburn glanced at the rope again. It was moving again—more vigorously this time. "Ah! I thought to myself. Somebody up there knows there's a class in here and they're playing a little joke. Then the movement subsided, so I went back to my lecture and didn't pay any attention."

Later, Fishburn's attention was drawn to the back of the room. The rope was dancing violently as if someone was yanking up and down on it. Still sure that it was only a workman playing a trick, Fishburn ignored it and finished the class. After class, Fishburn went to turn out the lights. "I glanced up to see the rope. The rope was not there." And the strange thing was, the knot in the rope was larger than the hole; it could not have been jerked through the hole. Intrigued, Fishburn looked around for plaster dust, but saw none. He decided to investigate.

Fishburn knew that the second floor was used for storage, but had never been upstairs; it was kept locked and off-limits to all but the physical plant crew. He made an appointment with security. "I wanted to check on the winch—that was the story I gave."

The next afternoon, he followed the guard outside. They entered through the only entrance, a side door with a separate key. Then the guard left him. The stairway was narrow and dark. It had been the servants' stair when the building was new. The upstairs was dirty and dangerously decayed. Items were stored in the rooms close to the stairs. Further away, rooms stood empty. Many of them looked as though nobody had entered them in years. Dirt and dust lay inches thick on all the floors.

Fishburn worked his way towards where the room that held the winch should be. He pushed open what he thought was the right door.

"I could tell that this was the winch room by the hole punched in the floor." Only there was no winch. Just an empty room with a dark outline in the dust on the floor—the outline of the frame that had held the winch.

Eerie as the upper floor was, Fishburn still clung to the logical explanation.

"Oh, I understand," he thought "They needed the winch for something and they came up here and got it." He turned to leave, but something made him pause at the door and look back. Suddenly he realized with a chill that there were no footprints in the dust except his own. The only marks in the floor were those of the frame. "There was no indication that anyone had walked across that floor."

Now Fishburn was really spooked. He called Physical Plant to ask if anyone had taken the winch. To his dismay, he found that not only had they not taken it, no one had been in the building that day. The winch was never found.

It got to be a tradition that after opening nights, when the stage manager had locked up and began the walk home, he would see the second floor blazing with light. Fishburn says this happened to him so many times he finally stopped reporting it to Security. "By the time they'd get there, the lights would be turned out," he shrugs. "They never found anyone or any traces of anyone." And when he and the physical plant crew inspected, they found that there was no electricity to the upper level—the wires had been cut and the fuses removed.

Not all of the doings at Fisher were supernatural. Fishburn explained, "It was an unwritten assumption that one of the things you had to do was break into Fisher Hall. It was sort of a rite of passage—to brave the ghost. So there were constant break-ins at night. It got so bad that Security stationed officers in the building all night. About every other night they'd have to arrest somebody."

Fishburn's theatre students inadvertently helped to put a stop to the break-ins—and to create a new legend about Fisher Hall. Fishburn got permission to store some large props in the basement. His playful students arranged the props—a coffin, department store mannequin, and four large candlesticks—to look like a corpse lying in state.

"We got a call from Security asking about 'the Devil Worship in Fisher Hall.' Some students had broken into the room in the middle of the night and were scared out of their minds. They came running over to Security to tell about all the coffins with dead people they'd seen! Security was kind of grateful to us so we left the coffin as it was."

Fisher Hall was demolished in 1971 and a new conference center was built on the site. There were a number of "incidents" while it was being built. There are rumors that things are still happening although University officials are spooked by any discussion of the matter. Perhaps things will always go bust in the night, as long as the Diamond Judge still wanders.

The Ghost on Stage

Dayton boasts not one but two haunted theatres. The home of the Dayton Philharmonic is Memorial Hall. Built in 1909, it was renovated in 1956 at the behest of a music-loving society lady who was tired of poor acoustics and neck-craning views. She made sure that there wasn't a bad seat in the house.

The renovation didn't do anything for an assistant custodian named Drake* who accidentally fell into the orchestra pit about 30 years ago, breaking his hip and dying shortly afterward. Ever since, there have been strange noises at the Hall that aren't the orchestra tuning up.

Doug Pascal*, a head stagehand at Memorial Hall, says that most of the stagehands take Drake's ghostly doings in stride.

"Drake's back!" they say when they hear noises where no noises ought to be.

Or "That's Drake," they remark, when lights come on mysteriously.

And "There goes Drake!", when they hear an invisible somebody walking across the overhead catwalks.

Pascal chuckles about Drake, the weird noises, and the flashing lights, which he attributes to electrical gremlins. He also tells of being alone in the building at 3 A.M. one morning:

"I went through the whole building, got everybody out and locked up. Then I went back to my office, changed my clothes—and heard a toilet flush in the bathroom above my office." Being a very security-conscious employee, Pascal *knew* he hadn't left anybody in the building. A bit sheepishly he says, "I left in a hurry. I didn't even check the building out. I just left." And left Drake on the job.

The Ghosts of the Victoria

The Eternal Curtain Call

From her sparkling glass and bronze doors to her pale green walls trimmed with gold, the Victoria Theatre, is a *grand dame*—the undisputed queen of Dayton's theatrical scene. The Victoria's green marble pillars and plush seats aren't the only attraction, however, says House Manager David Hastings. The Victoria boasts at least two ghosts.

The most romantic and well-documented ghost of the Victoria is "Vicky*," a flirtatious phantom who in life was an actress. In the early 1900s, she retired to her dressing room between acts to change into a black taffeta dress for her next scene. Another actor met her coming down the stairs. She stopped and said, "I forgot my fan." then went back up the stairs to her dressing room. She was never seen again.

The black taffeta dress she'd changed into was gone, as was the matching fan. There was no sign of foul play. It was as if a crack had opened in the wall and she had walked into it. Of course, the gossips' wagging tongues whispered that Vicky had run off with a lover. After all, actresses were no better than they should be....

Except that there were only two exits from her dressing room: down a stairway past the guard who saw her enter, or out a third-story window. The mystery was never solved, but her dressing room developed a reputation for being haunted. Vicky's ghostly face was sometimes seen, forming like a haze on the mirror. The room's door refused to stay shut. Could Vicky have been murdered in the dressing room and her body hidden until it could be smuggled out—possibly in a costume trunk? Or did the actress who created other realities on the stage, somehow walk into another dimension?

Vicky must have been an enchanting creature for she manifests herself in ultra-feminine ways: by the delicious rustle of her taffeta petticoats, by the elusive scent of her rose perfume that lingers where she has passed, by the light tap of her footsteps across the stage.

House Manager David Hastings has heard those footsteps and smelled her perfume. He has felt Vicky brush by him as she sweeps down the staircase. So have many other people. In 1990, as WDTN Channel 2 was taping a Halloween segment on ghosts, there was a noise from the balcony stairwell. Producer Martha Dunsky went to the area where the noise had been heard, thinking to shush the culprit, but found nothing. Instead, everyone heard the rustling of fabric. They thought it was a joke played by the stagehands—until they realized that they were alone in the theatre.

Vicky initially didn't like the plans to restore the Victoria. On the evening of the last show before the theatre closed for renovation, a distraught marketing director came to Hastings and told him about a vibrating chair in her office.

Hastings was skeptical, but went to check. Sure enough, the chair was vibrating.

"The ghost doesn't want us to change the Victoria," the marketing director told Hastings. Being a practical sort, he checked for motors all over the building and found nothing. He came back to the office. He sat in the chair. It gently vibrated beneath him.

During the two-year renovation, construction workers were baffled when their tools were moved mysteriously. Many reported a feeling that someone was behind them, although when they turned, no one visible was there. Strange shadows were seen flitting about in the gutted building.

When the restoration was finished, there was doubt that Vicky had stayed. After all, other ghosts had been dislodged from their haunts by renovations. Everything was quiet for a few weeks, but then a secretary wondered aloud if Vicky was still around. At that moment she smelled the rose perfume, stronger than ever.

Vicky roams the building at will, but she especially likes to visit the Victoria offices on the second floor and the reception room just outside. Formerly elusive, of late, Vicky has become bolder, coquettish, one might even say. Formerly only a select few smelled the perfume, but now many people are noticing it. It has been especially evident in the vestibule near the ticket window. Even the security guards comment that they feel like they are walking through a cloud of scent.

"Yes, the perfume has been real busy," Hastings says. "She's letting us know that she's still here. Perhaps that means that Vicky is more relaxed about the renovation and," he laughs, "getting back to her old haunts."

That was in the first week of May, 1991. On May 21, I got a startling phone call.

"I saw her," says the woman on the phone. She is cool, restrained. She is an employee of the Victoria whom I will call Kate*. She believes that she has just seen the ghost of the Victoria.

Early that morning Kate went to her supply closet inside the women's restroom on the third floor.

"I heard a noise, kind of a foreign noise. I stopped and listened, but didn't hear anything more, so I got some rags, and started to walk through the door to the hall. For some reason I stopped and looked towards the stalls, twenty feet away. The door to one of the stalls opened. I saw the dress. It looked like a woman seen from the back. I didn't see a head— everything up there was black. It wasn't the whole image of her, but I saw her dress. It was a black dress, tight-fitting at the waist, flowing into—not pleats, but loose folds. The dress didn't look stiff, but very soft. I saw it from about the armpits down. I didn't see arms.

"It was the biggest shock—I felt like the hair on my arms stood up about two inches, but I wasn't afraid, just startled. When I automatically shook my head to clear it, it took my eyes away. Then she wasn't there, but the stall door swung shut. 'O-kay,' I thought, 'I want explanations.' I walked out the door and I thought, 'No, I didn't really see what I just saw.' Then I went back into bathroom, turned on the lights, and checked the stall. Of course nobody was there. I turned off the lights, and moved around some to see if there was any reflection on anything that could have fooled me. There wasn't."

Did she try to talk to the ghost? "Yes, I did," Kate says a little sheepishly. "I talked to her out loud. I said, 'Are you ready to talk to me? Or are we just going to play awhile? Because if you're going to talk to me, don't scare me. I don't want to all of a sudden turn a corner and see you standing there.' Then I said to myself, 'Kate, you're talking to yourself.'"

She confides that she has named the ghost she doesn't believe in. "I call her 'Miss Victoria.' I'm the only one who calls her that; the others call her 'Betsy.'

"The Reception Room on the third floor is the place I've encountered her the most. When I'm vacuuming, she's brushed up against my hair. It's a real eerie feeling. There's *got* to be an explanation. There isn't any reason for that to happen. I've had things move; I've smelled her perfume. Brooms fall—brooms that I've put in corners so they won't fall and all of a sudden, boom! I'll find cleaning rags sitting in the middle of the hallway, doors will slam shut, lights come on."

Kate thinks that Vicky may be working up to a complete materialization a little bit at a time, "to get me used to her. If I talk about her, will that make her go away? If there is such a thing, if she needs to talk to somebody, I'll talk to her. Just so she doesn't scare me...."

Kate wonders why she has been singled out: "Why *me*? I don't *believe*. I've never been looking for her. It seems that she kinda likes me. I just hope she knows how to do windows."

Kate shakes her head. "The strange thing is I don't really believe. I'm a real good skeptic. but so many things have happened to me.... Usually I would have said, 'Nah!' but I know what I saw. I *know*..."

Then Kate says in wonder, "In two hours I will have myself convinced that this never, ever happened."

A Malicious Spirit

One of the other ghosts of the Victoria is a ghost of a trauma. At the turn of the century, a young girl named Lucille* was seated in one of the boxes at the Victoria. In those days folding screens were placed at the entrances of the boxes to keep out drafts and to hide the maid who accompanied the young woman as chaperon. Somehow the chaperon was lured away, and a violent madman dragged Lucille behind the screen and assaulted her. Other theatre patrons heard her screams and rescued her before she was murdered by the lunatic. The Dayton newspapers fumed that it was an outrage when young women couldn't attend a matinee in safety.

After the incident, Lucille and her family moved east. Lucille married and lived to be an old woman and died a natural death. But something of that violent assault lingered on to haunt the box. It was said that whenever anyone of a vicious temperament, anyone with anger in their heart came into the box, the temperature would drop.

For years Hastings, who had been an actor, thought that the box, which was called "the left box" in contemporary newspaper reports was at "stage left," or the right-hand box as you faced the stage. In the late 1970s, some mediums visited the theatre. They felt "angry energy" in the opposite box—the one on the left as you faced the stage, or "house left." This turned out to be the true site of the assault.

Five years later Hastings and his friend Steve* were checking the house before leaving for the evening. Steve is a psychologist and he didn't know the story of the box. As Steve entered the box, he let out a yell.

Hastings says, "I came rushing upstairs, calling, 'What happened? What's the matter?' I heard Steve exclaim, 'I feel like I've been slapped!' By the time I got to him, he was sitting in the back of the theatre, his face in shadow. 'Did you and Lucille get into an argument?' I teased him.

"He mumbled something about an insect bite. As he moved into the light, there, imprinted very clearly on his face, visible even through his beard, was the red mark of a hand print."

Why would Lucille single out Steve? I asked Hastings. Was he a violent sort of person? He smiled slightly, "He was a very *angry* person; one of the angriest people I've ever known."

The Other Ghost of the Victoria

Sometime in the 1880s, there was a suicide in the theatre. The man is said to have impaled himself on a knife fastened on the back of a seat. The blood ran down the Victoria's floor into the orchestra pit. The suicide's misty face was seen on the heavy velvet drapes that hung in the doors to the backstage before they were replaced by real doors.

If you visit the Victoria, you will enjoy the splendor of the turn-of-the-century decor. But think only good thoughts in the box at house left and listen for the rustle of Vicky's skirts as, a little late, a little breathlessly, she makes her invisible entrance—a lovely mystery to the last.

McConnelsville's Haunted Opera House

In the old river town of McConnelsville, the great stone arch over the theatre door proclaims, "1890 Opera House." Galen Finley, the owner of the McConnelsville Opera House Theatre, is reminiscing about how he came to own the Theatre:

"I went to the movies every Saturday night with my Grandma. We saw Ma and Pa Kettle, Roy Rogers, Abbott and Costello.... It was the only thing to do in town. I practically grew up in the Opera House." He worked as an usher in the theatre and "when the owner told me she was going to close it, she said, 'Why don't you buy it? I'll make you a good deal.'" Finley shrugs. "My dad said we'd done stranger things." So in 1962 he bought it with an eye to restoring its 1890s beauty.

Finley was a skeptic about things supernatural when he bought the theatre.

"We'd always heard it was haunted. I didn't believe it. It was the biggest joke in the world." He laughs. "Now I'm a believer. Trust me!"

The first incident happened the third day after Finley bought the theatre.

"I had an employee there and we were getting ready to clean. Both of us heard the piano and a lady singing, just as clear as could be. He looked at me and said, 'All right, who've you got planted backstage to put the fear in me?' I said, 'Nobody. I hear it too!' We looked at each other like, 'What?!' So we laid down our mops and went backstage. The stage hadn't been used for a long time. The drapes were all rotted. There were cobwebs everywhere, dust a foot thick. Nobody ever went back there. It was spooky. As we went through the door, we saw the piano sitting there, the lid down over the keyboard, covered with dust and cobwebs. And we got out of there."

That was only the beginning. Says Finley, "You constantly felt like there were people with you or watching you. You could hear people walking around you. I tried to use logic, to say it was floors settling or something. That didn't work."

For two years he worked on restoring the theatre. It is an elegant place with a Victorian sound dome and chandelier. The seats in the horsehoe balcony are red plush. The curtains are red velour with gold fringe. In the lobby, Finley stripped off layers of rubber linoleum and carpet to reveal the original multicolor tile work. Above the lobby doors are brilliant stained glass windows.

During the restoration, Finley held a party on the stage. Six people went in a group to the bathrooms, which were out front near the box office. When they came back they said to Finley,

"All right, who's the guy in the white suit you've got standing at the back of the auditorium?"

"What guy in a white suit?"

"Don't feed us that line. We've all seen him, all six of us."

Finley started out into the auditorium. There was no one there. He walked around the curtains at the back of the theatre and found the door to the theatre still locked.

From his guests' descriptions, the "guy in the white suit" sounded like an elderly gentleman who'd worked at the theatre for 30 years as an usher. He always wore a light tan or white suit and his name was Everett.

"We all know that Everett is there," says Finley. "Every so often he likes to flush the toilets. Then too, one night during the movie the main drape decided to close. It opened about four feet and stopped. I had to run back and open it by hand. Another evening, the switch just clicked by itself and the house lights went on and then off."

Everett isn't the only ghost at the Opera House. For a while Finley lived backstage. One night a friend of his was staying the night. The man leaped off the couch where he had settled down and said, "Look!"

Finley looked into the maze of ropes and catwalks and saw a "woman walking up to the hemp gallery where they flew the scenery. Both of us went and stayed at my mother's house." Says Finley, "It looked just like a transparent figure, like a fog going through. It was wearing some kind of a long gown."

Another time Finley was alone in the theatre at night: "I was playing the organ and I heard someone walking down the aisle. I thought to myself, 'I'll just go on playing until they're right behind me and then I'll scare them.' I continued to play, then I leaped off the bench and jumped into the aisle. There was nothing, no one—that I could see. I went right over the top of the organ and out the back door."

Finally Finley had a Catholic priest bless the theatre. Even the priest commented on how spooky the building was. There were fewer incidents after the priest's visit. But, says Finley, "They're coming back now. Or else they didn't all go." Finley laughs as if to say that it's OK with him. "Every old place ought to have a ghost! Some of the boys who work here can feel Everett's presence. They aren't scared of him. It's just knowing that there's something unseen—something that you know is there but that you can't see. We know we still have Everett. Everett has stayed."

The Ghost With the Best Seat in the House

The Sorg Opera House, Inc. in Middletown turned 100 years old in 1991. Age hasn't dimmed the beauty of this unique theatre, nor has it curtailed the activities of the theatre's original owner, Paul J. Sorg.

Paul J. Sorg, sometimes known as "The Last of the Robber Barons," was the second-wealthiest man in Ohio. He owned a paper company, tobacco concerns, and loaned money to James Cox so he could buy the *Dayton Daily News*, the flagship of Cox Enterprises. He served as a member of Congress and had a finger in every financial pie.

Sorg's wife Jennie was stage-struck. To please her, Sorg built the Opera House and gave her *carte blanche* to bring back top acts from New York. Trains used to bring theatre-lovers from Cincinnati to Middletown. The Sorg saw live opera, Otis Skinner, John McCormick, George M. Cohan, even a very young Bob Hope. From 1915 to 1986 it also showed movies, including the first talkie in Middletown, a horse opera called *In Old Arizona*. In 1929 it became a full-time movie house. After a 1935 fire, the Sorg was renovated and reopened in 1939. In that renovation, the second balcony was hidden by a false ceiling. The balcony still exists, frozen in time with its bench seating and the original rose and gold plasterwork.

There was a definite hierarchy to theatre seating. Blacks entered through a separate entrance and sat in the second balcony with the men in suits. No women were allowed there and it was an uncouth place. Restorers say they had to "shovel the tobacco juice out of the second balcony." The more genteel Orchestra and First Balcony sections required patrons to wear full evening dress.

Paul J. paid careful attention to such social niceties. He was a natty dresser, a "swell," as dandies were known in the 1890s. So it is not surprising that his ghost wears full evening dress as he sits in his favorite seat in the first row of the First Balcony.

Many people—janitors, caretakers, actors, and stage-hands—have seen the ghostly figure in 1890s evening dress. Those who have gotten a glimpse of the face say that it matches the portraits of Sorg in the theatre's lobby, down to the mustache. Whenever anyone approaches the figure to ask what it wants, it just disappears. Living or dead, as owner of the Opera House, Paul J. could hardly be expected to talk to his social inferiors.

Other witnesses believe they have seen and heard someone walking the catwalks above the stage—Barbara Hilgier*, for example. She has served on the Sorg's Board of trustees, she is a former secretary of the organization, and has done much technical work for the theatre, including rebuilding stage lighting for the all-volunteer group.

"The first experience I had alone," she says. "The tenor Robert White was in town and Baldwin had loaned us a beautiful grand piano. I had been cleaning up and I sat down to play. I always lock the theatre when I'm there alone so I was surprised to hear footsteps on the metal grid-platform above the stage where pulleys are hung." Hilgier emphasizes that the sound was not a vague creaking, but definite footfalls. "I left rather quickly.

"The year after this we had 'Cookie Cook and Friends,' a tap dancing ensemble. Three of us were there at about two in the morning, hanging lights and bringing in the sound system for the Saturday night show. The theatre was locked as usual, but all of us heard distinctive footfalls going across the back of the stage. We looked at each other and kind of quietly walked Indian file out of there."

The current owner has taken over Paul J. Sorg's favorite seat. It's his favorite too. Says Hilgier, "We just hope that Paul J. still enjoys the shows. The ghost has the best seat in the house!"

7

GRAVE MATTERS
Final resting? places

O grave, where is thy victory?
-I Corinthians 15:55-

The Ghostly Girl of Woodland Cemetery

With the bees buzzing lazily in the flower beds, the birds singing in trees overlooking a scenic pond dotted with white ducks, Dayton's Woodland Cemetery is a lovely place to spend the afternoon. One ghostly young girl has found it a lovely place to spend Eternity.

Patrick R.* of Dayton was quite matter-of-fact: "I see spirits all the time—all over the place." While interviewing him, I casually mentioned the Dayton cemetery.

"I've never seen a spirit there," Patrick said, "But I've got a buddy who's always saying to me, 'let's go up to the cemetery and see if we can see any ghosts.' But *I've* never seen one there."

He paused. "Come to think of it, I *did* see something kind of weird there." He turned to his wife Meg*, "You remember me telling you about that girl crying in Woodland Cemetery?" She nodded.

It was in September, 1990. He had taken a photography class and for the final project he wanted to do a series on tombstones. He cruised through Woodland Cemetery in his car looking for interesting sites to photograph. He drove past a young woman sitting on a fresh grave.

"She was crying, she looked real distressed. Whoever it was that died, she definitely was upset." He turns again to his wife, "You remember, Meg, I came home and told you 'That was so sad.' I couldn't figure out why nobody paid any attention to her. She had long blond hair and blue jeans and...."

I stopped him abruptly, searching in my papers for a newspaper clipping. I found it and began to read: "a girl with long, blond hair wearing a dark blue sweater..."

"She had it tied around her waist!" he broke in, excited.

"...jeans, and Nike tennis shoes..."

"She had her jeans rolled up. It was real hot; I was wearing shorts. I didn't know why she was dressed so warm. What are you reading?"

It was a story from the University of Dayton *Flyer News*[1] about Allan* a student who had an unusual experience at Woodland. UD folklore claims that Woodland has a tombstone that glows in the dark. This tombstone was visible from the north wing of Marycrest, Allan's dorm. Curious about whose grave it was, he decided to try and track it down the next day.

As he approached the grave that afternoon, he saw a young woman with long blond hair sitting on the stone. She wore a dark blue sweater, jeans, and Nike tennis shoes.

"I felt kinda dumb to go up to the tombstone she was sitting on, read the name and just walk away while this girl was watching me," Allan said.

He decided to try again the next day.

"There she was again," Allan said. "You know, the girl in the blue sweater, jeans and Nike tennis shoes, sitting in the same spot with the same clothes. I thought it was kind of freaky but she was probably thinking the same about me. After all, I really didn't have a good reason for being there."

Allan went away and came back the next day. The girl was still there.

"By this time, I was convinced she was a runaway or something, " he said, "Only, she was so clean, like her hair wasn't messed up, as if she never slept or something. And she was sitting in the same position, in the same spot on that tombstone. She didn't say anything. She just didn't move. Now that freaked me out."

He convinced a friend to come with him to Woodland the next day. They crept up on the grave from another direction, but this time the girl was gone.

"My friends all laughed at me, calling me a psycho, making me feel as if I'd really gone crazy," Allan said "Out of humiliation I never went back [to the cemetery]."

Patrick had heard the story of the glowing tombstone, but had never found the grave. He had not heard Allan's story until I told it to him.

Patrick was startled at the corroboration of the stories. At each detail he exclaimed, "Yeah, that's the girl!

"She was a good-looking woman, long blonde hair, thin build, sharp features, a red top, Nike sneakers and she had a blue sweater tied around her waist. I drove past her twice, three times. I couldn't figure out why nobody seemed to see her."

Patrick wonders if he can help the grieving ghost. He also wonders if anyone else out there has seen her. If *you* see the blonde spirit, try to ask her why she is so unhappy. But don't be surprised if, lost in her otherworldly grief, she doesn't see you.

A Chilling Cemetery Encounter

Patrick had another adventure in a cemetery in Bellbrook. On a night with a full moon, you can see the outline of a woman's head on one of the tombstones. Patrick took a group of nonbeliever friends to see if they could witness this phenomenon.

"It was the middle of summer—it was about 75 degrees. But in the cemetery the temperature dropped suddenly until it was real cold and frigid—about 50 degrees." Patrick smiles remembering his friends' reactions. "It made a believer out of them!"

The Tell-tale Tombstone

Sometime in the 1930s, Mrs. Grace Conners* of Carey was found half-strangled in her bed. Her husband, who had found her when he returned from working late, called the doctor. He hovered anxiously while the doctor eased her final moments.

As the doctor bent over Grace, she clutched his arm and, staring at her husband, whispered, "After I am dead I will tell who killed me." Then she died with her eyes fixed on her husband. The doctor smoothed her eyes closed and avoided looking at Connors.

"Burglars," muttered the husband "the back door was smashed in. It had to be burglars."

She was buried and Conners erected a handsome stone to her memory. A year passed. Conners married again and, small towns being what they are, gossip spread that he and the new Mrs. Conners had been very good friends even before Grace's tragic death. Conners pretended not to hear the whispers, but he couldn't avoid hearing about the strange pictures that had materialized on Grace's tombstone.

He hurried to the cemetery. Etched in the polished marble was a picture of a man with his hands around a woman's neck. The faces were those of Conners and his first wife. Even in miniature, the terror was apparent on the woman's darkening face.

Conners struck at the marble, but only succeeded in smashing his hand. He spat on the marble and rubbed savagely at the etching with a handkerchief. To his amazement, it melted away. Limp with relief, he turned to go. Looking back, he saw the faint lines forming their damning picture once again.

Conners walked home and hung himself. Then the picture on the tombstone changed, said the townspeople. The face of Connors grew dark and distorted, while Mrs. Connors' effigy smiled a twisted and triumphant smile.[2]

Tea for the Tomb

To the pioneers, the community of River Styx in Medina County was hell on earth. Founded in 1815, the area was described as a gloomy forest inhabited only by wild animals. Copperheads slithered amid the quicksands of its swamps and muddy river banks.

Such a place of shadowy terrors has its share of ghost stories. One concerns the return of a medium named Lottie Bader. A prominent medium in the Western Reserve area, Lottie died of consumption or (some whispered) of a broken heart after being accused of setting the neighboring Warrett family's house on fire.

Immediately after the blaze, Lottie held a seance where the ghost of a disgruntled farmhand claimed that he had set the mysterious fire. Most people accepted this explanation, except the Warretts, who spread rumors that Lottie and her family knew more about the fire than they rightly should.

After that, Lottie never held another seance. Once lovely, she grew thin, pale, and exhausted. As she lay dying Lottie said to her mother:

"I do not wish to be buried up in the graveyard with other people. Will you dig me a grave as near the kitchen door as possible so that I can be near you and where I can visit you from time to time?"

Sorrowing, her mother agreed. Then a short time before her death, Lottie asked her mother for tea and toast. When Mrs. Bader went to the kitchen she saw a headless woman at the stove making tea. The woman turned and said to her, "This you will have to do once a week the rest of your days."

Lottie died the next day, Friday. Exactly a week later at midnight the mother was awakened by heavy footsteps in the kitchen.

"Who's there?" she called in alarm. Clearly she heard her daughter's voice, "Mother, I am hungry, could you make me tea and get me something to eat?"

Mrs. Bader went to the kitchen but it was empty. In a stupor, she made the tea and toast. Again her daughter's voice said, "Put it on the table, Mother, and go back to bed."

The startled mother complied and the next morning Mrs. Bader found the food had been eaten. The story was the same on the next Friday and the next. Every Friday night for five years, until her own death, Lottie's mother made supper for her dead daughter, and each Friday the ghost ate and drank.

Eventually the body of Lottie was removed from the grave by the kitchen door and reburied in the township cemetery on the hilltop. The headstone reads simply, "Charlotte Bader, Died July 24, 1858, aged 25 years."[3]

The Haunted Monument

In a Marion cemetery stands a strange funerary monument with a life of its own. It is an impressive white granite column topped with a black granite sphere about three feet in diameter. The memorial was erected in 1887 as the centerpiece of the family plot of Charles Merchant and six members of his family.

The monument is not unique; most cemeteries of the period contain at least one similar granite ball mounted on a pedestal. And until 1905 it was just another tombstone.

One morning in July of that year a workman noticed that the heavy black sphere atop the Merchant memorial had been moved. The ball, weighing at least several hundred pounds, had turned several inches, exposing the rough spot on the bottom of the ball where it had been fitted into the top of the pedestal. The workman was puzzled. Pranksters would have needed a block and tackle or a crane to lift the heavy ball. Worried by this anomaly, cemetery officials poured a lead cement into the socket atop the sphere's pedestal and rolled it back into place. Two months later the big black ball had moved ten inches. Once again the rough base spot had rolled into view.

The curious swarmed to wonder and theorize. One of them, a geologist, considered the evidence and decided that the movement of the heavy stone ball was the result of unequal expansion, due to one side lying in the sunshine while the other side remained relatively cool. Other scientists took issue with this. They pointed out that if heat expansion caused the ball's turning, then it ought to turn *toward* the south instead of the opposite direction.

After a while, the flurry of media attention rolled along to the next attraction. The mysterious memorial still stands, its black granite ball with a rough spot near the top, poised atop a white stone pedestal. But there are no black and white answers. No explanation has yet been discovered. But the black marble ball in the Marion cemetery just keeps rolling along.[4]

Johnny Appleseed Returns

Johnny Appleseed was the stuff tall tales are made of. As he passed through the Ohio wilderness planting seedlings, he also passed into the folklore of the land. Stories about Johnny Appleseed emphasize his mysticism, (he is portrayed as a village idiot with a direct line to God), but he was also a shrewd entrepreneur, trading bags of seeds to settlers for land. When he died he was worth a fortune in real estate.

With apples only as far away as the grocery, we cannot comprehend what apples meant to the pioneers. No other fruit could be so easily planted or transported in the form of seeds or seedlings. Apples were for eating, for drying, and making into apple butter, cider, apple jack, and vinegar for pickling. In a frontier community, the first apple crop signified permanency, the budding of civilization.[5]

Johnny Appleseed was a devout follower of Swedenborgian doctrine which believed not only in Heaven, Hell, and the brotherhood of man, but in communication with spirits. So he would have seen nothing strange about the stories that every September he returns to the old family cemetery where his half-brother and other relatives lie buried on a hilltop south of Dexter City.

On September 25, 1942, his 168th birthday, a monument was dedicated to him along Route 21, a few hundred feet from the Noble-Washington County line. A few mornings later, a small boy was the first to see him. The boy had gone to gather hickory nuts brought down by the first frost. On his way he heard a calf, caught in a wire fence, bawling for help. The boy stopped to free the calf and went on his way to hunt hickory nuts. Then he saw Johnny, seated on a low branch of an apple tree near his family's graves.

"Son," said the apparition to the boy, "the apple tree, it does no one harm, but is loaded with good for everyone. Be like the apple tree and I'll always be with you." The startled boy ran for his parents, but they were too late or too blind to see the ghost.

A few mornings later a young woman on her way to help a sick neighbor saw the apparition. Then a mail-carrier, going out of his route to deliver a soldier's letter to his mother, saw Johnny too.

Everyone who sees him tells the same tale: Johnny Appleseed perches on a low branch of an apple tree, swinging his rough, bare feet. He wears ill-fitting pants, held up by one suspender, a mush pot for a hat, and a long grey beard. He munches one of his own apples and reads a New Church tract. And he smiles at those favored ones who see him—each a visionary like himself.[6]

8

A GHOST AROUND THE HOUSE
Household hauntings

The dead had no houses of their own...They might go every Saturday and visit the house where their widow or widower still lived with their children. They might temporarily occupy their old bedroom....
-Emmanual Le Roy Ladurie, *Montaillou-*

The word "haunt" comes from a Germanic word which means "to fetch home." Some people get so attached to a house or piece of property, that they just can't bear to leave—even when evicted by death.

The Spectral Schoolteacher

Linda Pierce* and her husband fell in love with the house in Kettering at first sight. A charming white one and a half story with a big picture window, it was surrounded by beautiful shrubs and shaded by a large old oak tree. It had been advertised as a rental, but the Pierces learned that it was part of the estate of a Miss Smith*, an old-maid schoolteacher who had taught at the old Dorothy Lane school. The house seemed perfect in every way, except one.

"We had small children," said Linda "and my husband would take them out a couple of nights a week so I could have some time off." It seemed that every time Linda was alone in the house, "funny things happened." One of these was the lights: they would flicker briefly or sometimes go dark for several minutes. Either was frightening.

Linda worried that there was a dangerous short in the wiring that might cause a fire, so Dayton Power & Light sent out some repairmen to check things out. Not only was the wiring fine, DP&L couldn't find any reason the lights should misbehave. Her husband scoffed at her fears—until the lights went out when *he* was home.

The lights malfunctioned for about six months. Then Linda happened to watch the *Phil Donahue Show*. The topic was psychic phenomenon. A light dawned about why the lights went off:

"I might have a ghost!" Linda thought, startled. The idea frightened her, but after listening to the show, "I thought it might be a real possibility that we had something like that going on."

Linda kept her suspicions to herself. After all, she told herself, the flickering lights didn't really hurt anything and they always came back on. Linda did a little sleuthing. She had assumed that Miss Smith had died in a hospital, but found that the woman had actually died in the back bedroom where her youngest daughter slept. Clue Number One: A ghost often haunts the site of death.

Then Linda actually saw Miss Smith. "I was awakened one night, I don't know why exactly. I sat up and looked into the hallway. I didn't see a face, but I saw the form of a woman, a tall, large figure floating several inches off the floor in the hallway." The figure moved quickly from the back bedroom towards Linda's room. It looked "foggy," and seemed to have "short cropped brown hair, like just to the ear." Somehow Linda was not frightened, but lay back down. When she sat up again, the figure was gone. Linda woke her husband. Annoyed, he told her to go back to sleep, certain there was nothing there.

But Linda was positive she had seen the figure. The next morning she sat in bed to confirm that she really could have seen out the door at that angle and that distance. From her bed to the door was only ten or fifteen feet. After thinking about her strange experience, she went over to her neighbor's.

"'Alison*,' I said to my neighbor, 'I want to describe to you what I think Miss Smith looked like.' When I got to the brown, short-cropped hair, Alison exclaimed, 'That's exactly what Miss Smith looked like.' She wanted to know if I had found a photograph or something. I said 'no, but I think I saw her at my house last night.'"

After that, all manifestations ceased. Linda thinks she knows why.

"I found out that the house had been Miss Smith's pride and joy—the only thing she cared for in the world." Clue Number Two: A ghost often wants to stay in a place it has loved very much.

"It was almost like she was coming around to look us over," Linda says "to see that we were the right kind of people to take care of her house. That night I saw her, I think I felt something like 'I want people to love this house'—which was possibly a projection from me. I wanted this woman to know that we were going to take care of her house and how much we loved it. I didn't really know how to relay this to her, but she seems to have gotten the message."

The Ghostly Interior Decorator

Sitting in its charming Victorian garden at 586 E. Town Street in Columbus is Kelton House, a handsome Greek Revival mansion, "living museum," and quite possibly a haven for the dead. Built in 1852 by Fernando Cortez Kelton, the house was occupied by his descendants until 1975 when Fernando's granddaughter, Grace Bird Kelton, died on Christmas Eve. Miss Kelton, a nationally known interior decorator, kept the interior much as it was in Fernando's day. Today Kelton House brings to graceful life a Civil War- era home. Run by the Junior League, the house is available for tours, meetings, weddings, and receptions.

It is said that Miss Kelton still keeps an eye on her beloved home—to the extent of rearranging the furniture and leaving out cleaning supplies when unhappy with decorating plans for the house. Footsteps have been heard in the attic by staff who were alone in the building. And a tour guide noticed a woman stray from her group. She followed the woman into one of the museum rooms, from which there was no other exit, only to find that the woman had disappeared.

One of two full-time office workers notes that "things in the offices are always being misplaced and turning up in the oddest of places and we've had file cabinets become mysteriously locked." Since there are only two workers, she notes, some of the incidents are difficult to explain. Overall though, they feel that their ghost is a friendly one.

One woman who helped restore Kelton house believed that the house was haunted by the ghost of Fernando Kelton who died there after he was injured in a fall from his office window. During Christmas week in 1978, she reports, "I heard the door being slammed four times and the furniture being dragged. I also heard some faraway rumblings in the attic."

Since all this took place during Christmas week, near the anniversary of Grace Bird Kelton's death, one wonders if the ghost wasn't Miss Kelton, redecorating for the holidays.[1]

Carrie Ann Carries On

Being more sensitive than most people, psychic Micki Adams realized she had a ghost almost as soon as she moved into her 1850s-era Yellow Springs house in 1986.

"I 'saw' her in the living room, looking out the window. She was very wistful and sad. I somehow knew this was because she was sickly and couldn't go out." Micki sighs empathetically. "She wanted to go out so much."

The apparition was a slight, hollow-cheeked young woman who looked like she was in her mid-twenties. She wore grey and brown 1920s clothing and her brown hair was cut medium short, "like her mother bobbed her hair," says Micki. "She tensed up when she saw me and I felt that she was afraid of me.

"I said out loud, 'Don't be afraid.' I wanted her to know that I wasn't going to try to get rid of her, that we could coexist. How much space could a spirit take up, anyway?" After Micki talked to her, the apparition went away, but she saw the young woman periodically after that. And the spirit told Micki about herself.

"She told me her name was Carrie Ann. She was very close to her father, which touched me because I was close to mine. She couldn't go out because she was sickly. I feel that she had tuberculosis—she certainly looked like she did, but she could have had allergies—this area is still called 'Sinus Valley.'

"Whenever her father left the house, he would always say to her, 'Carry on, Carrie Ann.'"

Without knowing the story, a visiting friend told Micki, "There was someone standing behind you the whole time we were talking."

Micki fired off a battery of questions: "Male or female? Fat or thin? Young or old?"

The answers all fit with what Micki had perceived. Feeling a little like "they're going to lock me up," Micki wanted to see if there was any earthly proof of Carrie Ann's existence. She visited the Xenia Library's Greene County Room, which specializes in local history.

"There were two Carries who lived on Xenia Ave. in Yellow Springs. Unfortunately the 1910 census didn't give house numbers, so I couldn't tell where on Xenia Avenue they were. But one was too old and was married and had kids. The other Carrie was not married and was fourteen in 1910, which would make her just about twenty-four if she was alive in the 1920s."

According to the census, Carrie's middle initial was *F*. So how could she be called "Carrie *Ann*," Micki wondered. Julie Overton, genealogy specialist with the Greene County Room, and an expert on names says that "Ann" was often a diminutive of "Francis."

"I don't know about that," says Micki, impressed by Overton's expertise, "but I wouldn't argue with Julie."

After Micki's research, Carrie Ann's visits diminished. Micki knows that Carrie Ann is still around, but "I don't see a whole lot of her. I do feel that she's comfortable." And still carrying on beyond death.

The Room With No Door

The ghost in Matt Goeller's house was basically a friendly one. In fact, she had only one flaw—she kept getting him in trouble with his dad.

"For years and years, my father used to get me up in the morning and say, 'Matt, you left the damn light on in the cabin room again.'"

Matt, a production manager at Dayton's WHIO-AM, chuckles as he remembers trying to convince his father he hadn't.

"Over and over and over he'd say I'd left the light on and I'd say, 'Dad, I didn't. I'm telling you I *didn't* leave the light on,' and we'd get into it. We went back and forth a million times!"

The cabin room was an unusual feature of their Oakwood mansion, built by a prominent Dayton family in the 1920s. Designed to make the owners feel like they were in a hunting lodge, the cabin room looked just like the inside of a cabin with log walls and a huge beamed ceiling. The walls were were covered with the heads of moose and other hunting trophies. There was also a large chandelier made out of deer antlers—the chandelier that Matt's father accused him of leaving on.

One day, Matt was finally vindicated. He was watching TV with his two younger brothers in the cabin room with the lights off. Then, "I have no idea why, but somehow that light came on by itself—without the switch thrown. And the TV went off too." Despite the fact that the same thing happened on two different occasions when his brothers were there to witness it, his father never really apologized and is still a little skeptical about the whole thing.

Could it have been an electrical quirk? Matt doesn't think so. "At the time this happened, we'd just put the house up for sale. An electrical inspection was done and everything was OK."

Matt always chalked up the disturbances to "our friendly pal Edna," as he and his family called the house ghost. "She was never nasty to us. We called her Edna because we got a boxful of keys when we bought the house. All of the keys were labeled with the kids' names: 'Doug's* Room,' 'Sissy's*

Room'—like that. We accounted for all of the keys except for one marked 'Edna's Room.' We never found the door that it fit."

An odd key—and, to match, the house has a room with no door. A window is visible from the outside, but inside, there is no way into the room. Peering through the window, all that can be seen, says Matt, is "just darkness. A black wall."

It is a chilling suggestion of the darkness of the grave. Perhaps, long ago, Edna was sent to her room, and has never left it.

Final Harvest

Next to his farm and his wife, the old Miami County farmer loved his white cat. That cat could do no wrong and the farmer insisted that the big barn door always be left open a crack so the cat could come and go as it pleased.

The old farmer died at harvest time, a fitting time to be gathered to his rest. Death or not, the crops still had to be brought in, so Will*, the old man's son, rented out the farm to George Crooks*, who cut and stacked the bales of hay in the barn. The white cat wandered in and out, hunting field mice and grasshoppers.

Since George didn't live on the property, Will asked him to lock the barn at night. The barn door was a heavy steel one that slid on a track, almost too heavy for one man to manage alone. It locked with a turn bolt and a padlock and should have been secure, but Will noticed that while George was kind to the white cat, he always seemed to forget to lock the barn.

George insisted that his last act every night was to lock that barn door. Still, every morning the big steel door was found open, just a crack. Tramps, thieves, or vagrants—that was the only explanation Will could think of. George swore that no one could get in after he locked up and pointed out that none of the expensive equipment in the barn had been taken.

George got rather touchy about it so the following year Will rented the farm to Adam*, a young man who had no patience with any suggestion of the supernatural. The white cat was included in the deal. One evening when he was outside, Adam heard a scraping sound. He turned around just in time to see the barn door sliding open. On another occasion the young man had secured all the doors and was walking away when the white cat got under his feet. He spun around to keep his balance—and saw that the hasp he had just locked was swinging back and forth, open.

In a panic he told Will what had happened. At last Will realized that in all the years of his father's life, the barn had never been locked. Perhaps locking the barn had somehow upset his father, offended his ideas about trust. Or maybe he was just looking after his cat. One day the white cat was found dead. After that the sliding barn door stayed closed—so long as Will didn't lock it. A few years later, Will sold off the property. He was careful to tell the new people about the door. They took the matter quite seriously. At first, they said, they noticed a "tension" in the barn, but after the animals were stabled there, "the old man" seemed to be happy and content. And they are careful never to lock the barn.

The Small Ghost of Middletown

Susan Gawron speaks apologetically about their ghost: "We have a *small* ghost." She sounds regretful that she can't tell me about any indelible bloodstains or clanking chains. "Nothing *major* has happened," she says, "just a lot of little things that my husband and I can't account for any other way."

Their Middletown house is a handsome Queen Anne painted in the original colors: yellow with green and white trim. Built in 1903, the house remained in the same family until the 1950s. Houses of this age have seen many births and deaths. Susan believes that their small ghost has been there a long time. She has never seen it, but Hoover, her cat, has.

"Hoover is very high-strung and he acts very strange sometimes. In the master bedroom, he's actually walked backwards while his fur puffed out so he was twice his normal size. I've seen him definitely staring at something invisible." At those times Susan has felt "a presence."

She believes that the presence is a child, a boy, although she doesn't know exactly why she thinks this, except that the manifestations have seemed "prankish." Her research has uncovered at least one little boy who died in the house.

Some of the occurrences certainly suggest a childish sense of humor:

"We got a new address book and we put it in the drawer, the same place we'd always kept it." One day Dan went to use it. "Gee, where's the address book?" he asked. They emptied the drawer and searched for several days, thankful that they hadn't thrown the old address book away. After five days, "one morning we came down and there it was in the middle of the kitchen table. I know we didn't eat on top of it for five days," Susan adds firmly.

Another time Susan missed a camisole. She asked Dan if he'd seen it. Naturally he hadn't and he joked, "I'm not wearing it." Because bedroom closet space is limited, Susan keeps her wardrobe in the other bedroom closet. A few mornings later she walked into the room and found the camisole carefully spread out on the floor. "I didn't walk on it for those days, either."

One of her husband's ghostly aggravations is his "little feud with the light in the attic." The entrance to the attic is through his closet and the attic light turns on with an old-fashioned and rather stiff turnknob. Says Susan, "He'll open the closet door one morning, look up and see that the light is on. He'll turn it off, then come home from work and find the light back on. This goes on for several days, then it stops until the next time, a couple of months later."

Susan has experienced another annoying manifestation. "On Tuesdays I used to work a half day, then I'd come home and do some housework. On the mantle in the parlor, I had a set of Heisey candlesticks that had belonged to my mother and a few other knick-knacks. About six months after we moved in, I came in to dust and the things on the mantle were rearranged—and not in a very attractive manner, either. I thought to myself, 'I can't believe Dan would do this.' and I put them back the way I wanted. The next Tuesday and the next, it happened again. Finally I said to Dan, 'Do you really think this looks attractive?' Of course, he hadn't moved anything.

"One Tuesday, I had a really bad day at work. I came home to find that the mantle was rearranged again and one of the Heisey candlesticks was balanced precariously half on and half off the mantle. I yelled out, 'I can't believe you would do a thing like this. These candlesticks mean a lot to me. They could have been broken! Just knock it off!' Then I started to storm out of the room and a candle came flying by my head. I guess the ghost didn't appreciate being yelled at. But the mantle hasn't been rearranged since."

Susan breaks off her story to apologize again, "I'm afraid these aren't very exciting stories—they're just small things that we can't really explain." Small and inexplicable—not unlike their very busy "small ghost."

The Ghost Followed Him Home

Roger Killian-Spencer* of Beavercreek, a Dayton suburb, has seen "entities" from the time he was a child, but when he was seventeen, a session with a ouija board conjured up an obsessive spirit who followed him home.

"The first time I talked to the spirit, my girlfriend and I had been using the ouija board, which I do not recommend *anybody* using!" he adds emphatically. They set up the board at a playground behind an elementary school in Beavercreek. First they talked to a male spirit who was coming across very faintly:

"In mid-sentence we could tell that something stronger was taking over. She spelled out her name: G-E-E-Z-E-L-L [pronounced Zhih-zell, like the ballet character, Giselle, who is captured by the spirits of the dead]. I asked her why she was talking to us.

"She said she had been following me. When I asked her why, she said at first that it was like an magnetic pull, then she claimed that we were interested in similar things."

Uneasy after these messages, Killian-Spencer stopped using the board. Then Geezell showed up at his house.

"I was going upstairs. I looked up and she was just standing there at the top of the stairs. I can't say that I was actually afraid, because I'm used to seeing unexplainable things. I immediately knew who it was. Our dog who was with me, was curious about her. He just sat there, ears cocked forward, looking up at her without barking.

"I was surprised when I saw her. I had always felt safe in my house because between my mother, who is a very determined woman, and myself, it would be difficult for anything malignant to get in.

"Speaking telepathically I told the spirit to go away. 'OK,' I said, 'you've proven your point, you're in the house. I don't want to deal with you right now.' She didn't say anything, just faded out."

Killian-Spencer continued up the stairs to his room.

"I probably walked through her. I felt a definite cold spot. I went in my room and felt certain that she couldn't get into it. My room is my sanctuary," he explained "kind of a bastion against—whatever. If I can't be safe there, I'm up the creek!"

After that first appearance, Geezell haunted the hall outside Killian-Spencer's room.

"She was in her mid-40s, about 5 foot 6 inches and well-proportioned for her height. I would say she was quite attractive. She had light-colored hair—ash blond or white—I could never really tell which. She was always transparent—I could see the wall behind her. She liked wearing lacy things— antique lace. All of her clothes seemed to be either white or grey in a form-fitting late Victorian, early Edwardian style with long skirts. I got the feeling that her clothes would have appeared racy at the time. Once she wore a cameo brooch that had her own profile carved on it.

She usually wore her hair loose on her shoulders. I only saw it up in a bun once; she had a widow's peak. Her face was remarkable, with very unusual steel-grey eyes. I remember the eyes particularly because of an evening when she brought somebody else with her. That night she was at her strongest, and she stood very close—about a foot from me.

"The gentleman she brought with her was about 5 foot 10 inches—not much taller than her. He had a very nondescript round face, a stocky barrel body. He wore simple clothes: a buttoned up shirt, trousers, no hat. He was balding a little, with darker hair than hers, and a mustache. He had a different kind of air—he was the one I was worried about. I never did find out what their connection was."

Geezell never stayed very long—an hour at the most, but Killian-Spencer often got migraines after speaking to her telepathically because of the intense concentration involved.

"Off and on I had dreams where she would speak to me. She didn't say anything memorable, we just talked about her and why she was here. She said that she was attracted to my energy.

"I think that as time went on her fascination with me became more obsessive and it became more of a game to see if she could get in my room, or catch me off guard. I often got very angry with her. I'm very protective of my sister and she sometimes insinuated that she would move out of the hall into my sister's room and show herself to my sister. At those times I would sit down and say, 'Fine, we'll talk.' She knew this was an effective tactic to get me to talk to her. She also tried to pressure me into using the ouija board *alone*. I wasn't that stupid.

"Gradually her games became more petty and I lost patience. At first I didn't feel any bad intentions from her, but I think that she became frustrated and that began to sour her. I demanded that she leave me alone. I threatened to do nasty things like kick her out of the house. Actually I was just bluffing.

"Geezell didn't know how much I could really do—which was to my advantage. I conned her until one night when I again used the ouija in the house because she was really starting to bug me. My best friend and my girlfriend pooled the things we know. And I thought between the three of us, we could kind of gang up on her.

"The board session didn't go very smoothly because I lost my temper, to the chagrin of both of my friends. I was to the point where I wasn't bluffing any more. Something told me that I had the energy to get rid of her. I was just sick of the whole thing.

"Geezell said goodbye in a hurry. My friends went home. That night I was doing some meditation and as I came out of the meditation before I went to sleep, I saw Geezell and the other gentleman standing at the foot of my bed. She was at her strongest.

"What bothered me the most was that they were actually in my room without alerting me. I think if I hadn't been in a trance, they wouldn't have gotten in. I was mad! I did something called 'expanding auras,' where you turn your aura from a natural mental defense into an offensive mechanism and extend your physical presence. They were forced outside the room on whatever 'semi-plane' they're on. I calmed down a little bit.

"But the gentleman came back into my room very easily. I got so upset that I don't remember exactly what I did. I think I did the same thing again, only three or four times stronger. I could feel that it worked. He was *gone*. But I could still see Geezell out in the hall. At that point I asked her to come back in to my room so we could discuss this. I didn't worry about her being stronger than me any more. I knew she couldn't defeat me.

"I put a hex on her. It stuck her out in the hallway and it kept her there. After that I never felt her energy as strongly as at first. I last saw her in late July of 1989."

The family moved from the house in spring of 1991. Killian-Spencer recently walked by the house.

"It struck me that she's still stuck there, she can't move, she's tied to the house. But the hex isn't everlasting, I don't think. It was made in the heat of the moment. If I were to undo the hex now, would she get angry at the house? Would she get angry at me or follow me? I don't know...."

The Ghost in Possession

Galen Finley, owner of the haunted McConnelsville Opera House also owns a haunted house. It was built in 1843 for Frances Gage, a figure in the Women's Rights movement, who hosted Susan B. Anthony at the house. As a young man Finley did odd jobs for William Bash*, the owner of the 11-room house. After Bash died, his daughter sold the house to Finley along with all the furniture, paintings, and a grand piano because she couldn't bear to see the furnishings sold separately. Her father had loved the house and she knew Finley would too. But Bash was reluctant to relinquish possession.

"When I moved in," says Finley, "anyone else could go out in the hall and nothing would happen. But when I'd appear in the hall or even near to it, the closet door under the stairs would open every time. Finally one night I started up the steps and the door opened. My mother and another friend were washing the windows on the front door. When this happened, Mother turned around and addressed the old man who had owned the house: "William Bash! Now, William, enough is enough. My son is restoring your home back to its original grandeur. And you should be thrilled to pieces and sit back and enjoy yourself because your home is going to be back as it was in your heyday when you were a wealthy man. Leave my son alone!" Finley chuckles as he remarks, "Nothing's happened since."

The Ghosts of Patterson Homestead

It has been said that ghosts happen where there has been a lot of *living*. There has been a lot of living in Dayton's Patterson Homestead. And, so it seems, quite a few ghosts.

Built as a farmhouse in 1816 by Col. Robert Patterson, Dayton's Patterson Homestead is a handsome three-story Federal-style brick building, restored as a family home of the 1816-1868 era. Antiques and family memorabilia are displayed on the first two floors with its graceful staircase and tall windows. The third floor, which is not open to the public, still has the remnants of family apartments. Trees and bushes set off the full beauty of the house which overlooks a sweeping lawn on Brown Street. Festivals, speakers, and tours keep the house lively.

Early in 1989, Kirby Turner, the Director of the Montgomery County Historical Society, was working in the basement while a woman's group held a meeting in the auditorium. Turner heard heavy footsteps on the stairs behind him. Thinking in irritation that he'd have to shoo the intruders away, he whirled. And there was nobody there.

"There was no question in my mind that there *had* been somebody on the stairs," he says. Right away, he went up the stairs to check the kitchen, with negative results. He even walked over to the meeting room to ask if anyone had strayed into the basement. Negative again. Says Turner, "It took me a while before it hit me that it was something unnatural." He recollects that the footsteps were heavy ones, like a man wearing boots. And he is certain he heard them.

On a cold April Sunday in 1989 a volunteer named Danielle* found herself trapped by a mysteriously jammed door. She had just finished a tour and had gone to the kitchen for a cup of tea before her next group when the door into the kitchen slammed shut violently. Thinking that a breeze had caught the door, she pushed and pushed on it, but found that it was completely jammed. Then she heard her tour party knocking on the front door.

"Oh no," thought Danielle "I'll have to go out the back kitchen door and around to the front to let them in." At that, a door leading from the adjoining pantry into the dining room slowly swung open. Danielle was baffled. The door to the dining room had been kept locked as long as she had been there. It took two people to unstick the jammed door in the hall.

Another mysterious breeze arose when Mrs. Dorothy Patterson visited the house. As she walked through the front hall, a strong wind came out of the parlor on the left, as if someone were breezing by.

One of the most puzzling incidents concerned some gingerbread men, Christmas decorations, which had been dipped in a foul-smelling formalin-based preservative and hung on a line in the basement to dry. The next day Patterson Manager Mollie Williams went to the basement and found all but one of the cookies yanked off the rope, lying on a table beneath. At first she suspected rats or mice had chewed through the strings, but the strings had been vigorously jerked apart, not gnawed. Mollie Williams and Kirby Turner are the only persons with keys to the house and they were mystified. Did one of the Pattersons object to the smell of the preserva-tive, which might have reminded him of embalming fluid used during the Civil War? Or did it offend some ghostly, but still-fastidious Patterson housewife?

Patterson has its own ghost of Christmas past. During a Christmas tea eight people were being given a candlelight tour. On the second floor, one of them came to Mrs. T.*, the tour guide, saying,

"Didn't you say we weren't supposed to go up to the third floor? I just saw someone walk up those stairs." Mrs. T.

quickly counted heads and immediately rushed to the stairway. From the side, she saw the legs of a man wearing tall polished boots ascending the stairs. As she reached the bottom of the stairs, she saw the man looking down at her from the third floor. It was a man in military uniform wearing riding boots—perhaps Frank Patterson who was killed while testing aircraft at Wright Field. And then, he wasn't there.

Patterson volunteers have smelled ghostly odors like a light flower perfume, fresh-baked cookies, and boiling green beans in the empty kitchen. When I toured the house I felt "someone" on the entire third floor, one of the second-floor bedrooms, and in the basement. Psychic Micki Adams felt "an intense sadness" in the front bedroom—a woman rocking her sick child. Medium Kathleen Cook saw a man at the desk in the front room downstairs. "He was just sitting there watching everybody. I didn't ask him anything." She felt spirits in other rooms and heard children laughing and playing. Many volunteers have experienced the feeling of "a presence."

A benign presence, thinks Kirby Turner. "Like 'they' are watching over the house, interested in what's going on." Manager Mollie Williams, who has been so effective in making the house a popular attraction, says that people used to complain about Patterson Homestead being "so cold." Now, they say, the house feels much warmer. As if a ghostly someone approves?

9

RESTING IN PIECES
Dis-embodied spirits

Are we not spirits that are shaped into a body?
-Thomas Carlyle-

Some ghosts have a difficult time pulling themselves
together. Decapitated, fragmented, or shattered, they wander,
searching for their better halves with lanterns and candles, or
simply groping in the dark. Come the Last Day and the
resurrection of the body, perhaps they'll find themselves.

Ohio's "Sleepy Hollow"

Bellbrook was once called "Ohio's Sleepy Hollow"
because of the reputation it had for ghosts and strange legends.
It, too, had a headless ghost.

James Buckley was an Englishman who built a sawmill
along Sugar Creek (then known as Possum Run Creek) in
Bellbrook. The sawmill prospered and Buckley became a
wealthy man. Someone who coveted the gold coins hidden in
his cabin, waylaid him on the road, struck off his head, and left
the corpse bleeding in the dust. The head was discovered in the
road, filthy and unrecognizable, the hair matted with blood.

The murderer was never caught and it was whispered that Buckley's cabin was haunted. Local residents avoided it, so the new owner rented it to an unsuspecting Dayton couple. Shortly after they moved in, the wife ran into the village, screaming that a man with his head under his arm was standing at her door. Buckley's ghost walks down by Little Sugar Creek, holding out his arms, imploring passersby for help.[1]

Deep Cut Ghost

Many headless ghosts began their careers by being robbed and murdered. Now they wander, seeking their heads—and revenge on their killers. The headless ghost of Deep Cut (between Old Washington and Cambridge on U.S. 40) was a laborer who worked on the National Road. He saved most of his earnings—a fact noted by several of his workmates. One payday he disappeared and was never seen again until his apparition began frightening horses on the road. His murderers had shoveled his headless body under tons of road fill. It now lies entombed under concrete and asphalt, but the laborer's ghost still stumbles across Route 40, caught in the headlights of passing cars.[2]

The Headless Conductor of Moonville

A headless railroad conductor walks the line near the ghost town of Moonville in Zaleski State Forest. Moonville sprang up around the local iron furnaces over 100 years ago, but all that is left is an old railroad tunnel and some traces of where the tracks once ran.

The story goes that a B & O conductor was having an affair with an engineer's wife. Insane with jealousy, the engineer asked the conductor to check something under the train, then ran over him, slicing off his head.

The track still exists today. It's the most god-forsaken stretch on the B & O Railroad between St. Louis and Parkersburg, according to George Tolliver, who remembers walking the tracks between Mineral and Moonville. The railroad tracks went through two tunnels and over four trestles. There were no roads so you had to walk the tracks to get between the two villages. If you got trapped in a tunnel or on a trestle, it would be your last trip, Tolliver recalls, noting that he himself nearly died on a trestle about 80 years ago. He's heard many tales of the ghost, most describing him as "a colored man, eight feet tall, looking like he was walking on stilts, a miner's cap with an oil lamp on his head with flame flowing back over his shoulder...always walking down the track."[3]

Others have heard the conductor's last screams. Some see his red and green lantern bobbing along the tracks as he weaves through the forest looking for his head. When he finds it, the engineer will have hell to pay.[4]

Ghost on Lady Bend Hill

Lady Bend Hill on Route 40 in Belmont County is haunted by the ghost of a headstrong—and headless woman who died after an argument with her lover. The young woman galloped away in a rage, even though a storm threatened. She was decapitated by a bolt of lightning and her body was never found. Now she startles motorists on the third bend from the top of the hill, appearing as a headless woman mounted sidesaddle on a ghostly white horse, which streaks down the road like lightning. A stagecoach driver who saw her on New Year's Day, 1896, a day of record-breaking cold, related that he saw a headless woman rider floating in the icy air. He whipped his team, but was senseless with fear by the time he reached his destination.[5]

The Headless Indian

The Riddle School, on Township Route 593, was built in 1886. Now the Katotawa Community Club, it was named for Katotawa, an Indian who was very friendly towards early Ashland County settlers. Despite this, a settler who believed that "the only good injun is a dead injun," beheaded Katotawa and threw his head into a stream. On dark and misty nights, Katotawa's headless ghost, blood spurting from the ragged stump of his neck, wanders blindly by the stream which now bears his name.[6]

The Hundredth Skull

In the early part of this century Bill Quick, trapper and frontiersman, lived in a cabin on the upper Scioto, not far from the present town of Kenton. As he returned from hunting one evening, he found his cabin ransacked and his father dead in a pool of congealed blood, a raw strip of flesh where his hair had been.

Quick swore an oath on a jug of hard cider that he would revenge his father's death a hundredfold. All the Indians grew to fear him—the death that walked in darkness. They never knew how or when he would take his revenge: by a knife flashing death from beyond the trees. By a bullet as they lay down their weapons to paddle across a river. Or by ax that clove off their skulls as they slept—hideous fruit to be placed in a sack and carried home.

Bill Quick worked as well as his name, but unlike his enemies, the scalp was not enough. He took the whole head, burying it in the ground until it was as bright as a wolf's tooth. Then he would add the skull to the row of ninety-nine ghastly trophies grinning down at him from a ledge in his cabin.

But the terrified Indians were moving to safer lands by the lakes and the ones who remained were warier. Before Quick could complete his revenge, he was seized with Black Water Fever. He called his son Tom to him and pointed a shaking finger at the skulls.

"Finish what I have started," he whispered. "If you fail, my father and I will rise from our graves and haunt you until the hundredth skull is taken."

Trembling, Tom promised. Bill Quick died and was buried. Unlike his father, Tom was a poor shot and had no taste for blood. Day after day he put off fulfilling his promise. He sat in the cabin and drank, until it seemed that the skulls gibbered and clacked their teeth at him in chattering mockery.

Soon everyone knew that Tom was sworn to kill an Indian and everyone laughed at the sluggard. One night, when Tom had been drinking more heavily than usual, a group of his friends reported that a band of Indians was in the area. They ridiculed him and taunted his manhood until he picked up his rifle and staggered out of the cabin in search of the last skull.

Riding home, his friends heard a shot fired; they laughed and cheered. The next morning they called upon Tom to congratulate him. Knocking brought no answer; they pushed the door open. The hundredth skull stood in the place reserved for it, polished as bright as ivory, with a bullet hole in the forehead. Tom Quick's headless body lay beneath it.[7]

The Ghostly Hand

In April, 1958 a ghostly hand drove a family out of their apartment on Mason Court in Cleveland. The Lees* moved into the apartment in November of 1957. Immediately they were disturbed by mysterious moans and groans and screams from the basement. The following March Mrs. Lee bravely decided to investigate.

She descended through the trap door into the basement. It was a nightmare of clutter, with piles of broken furniture lurking like monsters in its darkened corners. Mrs. Lee slowly walked around, wondering if they had just imagined the noises. In the gloom something stark white caught her eye. It was a bloody hand thrust rigidly through the debris, the stiff fingers clawing at the air. Mrs. Lee went berserk and ran screaming from the house.

Lee thought his hysterical wife was exaggerating. There *had* to be some perfectly normal explanation. Sitting in the kitchen, trying to soothe her, he watched as the basement trap door lifted under his wife's feet and she fell. "Who's there?" Lee shouted, trying to see through the dark below the floor. He searched the basement. There was no one there. Lee raced upstairs and nailed down the door.

The next day the family moved out. Lee couldn't get anyone to believe his story, so on March 31 he took some friends to the apartment with him. As Lee told his story in the kitchen, the trap door burst open, splintering the wood where it had been nailed down. Terrified, they all ran into the living room. There they saw ghostly fingers wiggling at them through holes in the floor.

Lee called the police. They saw the holes in the floor, the wrecked trap door, but they found nothing tangible to account for the any of it. One police officer said he heard something that sounded like dirt being shoveled in the basement. The Lees never returned to the house.

Lee later talked with the neighbors who told him that a husband and wife had lived in the apartment years ago. They quarreled violently; the husband told the neighbors that his wife had run off and then he moved away. The wife was never seen again in her entirety. The rumor was that the husband had murdered and dismembered his wife and hidden the parts in the basement. The case was investigated by ghost hunter Hans Holzer in 1963, but the only spirits he found were fumes hanging around a drunk who was sleeping it off in the house.[8]

The Half-There Haunting

One night in November, D. Bellows* was the only person working late at Creek Realty* in Beavercreek. He was getting some copier paper out of the cabinet in the back room when he heard a noise: "a knock or a bump, like the front door opening." He started to straighten up.

"Hello?" called Bellows, thinking that a colleague had come in the back door. As he spoke, in the doorway he saw a person dressed in "a calf-length black dress and high-button 1890s shoes." The trouble was, the person was only half there—from the thighs down.

"Between the time I said 'hello' and completely straightened up was only a microsecond, but it was gone. I walked into the hall to see where what I'd seen had gone. I felt a cold draft go across my face, but the back door was shut."

Bellows explained that the pneumatic door closer took eight seconds to close and he had only taken about two to cover the eight feet to the back door. He stood there, baffled. Then, jarringly, the phone rang.

In shock, Bellows croaked, "Hello?" instead of the standard, "Good evening, Creek Realty."

"Have I reached Creek Realty?" asked the caller.

Completely rattled, Bellows blurted, "I'm sorry, I just saw the ghost."

The caller, who was one of his co-workers, laughed. At her suggestion the ghost was dubbed Esmerelda. Someone else in the office suggested that the ghost was a "displaced phantom." A historic log cabin next door had just been torn apart for removal. Bellows couldn't bring himself to ask if any leg bones had been found in the rubble.

Nonplussed, Bellows still shakes his head about the event. "I didn't want to, expect to, or need to see anything like that. It was really weird. I don't talk to things I don't see," he says emphatically. Which, to D. Bellows, means that something only half there—or possibly present only in spirit—visited Creek Realty that November night.

The Spectral Skeleton of the Great Black Swamp

In *Myths and Legends of Our Native Land*, Charles M. Skinner tells a grisly tale of a dismembered skeleton in the Great Black Swamp.

Two miles south of Munger, Ohio, in the heart of what used to be called the Black Swamp, stood the Woodbury House, a roomy mansion long gone to decay. John Cleves, the last to live in it, was a man whose evil practices got him into the penitentiary, but people had never associated him with the queer sights and sounds in the lower chambers, nor with the fact that a man named Syms, who had gone to that house in 1842, had never been known to leave it. Ten years after Sym's disappearance it happened that Major Ward and his friend John Stow had occasion to take shelter there for the night—it being then deserted,— and, starting a blaze in the parlor fireplace, they lit their pipes and talked till late. Stow would have preferred a happier topic, but the major, who feared neither man nor devil, constantly turned the talk on the evil reputation of the house.

While they chatted a door opened with a creak and a human skeleton appeared before them.

"What do you want? Speak!" cried Ward. But waiting for no answer he drew his pistols and fired two shots at the grisly object. There was a rattling sound, but the skeleton was neither dislocated nor disconcerted. Advancing deliberately, with upraised arm, it said, in a husky voice, "I, that am dead, yet live in a sense that mortals do not know. In my earthly life I was James Syms, who was robbed and killed here in my sleep by John Cleves." With bony finger it pointed to a rugged gap in its left temple.

"Cleves cut off my head and buried it under the hearth. My body he cast into his well." At these words the head disappeared and the voice was heard beneath the floor, "Take up my skull." The watchers obeyed the call, and after digging a minute beneath the hearth a fleshless head with a wound on the left temple came to view. Ward took it into his hands, but in a twinkling it left them and appeared on the shoulders of the skeleton.

"I have long wanted to tell my fate," it resumed, "but could not until one should be found brave enough to speak to me. I have appeared to many, but you are the first who has commanded me to break my long silence. Give my bones a decent burial. Write to my relative, Gilmore Syms, of Columbus, Georgia, and tell him what I have revealed. I have found peace."

With a grateful gesture it extended its hand to Ward, who , as he took it, shook like one with an ague, his wrist locked in its bony clasp. As it released him it raised its hand impressively. A bluish light burned at the doorway for an instant. The two men found themselves alone.[9]

Ghastly Ghostly Odors

The ghost of an odor? It seems impossible, but phantom scents are a notable, if elusive, form of psychic manifestation. A whiff of rose perfume announces the presence of the ghost of Dayton's Victoria Theatre; a ghostly gingerbread smell haunts the Stetson House in Waynesville. Guides at the Patterson Homestead in Dayton have experienced homey but mysterious odors of baking cookies and fresh green beans. But not all phantom scents are so pleasant.

Two women students, Christy* and Lisa* experienced an appalling odor in their dorm room at Miami University. The dorm, originally part of a women's college, had burned down several times. Reputedly a male student, who had been visiting his girlfriend illicitly, died after he concealed himself in a closet when the alarms went off. This is the stuff of student folklore, but what these two women experienced was all too real.

It began with a horrible odor in their closet. Lisa described it as "sickening. Like rotting sausage." It was both sweet and corrupt—the smell of decaying human flesh. Christy first thought that there must be a dead mouse in the wall. But the horror did not confine itself to the closet. It lingered there for a day or two, then moved into the room itself.

Christy and Lisa were appalled by the stench. Their friends also noticed the smell, which was strong only in a certain area.

"You could walk through it," said Lisa "like through a circle, and come out on the other side." The circle, with its unbearable odor, moved around the room, changing its position daily. It edged closer and closer to the door. Then, at last, it moved into the hall just outside the girls' door and, mercifully, disappeared.

Dead and Gone

From the *Western Star*, August 27, 1891, comes a story about the most disembodied of phantoms:

> Charles J. Reed, a young man of twenty-five years, living at Xenia, O., fell dead, recently, while walking across the dining room in his father's house. The family were present at the breakfast table when Charles entered the room. He had passed the table but a few steps, when he fell heavily to the floor, and never again breathed. The body was carried into a bed-room, and after vain efforts at resuscitation, left lying on the bed with composed limbs and covered face. In the meantime the boy had been dispatched for a physician, who arrived some twenty minutes after death. He afterward remembered that when he arrived the weeping relations—father, mother and two

sisters—were all in the room out of which the bed-room door opened, and that the door was closed. There was no other to the bed-room. This door was at once opened by the father of the deceased, and, as the physician passed through it, he observed the rigid outlines of the body under the sheet that had been thrown over it, and the profile was plain-discernible (sic) under the face cloth, clear cut and sharp, as profiles of the dead seem always to be. He approached and lifted the cloth. There was nothing there. He pulled away the sheet. Nothing. The family had followed him into the room. At this astonishing discovery—if so it may be called—they looked at one another, at the physician, at the bed, in speechless amazement. A moment later the three ladies required the physician's care; all had fainted and fallen to the floor. The father's condition was but little better; he stood in a stupor, muttering inarticulately, and staring like an idiot. Having restored the ladies to consciousness, the physician went to the window—the only one the room had. It was locked on the inside with the usual fastening attached to the bottom bar of the upper sash. No inquest was held—there was nothing to hold it on; but the physician and many others who were curious as to the remarkable occurrence made the most searching investigation, but without result. Charles J. Reed was dead and "gone," and that is all that has ever been known of it to this day.[10]

OUR HAUNTED PRESIDENTS
The Harrison Horror to Harding's Doom

In the democracy of the dead, all men at last are equal.
There is neither rank or station nor prerogative
in the republic of the grave.
-John James Ingalls, Senator from Kansas-

The Harrison Horror

In his *Devil's Dictionary*, the acid pen of Ohio author
Ambrose Bierce defines a grave as: *Grave, n. A place in which
the dead are laid to await the coming of the medical student.*
For the descendants of William Henry Harrison, 9th President
of the United States, this would have been a grim joke indeed.

Harrison died in 1841, a month after taking office and was
buried at North Bend. On May 28, 1878, his son, the Hon.
John Scott Harrison, died suddenly at his home in Cincinnati,
and was laid to rest with all the pomp due a United States
Senator. "The remains," wrote the *Cincinnati Commercial* in
admiration, "were enclosed in a handsome metallic casket, with
heavy silver handles."

But "Old Hickory" must have spun in his grave at subsequent events. On May 31, 1878, *Commercial* subscribers were stunned to read:

> We have never been called upon to speak of a more shocking outrage than that of the robbery of the grave of the Hon. John Scott Harrison. But yesterday the Commercial contained a report of his funeral services. His remains were carried by old citizens, who were his near friends and placed in a spot sacred in the history of the country. The grave was prepared with extraordinary care. The iron casket was placed in masonry and covered with an immense stone and cemented, before the earth was thrown in. It was ascertained that the son of a poor widow [actually Benjamin Harrison's cousin, Augustus Devin] had been removed from his grave in the neighborhood and one of Mr. Harrison's sons came to the city on the generous errand of seeking the body of the widow's son, and not knowing the desecration of his father's grave, found that honored father at the Ohio Medical College *(Sic)*, with a rope about his neck, until wanted in the dissecting room....
>
> It is doubtful [clucked the paper] whether the law would be allowed to take its course in case the guilty were speedily discovered.
>
> General Benjamin Harrison [born at North Bend and later our 23rd President] is in the city and is resolved to ascertain who are responsible and to cause their punishment.[1]

Unfortunately outrages of this sort were commonplace. Medical students needing specimens for their anatomy classes were limited by law to the bodies of tramps and paupers. But there were never enough bodies, which meant that the "Resurrectionists" as they called themselves, had the market in dead bodies virtually sewed up.

They had to work fast, before the body decayed and became worthless for dissection. After the mourners had gone and the watchmen were looking the other way, as they were frequently paid to do, the loose dirt was shoveled out and the coffin lid ripped off. Silver handles and name plates were pried off and pocketed.

A sharp hook was plunged into the stiff flesh under the corpse's chin, ensuring that vital internal organs that students needed to study would not be damaged. Then the resurrection-ists climbed to their winch and cranked the corpse out of the ground. The body was dumped in a sack, and the resurrection-ists replaced the coffin lid, the dirt, and as many signs of their desecration as they could while hurrying in the dark.

To avoid detection corpses were often preserved in brine and shipped out of state in barrels marked "pork" or "beef." Otherwise, students dissected at full speed, first skinning the head and removing scars or other distinctive marks that would help to identify the body if they were raided.[2]

On June 1, 1878, a full half-page of gruesome details was released under the heading "THAT HORROR, The Theft and Finding of J. Scott Harrison's Corpse."

"[The body] was, in medical parlance, 'in pickle.' That means immersed in brine, after an injection of chloride of lime into the veins, for preservation during the summer."

The janitor of the medical school was implicated and arrested. The $10,000 bail was posted by a faculty doctor. Benjamin Harrison, in an interview printed in the June 1 *Commercial*, condemned the faculty of the Medical College: "They say they are shocked about it. They have the guilty parties under their wing. If they do not point them out, then they themselves are as responsible as if they themselves had been guilty of the outrage."

Following this interview was a testy rebuttal from a representative of the faculty expressing regret for the mistake, but complaining of a shortage of bodies for the anatomy room. Said the doctor:

"The men engaged in the business of procuring subjects are, of course, unknown to the Faculty. They bring their material to the College, receive the stipulated price and disappear as mysteriously as they came."[3] After naming the shiftless Bob Roundtree, "whose record is not of the best," as the probable resurrectionist, the paper goes on:

If cemented walls, carefully and skillfully
constructed and vast weights, requiring the strength of
many men to lift, and...prepaid watchmen could not
save their loved and honored parent's grave from
desecration and dishonor, what could? This is the
question that many people have asked themselves in
the last twenty-four hours. What can we do...to save
our loved and lost ones from the ignominy of the
"chute" and windlass and dissecting knife...?

The paper envisioned a grisly scenario:

It was not pleasant...to meditate that the body of
the mother who had borne and nourished him and who
he had loved and revered was liable to be hooked
under the chin and dragged from its last resting place
and carted through the streets naked by ruffians, and
hauled up the "well" in the medical college and
exposed to the knife of careless, reckless young
students who carved the sacred remains with pipe in
mouth and the ready jest and laugh on tongue.[3]

Such horrific passages were why many Victorian women
were forbidden by husbands and fathers to read the newspapers. Appalling though the details were, no doubt Papa would
have been equally shocked at the notion of the students
smoking without permission in the presence of lady—even a
deceased one.

As a result of public outcry, stiffer laws were passed
against resurrectionists. The body of John Scott Harrison was
once again quietly laid to rest. But for the rest of his life,
Benjamin Harrison could hardly utter the word "father" without
reliving the anguish produced by The Harrison Horror.[4]

The Lincolns and Spiritualism: The Ohio Connection

Was Abraham Lincoln a spiritualist? That question has
been asked ever since the 15th President attended seances in
the White House and had recurring dreams and visions,
including one of his own death. Soon after Lincoln was elected

President, he was shown an article in *The Cleveland Plaindealer* that hinted that he accepted the possibility of spirit communication. He said in reply: "This article does not begin to tell the wonderful things I have witnessed. Half of it has never been told."[5]

Some of the "wonderful things" that he witnessed included a levitating piano and a message from Daniel Webster through medium Nettie Coburn Maynard that Lincoln should issue the Emancipation Proclamation.[6] When news of this seance was publicized, "A Citizen of Ohio" (David Quinn) wrote an indignant book called *Interior Causes of the War: The Nation Demonized and its President a Spirit-Rapper.*

The *Plaindealer* also told the story of a medium named Conklin who, at a reception in Cleveland, recognized Lincoln as a client who used to "come alone, sit silently, question mentally, and depart as he came, unnoticed." Conklin told of how Lincoln received a spiritual message from a friend whom he had left recovering from an illness. He had no idea that the friend had died until the friend's death was confirmed the next day.[7]

If Lincoln was reputed to be a spiritualist, his wife Mary Todd Lincoln was a confirmed believer. While Mrs. Lincoln showed an interest in spirit communication, it wasn't until after the death of her son Willie in 1862 that an Ohio woman, Lizzie Keckley, introduced her to the mediums of Washington.

In the 1860s, thousands of Americans tried to raise the dead during the War that took a horrendous toll in young life. During these years one of Mrs. Lincoln's closest friends was Elizabeth Keckley, a mulatto seamstress who wrote the first "backstairs at the White House" book, much to the horror of Mrs. Lincoln and her sons who felt betrayed by the book's intimate confidences, harmless though they seem to us.[8]

Keckley was an ex-slave who sewed for Varina Davis, wife of Confederate President Jefferson Davis and other eminent ladies who introduced her to the First Lady. Tall, regal, and lady-like, Keckley had excellent taste and reasonable prices—traits which endeared her to Mrs. Lincoln. After weathering some of Mrs. Lincoln's rages and whims, Keckley became a trusted friend and confidant. Mrs. Lincoln described her as "although colored,... very industrious...very unobtrusive and will perform her duties faithfully."[9]

Mrs. Keckley's son, who attended Wilberforce University, had died in the Civil War. The anguished mother turned to spiritualism hoping to contact her dead son. Linked as they were by the loss of their sons, Mrs. Lincoln eagerly allowed Mrs. Keckley to introduce her to the spiritualists of Washington.

Mrs. Lincoln desperately wanted to believe that Willie was close by. As she told Charles Sumner, "a very slight veil separates us from the loved and lost and to me there is comfort in the thought that though unseen by us they are very near."[10] She told her sister, Emilie Todd Helm, that Willie came nearly every night to stand, smiling, at the foot of her bed.

At a seance arranged by Mrs. Keckley, Mrs. Lincoln saw the spirit of Andrew Jackson who told her that he was now Willie's guardian and that she should not trouble herself anymore. From that day forward Mrs. Lincoln grieved a little less for her dead son.[11]

In later life, Mrs. Elizabeth Keckley settled in Xenia and presented several relics of the Lincolns to Wilberforce University.

The Phantom Funeral Train

Lincoln's funeral train passed through Ohio on its melancholy journey to the President's final resting place in Illinois. At Cleveland, the body lay in state in a Chinese pagoda of black velvet sprinkled with silver stars. In Columbus the casket lay under the cupola of the State House and rode on an oriental temple-style hearse with roses scattered under its wheels, accompanied by floats with young ladies in black scarves ensconced among branches of evergreen—a kind of funereal Rose Bowl parade.[12]

The train stopped at Urbana in darkness. "A pilot car 'beautifully draped,' had preceded the cortege the whole way to make sure that no obstruction should endanger "*the* train containing the remains and the Escort." A gun was fired at intervals while the people stood in the light of bonfires and blazing torches in perfect silence, gazing at the pilot car. At the end of fifteen minutes, it "moved off into the darkness and the next moment the train came in just as solely and noiselessly." After fifteen minutes, the train moved quietly away, leaving the people more aware than ever of the "great calamity."[13]

As reported in the Albany *Evening News*, Lincoln's train still travels those tracks:

> Regularly in the month of April about midnight the air on the tracks becomes very keen and cutting. On either side of the tracks it is warm and still. Every watchman, when he feels the air, slips off the track and sits down to watch. Soon the pilot engine of Lincoln's funeral train passes with long, black streamers and with a band of black instruments playing dirges, grinning skeletons sitting all about.
>
> It passes noiselessly. If it is moonlight, clouds come over the moon as the phantom train goes by. After the pilot engine passes, the funeral train itself with flags and streamers rushes past. The track seems covered with black carpet, and the coffin is seen in the center of the car, while all about it in the air and on the train behind are vast numbers of blue-coated men, some with coffins on their backs, others leaning upon them.
>
> If a real train were passing its noise would be hushed as if the phantom train rode over it. Clocks and watches always stop as the phantom train goes by and when looked at are five to eight minutes behind.
>
> Everywhere on the road about April 27 watches and clocks are suddenly found to be behind.[14]

I read this account in a book of Ohio folklore at my grandparents' house in Galion when I was about five years old. Directly across the street from their house ran the railroad tracks and I was convinced that some balmy April evening that black train with its grinning skeleton musicians would glide by before my horrified eyes. Have any of you out there seen it?

Mrs. Satan; Madam President

As the first woman candidate for President, Victoria Claflin Woodhull got mixed reviews: "In the annals of emancipation, the name of Victoria Woodhull will have its own high place as a deliverer," said Elizabeth Cady Stanton. The Pittsburgh *Leader* characterized her as "one of the most remarkable, albeit terrible and dangerous women who ever lived." Her enemies called her "The Woodhull," a form used for courtesans; she was caricatured by Thomas Nast as "Mrs. Satan" with horns and bat wings, for she espoused free love and the rights of women to decide their own destinies. She herself was convinced that her own destiny was prophesied by her spirit guide.

Born in 1838 in Homer, Victoria possessed psychic powers from the time she was a child. It ran in the family: her mother Roxanna, and sister Tennessee were both healers and mediums. Tennessee, age 5, was nearly run out of town after she predicted a fire in a seminary *too* accurately. She also frightened the local children by reading their minds.

Victoria's gift appeared at age three. She fell into a trance after a neighbor died and reported seeing him in the other world. She played with the ghosts of her baby sisters who had died before she was born. Sometimes she saw the devil who, despite the fact that he hid his face behind a red silk handkerchief, was betrayed by his cloven hooves. In later years, when The Woodhull was at the height of her notoriety, neighbors recalled seeing Victoria, Tennessee, and Roxanna stirring a kettle in their back yard, like the three witches in *Macbeth*.

Their opportunistic father, Buck Claflin, who had heard of the sensation that the rapping Fox sisters were making in Cincinnati, set the girls to telling fortunes in the parlor of their Mt. Gilead boarding house. Indignantly Victoria told her father that their gifts didn't work that way, that she couldn't just switch the power on and off. "Never you mind." snapped Buck, "Fake it if you have to; just be sure you give the customers their money's worth."

It was in Mt. Gilead that Victoria saw her first vision of her spirit guide, a beautiful young man in a dazzlingly white tunic who brought her a message:

"You will know wealth and fame one day," he promised.
"You will live in a mansion, in a city surrounded by ships, and
you will become ruler of your people."

Victoria took this prophecy very seriously during the lean
years of telling fortunes, laying on hands, and hawking her
father's herbal concoctions at medicine shows where her sister
Tennie was billed as "The Wonder Child." To escape this
tawdry life, she married the alcoholic Dr. Woodhull. They
moved to Indianapolis, where as Mrs. Victoria Claflin
Woodhull, Spiritual Healer, she quickly became the psychic
toast of the town. Victoria made the lame to walk, the deaf to
hear, and, incidentally, solved a bank robbery

Encouraged by these successes, she moved to Cincinnati,
then Chicago with Tennessee. "The Wonderful Child has
Established a Magnetic Infirmary" proclaimed the placard.
The spiteful called it a house of assignation. Dr. Woodhull had
quietly vanished.

When the spiritualist Col. Blood came to Victoria for a
consultation, she immediately fell into a trance and stated that
she and the Colonel were destined to marry. According to
Victoria, they were betrothed on the spot by "the powers of the
air." With Blood's encouragement, Victoria was soon elected
president of the National Association of Spiritualists.

Another move followed, this time to Pittsburgh where
Victoria met once again the beautiful young man in the white
tunic.

"Go to New York City," he said, "to 17 Great Jones Street.
There you will find a house ready and waiting for you and
yours." As he spoke, Victoria was given a tour of the house in
a vision. This time she was determined to get some answers
from the figure.

"Who are you?" she demanded "All these years, I have
never known. Tell me who you are!"

The figure stretched out a hand and wrote with his finger
on a table top. The letters glowed with a supernatural light:
DEMOSTHENES.

Just why the noted Greek orator would care about a
clairvoyant from Ohio was never explained, but Victoria
followed the figure's instructions and went to New York in
search of Great Jones Street. In later years she enjoyed telling

how she found the house of her vision at the address given, how she waited in the parlor to discuss renting the house, how she saw a book on the parlor table. Stamped in gold on the book's cover was the title, *The Orations of Demosthenes*. She felt "a blood-chilling astonishment" at this confirmation of her spirit guide's identity.

Tennessee and Victoria blossomed in New York. They opened a brokerage office on Wall Street. Known as "the Bewitching Brokers," they were the first businesswomen in the history of the Market. Through their financial dealings, they became acquainted with Commodore Cornelius Vanderbilt, who had taken up spiritualism since the death of his child.

Vanderbilt was enchanted by Tennessee and called her "my little sparrow." For her part, she referred to him as "old boy" and turned down his repeated offers of marriage. Victoria gave Vanderbilt spirit-advice on the stock market, but when she conjured up the spirit of his dead wife, the Commodore flatly refused to communicate with her.

"Business before pleasure," he ordered. "Let me speak to [the late financier] Jim Fisk."

In Victoria's later years, all of Demosthenes' prophecies seemed about to come true. After all, she *had* led her people— the spiritualists. The Woodhull was the Equal Rights Party candidate for President in 1872, advocating a platform of women's suffrage, one sexual standard for men and woman, the legalization of prostitution, and "free love."

Then something went wrong. She lost the election by a landslide. She exposed the Reverend Henry Ward Beecher's adulteries, was jailed for violating the obscenity statutes and tried for libel. Desperately denying that she had ever advocated free love, she married a rich Englishman and died in her sleep at the age of 88. If she felt that her spirit guide had abandoned her, she did not entirely abandon the spirits. If her daughter Zulu had not survived her, her fortune would have gone to the Society for Psychical Research.[15]

U.S. Grant: E.S.P. in the Family

Eighteenth President, Ulysses Simpson Grant, born at Point Pleasant, was surrounded by women who could predict the future. It was an accepted fact in the Grant family that Julia Dent Grant was psychic. When the Grants were married, Julia declared that she was marrying a future President of the Republic, something that seemed very unlikely given Grant's previous record.

Julia's *Memoirs* are filled with psychic dreams and visions. During the Civil War, Julia saw a vision of Grant in peril:

> I went into my room to rest for a few moments, when I distinctly saw Ulys a few rods from me. I only saw his head and shoulders, about as high as if he were on horseback. He looked at me so earnestly and, I thought, so reproachfully that I started up and said, "Ulys!" My friend in the next room said: "Did you call?" and when I told her, she said I was only a little nervous thinking of him and would soon meet him. I started that evening with my little ones. We heard of the battle of Belmont, however, before we left. Ulys met me almost before the train stopped. I told him of my seeing him on the day of the battle. He asked at what hour, and when I told him, he said: "That is singular. Just about that time I was on horseback and in great peril, and I thought of you and the children, and what would become of you if I were lost. I was thinking of you, my dear Julia, and very earnestly too."[16]

Julia had a terrible premonition on the day that Lincoln was assassinated. In fact, she prevented her husband from going to the theatre with Lincoln, which probably saved his life.

In 1871, during Grant's first term in office, the Grants were expected at a reception in Chicago. Julia dreamed of a big bird with smoke arising from its wings and insisted that the family leave the city. Grant thought she was being fanciful, but they made their excuses and left Chicago—right before the city burned.

Grant's sister, Mary Grant Cramer, was a spiritualist and clairvoyant who predicted Julia's death. Says Mrs. Cramer:

"The dream was exceedingly vivid. I thought that Mrs. Grant came to my bedside and placing her hand on my shoulder—said impressively, 'Mary, I have come to talk with you and to say good-bye, because I am not going to be with you much longer.'

Mrs. Cramer told of her dream at the breakfast-table the next morning and was amazed to hear a visiting friend of the family, Mrs. Katherine Lawrence, say that she, too, had had a weird dream the night before. She dreamed that she, Mrs. Cramer and her sister, Mrs. Virginia Grant Corbin, were standing together at the door to Grant's tomb on Riverside Drive in New York City. A crowd was gathered, waiting for some kind of procession to arrive.

Julia Dent Grant died eight days later. The *New York Sun* and other papers carried the story of the prophetic dreams.[17]

The Grant's daughter Nellie seems to have inherited the family trait as Julia told in her *Memoirs*:

The next morning Nellie was having her boots laced by the nurse when she looked up and said: "Mamma, when are we going to our home?" "Why, Nell," I said, "this is our home; we are going to stay here always. Those nice, kind ladies and gentlemen that received us yesterday gave this nice house to your papa, and this is our home." [The Grants had just been presented with a handsome house in Philadelphia.] She looked up, rather mystified I thought, and said: "No, mamma, no, this is not our home. I have just come from there. Our house is a great, great house (with a struggle to say what it was like) like...like...the picture in my geography of the...the...Capitol in Washington; I know mamma, I was there." "No, no little girl, this is all ours. You have been dreaming, little one."[18]

Grant himself has been seen planning his Civil War strategy at Fort Monroe, Virginia.[19]

The Haunted Ring of Mrs. Rutherford B. Hayes

Rutherford B. Hayes, 19th President of the United States and his wife Lucy were reburied at Spiegel Grove in 1915. While the workmen were moving the caskets the following curious incident occurred:

> He [Webb, son of Hayes and Lucy] came to tell me [his cousin, Lucy Elliot Keeler] at the first opportunity—that he found the original caskets almost intact and in excellent condition....The old coffin [of Mrs. Hayes who died in 1889] sagged open at one end and out rolled —in his hands—his *mother's wedding ring*. He showed it to me—engraved with her name from RBH. It seemed to me like a last message from Aunt Lucy to this devoted son of hers![20]

The ring is now on display in the museum at the Rutherford B. Hayes Presidential Center.

James A. Garfield: Our Most Haunted President?

Garfield was possibly our most haunted President. He was born Nov. 19, 1831, under the sign of Scorpio whose denizens have a strange fascination with the secrets of life and of death.

His psychic leanings ran in the family. His grandfather, who was known as "James the Astrologer," had great mathematical and clairvoyant gifts. Garfield's mother Eliza told the family stories of his uncanny predictions.[21] Garfield's sister Mary was also credited by the family with the gift of second sight.

All his life, Garfield had an acute sense of his own destiny. Torn between orthodox religious beliefs and a certain mysticism, around 1837, Garfield began to have what he believed were visitations from his dead father's ghost. Like a more benign version of the Ghost of Hamlet's father, the spirit advised him which college to attend. Later, he supposedly told Garfield to accept the command of a volunteer regiment which he had been offered.[22]

In 1851 the intense interest that spiritualist had been generating prompted Garfield to visit a seance in Cleveland where he asked the medium to contact his father. A series of raps purporting to come from his father, Abram, who died when Garfield was not yet two, half-convinced Garfield that he had indeed communicated with the dead:

> June, Wednesday 4 1851: I went to the Dunham House [in Cleveland] where Miss Fish of Rochester [sister of spirit-rappers Margaret and Kate Fox] is attending to the "spirit knockings" (so called). I paid the door keeper $1.00 and was conducted into the room where the ladies (Miss Fish and two others) were. The company (16 in number) were seated around a table the ladies sitting at the head. After the company were seated, one of the ladies asked if the spirits would communicate with us by rapping. Immediately the rapping commenced on the settee or the wall and then on the table where we were sitting. The manner of proceeding was as follows: An individual first asked if there were any spirits that would communicate with him. If there were, it was indicated by two or three raps! If the answer was a name, the ladies would call over the alphabet and when they came to the right letter it would rap! Or you might write a list of names and when you came to the right one it would rap! There were many questions and correct answers infallibly given. I was a perfect stranger to every person in the room. I called for the spirit of my father. It (what professed to be it) responded by rapping. The rapping of no two spirits were alike. I asked my father his name. I called over several names and when the right one was named it rapped! In this way it told me my own name, that I had one brother living, told me his name, said I had one brother in the spirit land, name given, age also, told me how many years he (father) had been dead. There were many other tests and correct answers. There was intelligence in the answers given to my questions, that no persons (not even myself) in the

room possessed. So it is impossible that the girl could
have made the rapping for she did not possess the
intelligence. 'Tis a mystery however, and I'll not
speculate upon it.[23]

Other experiments did not confirm Garfield's belief and,
indeed, he defeated a noted spiritualist in debate. However, he
retained a lingering notion that it was possible to communicate
with the world beyond. He attended a seance held in Eliza's
house, with her granddaughter, Eliza Trowbridge, acting as
medium:

> July Sunday 18, 1852: Heard the Spirit rappings at
> Mother's, Eliza Trowbridge being the medium. Had a
> long conversation with what purported to be the spirit
> of my Father. He (or it) was pleased with the course I
> am pursuing in regard to study. Told past events
> correctly, but I have no confidence in the prophesies.
> It said that I would attend school four terms more, and
> would be married in one year. It also said I would go
> home again in three weeks. With regard to the first, I
> hope to go more than four terms. The second must not
> be true, and the third I do not expect.[24]

Garfield was elected our 20th President in 1880. On his
dead father's advice, he set his course to reform the civil
service, alienating many of his supporters and causing his own
death at the hand of a disappointed office-seeker who shot him
in July of 1881.

Garfield was one of those numerologically unlucky
Presidents doomed to died in office when elected at 20-year
intervals: William Henry Harrison, 1840; Abraham Lincoln,
1860; Garfield, 1880; William McKinley, 1900; Warren G.
Harding, 1920; Franklin D. Roosevelt, 1940; and John F.
Kennedy, 1960. Garfield had a premonition that he was going
to be killed. He told his fears to a close aide who later testified
that Garfield knew he was a dead man. A few months before
the shooting, Garfield took out an insurance policy on his life
for $25,000. And only a few days before he was shot, Garfield
sent for Robert Lincoln, President Lincoln's only surviving son

and went over every detail of his father's assassination and funeral arrangements.[25]

While Garfield was president of Hiram College, he lived in a two-story frame house where he courted and won Lucretia "Crete" Rudolph. In the same house, they began their married life together. This house was bought in the 1960s by the Norman* family to keep it from being demolished. The Normans think that Garfield, his wife and friends sometimes return to the house.

The Normans first experienced electrical and plumbing problems: the dining room light turned on and off as it pleased so did water taps, upstairs and down. Irritated by the flickering lights, Mrs. Norman finally snapped, "That's enough of that!" After that the dining room lights behaved normally.

Then the Norman's furniture got into the act: a rocking chair rocked by itself, their pump melodeon played—and pumped—by itself, and a broken cuckoo clock somehow managed to chime. Clocks stopped and lamps came on precisely at 3:20 A.M., although nobody knew why.

A puddle of water materialized in front of the family in the dining room. A candle snuffer was seen to fly twelve feet from the mantle where it was lying. The Normans left tape recorders running, which recorded nonexistent flute music, raps, and the chiming of invisible glassware. Many people heard these sounds, but the sounds gradually faded off the tapes.

Out of curiosity, the Normans called in Charlotte*, a local psychic who specialized in automatic writing. At Charlotte's first session, someone wrote in small, dainty handwriting similar to Crete Garfield's. Next came a spirit named "Andrew" who said he "represented a whole group of free spirits who knew they were dead, but who enjoyed coming to the house."

Andrew got to be a regular fixture. He asked Joan*, the Norman's daughter, to string cranberries and popcorn for the Christmas tree. Thinking it would be a charming, old-fashioned touch, she did, even though it took her three days. Until she got the strings on the tree, the lights on the Christmas tree flashed on and off—even though they were not the blinking kind.

The visiting spirits were apparently not very happy with the Norman's ideas about furniture arrangement. The family often found their furniture rearranged. Putting it back made no difference, somebody kept changing it around. Years later, the Normans read Crete's diary, quoted in *The Garfield Orbit*, which showed that the Garfield's furniture *had* been in those locations.

One spirit was disturbed about something more serious than interior decorating. One night during an automatic writing session, a lighted candle flared up into a huge flame. At this the psychic changed her pen to the left hand, which wrote, "I am James Garfield. If you need proof, look at the candle. I am unhappy because so-called friends had me murdered." Later the Normans found a crossword puzzle mysteriously filled in by someone who used the odd, left-handed *E*s seen in Garfield's handwriting.[26]

William McKinley Returns

William McKinley, 24th President of the United States, born at Niles in 1843, was another President whose assassination generated many premonitions—as though a momentous event like the murder of a head of state creates a shock wave in the psychic atmosphere, like the preliminary tremors before an earthquake.

In 1900 it was whispered that the spirits of Queen Victoria and President McKinley were seen in the room where President Lincoln had a prophetic dream about his assassination. Queen Victoria and President McKinley both died within the year.[27]

Ohio's own Ambrose Bierce wrote a weirdly prophetic verse when William Goebel, a contender for the governorship of Kentucky was assassinated:

The bullet that pierced Goebel's breast
Can not be found in all the West;
Good reason, it is speeding here
To stretch McKinley on his bier.[28]

This bit of poetic nastiness brought Bierce under suspicion of murder after McKinley's death.

During luncheon the day before his assassination, McKinley asked a waiter uneasily, "What's on the other side of that door?" It was the door he was to walk through to his death.

Twenty-four hours after McKinley's death, part-time bartender John Nepomuk Schrank had a grisly dream. In his dream Schrank saw McKinley rise from his coffin, point an accusing finger at Roosevelt and name his Vice President as his murderer.

Schrank brooded over this dream for eleven years. On September 14, 1912, the anniversary of McKinley's death, Schrank was writing a poem when the ghost of the assassinated McKinley appeared before him. Schrank wrote about his vision:

> Sept. 15, 1901—1:30 AM in a dream I saw President McKinley sit up in his coffin pointing at a man in a monk's attire, in whom I recognized Theo. Roosevelt.
> The dead president said This is my murderer, avenge my death.
> Sept. 14, 1912, 1:30 AM: While writing a poem someone tapped me on the shoulder and said Let not a murderer take the presidential chair, avenge my death. I could clearly see Mr. McKinley's features.
>
> (signed) Innocent Guilty

Schrank then went out and shot Roosevelt, who was wounded, not killed, and insisted on giving his scheduled speech. It is not recorded if McKinley's ghost ever visited Schrank again.[29]

"A great life never dies." said President McKinley at the dedication of Grant's tomb. McKinley took this pronouncement very personally. Noted for his oratory when alive, President McKinley spoke after his death at seances held by

Judge Albert Munson, the founder of the GOP in Medina and one of McKinley's staunchest political supporters.

Munson's "Spirit Father," or spirit guide, was his late father, Lyman Munson. His Spirit Father told Munson that if he wrote letters to McKinley, replies would come via sealed letters.

Medium Annie L. Chamberlain, whose control called herself Electa, was able to summon the spirit of McKinley who stated that "I hardly realize the change that has come so suddenly to me. I am not dead. I still live....I am too bewildered with astonishment to give expression to my feelings." At this point Electa broke in to say that McKinley's "Spirit Attendants took him in charge, not permitting him to be further interviewed at this time. He has learned but little as yet of spirit life and has many things...to unlearn...."

Through Electa, Munson was told that he had helped McKinley adjust to the afterlife. McKinley also praised Munson warmly for his political support: "You mistake in words Dear Judge when you say you have an humble part, which should read the *most important part* in the 1884 campaign. You surely turned the tables for me then and I have ever since blessed and honored you for it."

Once fully acclimated, McKinley asked Electa to tell Munson about life in the hereafter: "We have been having glorious festivities lately. Eminent orators discoursed to us. An area of many hundred miles was filled with eager listeners and so clear and lambent was the air that each inflection of the speaker's voice was heard throughout the vast throng."

Truly a politician's idea of Heaven.[30]

The Doom of Warren G. Harding

Warren G. Harding, 28th President of the United States, looked every inch a President. He was matinee-idol handsome, with a imposing head of silver hair. Standing six feet tall, broad-chested, and possessing an air of simple majesty, when he stood up to make one of his resounding speeches, he was a most impressive figure.

But behind this presidential presence was a man of simple tastes: relaxing with his stockinged feet up on his desk, poker with his friends, cold beer on a hot summer day, and pretty girls. Left to himself he would have stayed a small-town newspaper editor and enjoyed his common pleasures. But his friends, and his wife, Florence had a different idea.

Harding found that he had a talent for public speaking—an ability to speak eloquently for hours and say nothing at all. Harding's cronies saw in him more than a good poker partner—they saw a political asset that could take them all the way to the White House. Women had the vote, they reasoned, and, being charmingly irrational creatures, would cast it for the handsome, courtly senator from Ohio.

The political ambitions of Harding's friends were seconded by Florence Kling Harding. A divorcee, five years his senior, she had prodded the easy-going Harding into marrying her, then insinuated her way onto his newspaper's staff. Relentlessly she pushed him into positions higher than his inclinations or talent. She called him "Wurr'n." He called her "the Duchess," a title she seems to have accepted in all seriousness as her due. She managed all his affairs—except those with women, which Harding seemed helpless to resist.[31]

The Duchess had a mystic streak that led her to consult psychics about her husband's future. When Harding was running for President, she visited Madame Marcia, a fashionable Washington clairvoyant who told Mrs. Harding that she was "a Child of Destiny." When the Duchess paid her first incognito visit to Madame Marcia, she asked Madame to cast a horoscope for a person born November 2nd, 1865 at 2:00 P.M. Citing a need to consult the spirits, Madame Marcia sent her away and consulted *The Congressional Directory*. When the Duchess came eagerly to her next visit, Madame Marcia, who knows all, sees all, was able to announce that the man in question would rise to great eminence, that he was "sympathetic and kindly, intuitive, free of promises and trusting to friends, enthusiastic, impulsive, perplexed over financial affairs. Many clandestine love affairs; inclined to recurrent moods of melancholia."[32]

Brooding over those many clandestine love affairs, the Duchess wanted to know more. After a little more research, Madame could confidently tell her that if the man born on November 2nd chose to run for President, nothing on earth could stop his being nominated and elected.

"But," she added darkly, "he will not live through his term. It is written in the stars...Following the splendid climax in the House of Preferment, I see the Sun and Mars in conjunction in the eighth house of the zodiac. And this is the House of Death—sudden, violent, or peculiar death."[33]

Either the Duchess saw this as a small price for "Wurr'n" to pay for her ambitions or perhaps she felt it would be ample revenge for those many love affairs. When Harding was nominated for President, the Duchess may have had a qualm or two. To a reporter she exclaimed, "I can see but one word written over the head of my husband if he is elected and that word is "Tragedy." [34] She may have only meant that her husband would be out of his depth in the Oval Office, but the imaginative Gaston Means hints that the Duchess foresaw a tragedy of her own making, that she poisoned Harding to save him from being impeached.[35]

In *The President's Daughter*, Nan Britton, reputedly Harding's mistress and mother of his child, claimed to have a premonitory dream the night of the President's death:

Thursday, the 2nd of August, 1923, I dreamed a strange and terrible dream...I was conscious...of *a something* above me...[that] seemed to be floating through the air....*What* was I seeing! God! A coffin! A coffin draped with...American flags, and heaped with red, red roses!...The whole, mounting majestically, lifted by an invisible force, upward, onward, protectingly shrouded by white, white clouds!

So he had come to me!...that I might be the first to know he was leaving this earth! He himself, tired unto death, lay hidden beneath the folds of the crimson-striped flag he had so loved, revealing to me only the symbol of his going, the beautiful cradle of his last restful sleep! Perhaps he had been too tired, too tired to bend over me, too tired even to murmur before he went away, "I love you, dearie!" But I knew. I understood. He meant to waft me sweet kisses in his sleep....the coffin [was]...going upward, heavenward, away from me—away from *me*! Oh, God! No, not away....Even as one transfixed I lay, moving only pitifully frightened eyes to watch the coffin fade slowly out of sight, protectingly enveloped in the white, white clouds...![36]

ETERNAL REST GRANT UNTO THEM, O LORD
Haunted houses and servants of God

*Neither religion nor reason requires us to give
up a belief in ghosts.*
-John Wesley-

*"Requiem aeternam, dona eis, Domine. Et lux perpetua,
luceat eis."* So reads the traditional Latin of the Mass for the
Dead: "Eternal rest grant unto them, Lord, and may eternal
light shine upon them." Many people who have come through
near-death experiences speak of being bathed in a beautiful
Light. Mediums who send earth-bound spirits on their way
instruct those spirits to "Go to the Light." But some souls exist
in the outer darkness, unable to find their way to eternal day.
The Catholic church recognizes this state as purgatory; some
spirits call it hell.

The Ghost of the Old Priory

One such tormented spirit was a priest I will call Father
Ambrose*. He was a priest of St. Joseph's at Somerset, the
oldest Catholic church in Ohio. Also known as the Old Priory

after the Dominicans who ran a seminary there, the church sits on a slight hill. With its facade darkened by time and a spire that towers over the countryside, St. Joseph's seems a brooding fortress, keeping the Devil at bay.

Father Ambrose, like every priest, often said masses for the dead. The custom was for the bereaved to give the priest the name of the deceased and a token stipend of a dollar. The priest would say the requested number of masses, which, hopefully, would shorten the loved one's time in purgatory.

Father Ambrose died suddenly one day and was buried. Shortly after his death, something strange began to happen at the Old Priory. Repeatedly, the candles lit on the altar would be suddenly snuffed by an invisible hand. The attending priest would motion to the server to re-light them, whereupon they would flare up again. People began to wonder whether the Old Priory was haunted by an evil spirit—until the ghost of Father Ambrose returned.

He was seen fleetingly in the hallways. He haunted the priests' cells, looming as a dark figure at the foot of the bed. Most frequently, he appeared in the sacristy when the priests were robing for Mass. He looked sorrowfully at them, but he never spoke.

His brothers wondered if Father Ambrose had committed some sin that had gone unconfessed. They said Masses for him. Father Ambrose appeared again in the sacristy, looking more mournful than ever. The candles still went out.

Puzzled, the community talked it over and decided that Father Ambrose had died before he could say some masses that he had been paid for. Each priest added a new Mass intention: "For an unknown intention of Father Ambrose's." On the altar, the candles blazed up brightly. The spirit of Father Ambrose, his obligations satisfied, was never seen again at the Old Priory.

Still in the Habit

Sister Mary Dominic* had seated herself at dinner in the refectory in the Dominican convent in Lancaster, when she realized that she had left the light on in her cell. She excused herself and left the refectory just as the soup was served. The nun hurried silently up the corridor to the staircase that led up to the nuns' cells. Sister Mary Dominic switched off the light in her cell, and, tucking her hands under her scapular, hastened back to dinner.

On her way down the stairs, she passed another nun coming up. Even though the starched headdress made it difficult to have any real peripheral vision, she recognized the elderly Sister Mary Francis* stumping up the stairs. Sister Mary Dominic got as far as the door of the refectory when she realized that there was no empty chair in the room but her own. She glanced furtively about her. No nun was missing from her place.

Mechanically she ate her soup and wondered what in the world Sister Mary Francis, dead for several weeks, had forgotten. Perhaps, she mused, after a lifetime in the convent, the nun was simply following the Rule by force of habit.

The Fear of the Lord

"Come children, harken to me: I will teach you the fear of the Lord, Psalms 23:12." These haunting words are carved above the door to Nazareth Hall in Grand Rapids. A more fitting motto might have been "Abandon Hope All Ye Who Enter Here," for the former boarding school has a whole host of sinister stories woven about it, as thick as the trees that now encroach on the abandoned building.[1]

The Academy, which boasts a tower and massive brick chimneys, was built in 1927 as a boys' boarding school. Run by the nuns of the Ursuline Convent of the Sacred Heart, it closed in 1982 for financial reasons and has been sitting for sale, empty, ever since. Young trees have crept up to the walls of the Academy, while vandals and ghost seekers have broken windows and damaged the interior.

One of the many tales about the Academy states that several students were molested by a priest. One of the boys hung himself on a tree on the Academy grounds. His despairing soul, shut forever out of Heaven, roams the estate.

Another story tells of a teaching nun who went insane and slaughtered a number of innocents, then turned the knife on herself. One law enforcement officer declares that the story is without foundation, that no nun and no children ever died at Nazareth. He also wishes that thrill-seekers would stop trying to break into the Academy.

Several college students who invaded the premises wished they hadn't. First they heard moans, then a dark-robed figure leaped out of the blackness and chased them down the hallway. Another student saw a lantern-like light bobbing in one of the upstairs windows around midnight. An earthbound nun seeking new victims? Or trying to find her way out of Hell?

"The Sweet Bye-and-Bye"

The famous minister, preacher and inspirational writer Norman Vincent Peale was born in Bowersville in Greene County in 1898. As a man of God, he is well-acquainted with miracles. He describes his encounters with the world beyond in *The True Joy of Positive Living, An Autobiography*:

> ...I was seated on the platform of a large auditorium in Sea Island, Georgia. Some ten thousand persons filled the building. They were singing hymns...I watched...several hundred, come streaming down the aisles, singing that old hymn "At the Cross, at the Cross." Then I "saw" him, my father who had died at age eighty-five long before. He came striding down the aisle, singing. He appeared to be about forty years old, in the prime of life, no more arthritis, no sign of stroke or enfeebled body. He was vigorous and obviously happy, and gave every evidence of enjoying life.
>
> I was spellbound, completely lost in what I was "seeing." The huge audience faded away. I was only with him. Getting closer, he smiled that great old smile of his and raised his arm in the old-time familiar gesture as he moved strongly forward on sprightly step. I arose from the chair, advanced to the edge of the platform, reaching for him. Then he was gone, leaving me shaken, somewhat embarrassed by my actions but happy at the same time.[2]

Not only did Peale experience the presence of his parents after their deaths, but he travelled back in time to when they were young. On a visit to the old family home in Norwood, it seemed to Peale

> that I was removed from worldly reality and was once again a small boy standing on that sidewalk, holding the hand of my little brother Bob. The two of us were dressed up as children were in those days. We were waiting for Mother and father. Then the door opened, and they came down the steps. Mother was wearing an old-fashioned dress that reached her shoetops....The dress seemed to be made of a lacelike material with a full skirt and a narrow waist, and a high collar giving a choker effect. Her hair was piled high and a hat added grace and charm. She seemed about 35 years of age. Father appeared to be about 40 and was dressed in a suit of a dark blue serge, a derby hat atop his head. He took Mother's arm, and with his accustomed vigor and old-style courtesy, was escorting her down the steps. They were smiling at us.
>
> The experience was so completely real and I was so lost in it that I started to rush forward to them. That broke the spell and the vision vanished....Perhaps we live in an unobstructed universe where those we have loved long ago and lost for a while may now and then brush our lives with their loving presence. And perhaps such a gracious experience is meant to say, "We shall meet again," as an old hymn expressed it, "in the sweet bye-and-bye."[3]

What conclusions does this Spirit-filled man draw from his experiences? 1) Our loved ones who have died in the Lord are not dead; 2) they live and grow and are well and happy. and 3) their love for us continues; 4) they are near.[4]

The Bishop's House

Episcopalian Bishop William Montgomery Brown was a legend in his own lifetime. Known as "The Red Bishop" or "Bad Bishop Brown," for his radical beliefs, he denounced what he called the "supernaturalistic fictions of the Bible" and "belief in a supernaturalistic God." In 1924 Brown was tried in the first heresy trial to be held in over a thousand years, convicted and defrocked. Outraged by social injustice, Brown espoused Communism in his later years, styling himself "Episcopus in partibus Bolshevikium et Infidelium." (Bishop to the Bolsheviks and Infidels)

The Bishop was a tall, well-built man with a stately air. With his shoulder-length cascade of white hair, he radiated wisdom and kindliness. Many stories are told of his generosity and his charities. If a tramp called at the Rectory, the Bishop would give him a cake of soap, then send him to a local men's outfitters with a note telling the shopkeeper to give the tramp a pair of pants or a shirt and put it on his bill.

Bishop Brown could well afford to be generous. In 1885 he married the immensely wealthy Ella Bradford, heiress of a prominent Cleveland woman. They first met when Ella's mother had seen promise in Brown and, as his patroness, had sent him to be educated at Kenyon College.

The Bishop and his new bride could not have been more different. He was tall and massive; she was small and dainty. He loved vigorous outdoor exercise; she preferred the parlor. He enjoyed entertaining and meeting people; she was shy and retiring. A photograph taken on his wedding day shows a confident, poised leader of men; her portrait, in satin and tulle, is that of a diffident, almost timid figure. Yet, despite Mrs. Brown's ill-health and their childlessness, the marriage, which lasted until her death in 1935, was a happy one. He called her "Precious."

As a wedding present, Ella's mother built the couple a lavish rectory in Galion that dwarfed the tiny Episcopal church across the street. Dubbed "Brownella Cottage" after the new bride, the house was surrounded by a lacy iron fence. The Bishop added a glassed-in walkway to the little house that served as his study so that he would have a place to take his constitutional on damp days.

After the Bishop's death in 1937, it was discovered that he had willed the bulk of his fortune to the Communist Party. Since the Party was outlawed in Ohio, legally it did not exist, although it tried unsuccessfully to claim the money. The trustees gave the interest on the estate to Galion Hospital and Kenyon College, but there remained the problem of the house. Brown had told his secretary that he had wanted Brownella Cottage to become a home for student nurses. There was already housing for nurses at the hospital, so Brownella Cottage stood, untouched, for 35 years while the trustees debated what to do with it.

My grandparents lived in Galion and as a child I was fascinated by the cottage. A caretaker lived on the grounds. He mowed the grass and weeded the beds of tiger lilies that rioted around the iron fence. The trim of the house was a deep green that blended in with the tall shrubbery and ivy that overgrew the structure. From the sidewalk I could see the chairs in the enclosed porch, shrouded in dustcloths like overstuffed corpses. Once in a great while I would see a light in one of the windows. Accidentally left on by the caretaker, said my grandmother, but I knew it was the Bishop's ghost. My greatest ambition was to visit the house, but I was told that nobody was allowed in, except for the caretaker and the trustees of the estate, which made it all the more mysterious.

In the early 1970s, the Cottage was donated to the Galion Historical Society. Lovingly restored by Historical Society volunteers, Brownella Cottage is a charming architectural time-capsule. The rooms have been repainted in the pale green, dusty rose, and robin's egg blue of the early 1900s, with stenciled borders that copy the original wallpaper patterns. The house's furnishings are intact.

The tiles in the entrance hall spell the Latin greeting "Salve." The Bishop was fond of music, so the music room, with piano, reed organ, and wind-up music box, adjoins the central reception area with its coffered wooden ceiling. Mrs. Brown's favorite sitting room with a tower room heated by a unique circular radiator, looks out onto one of the house's six porches.

In the kitchen stands a magnificent zinc-lined oak icebox with brass hinges and mirrored shelves. Even the original house telephone is there—each button labeled: "E. Brown," "Study," "Carriage House" in faded ink. The Bishop's book-lined study is decorated with ecclesiastical motifs—stenciled crosses on the walls, "Alpha" and "Omega" spelled out in the tiles on the hearth.

Upstairs are bedrooms crammed with high-backed beds and mirrored dressers. There are the latest modern innovations—a bathroom with a corner marble sink and closets whose lights go on automatically when you open the door. Upstairs, too is the turret room decorated in sea-green and eau-de-nil brocade, where Ella's creamy satin bridal gown and tiny embroidered side-lace boots are preserved in a glass case like a coffin. She died in this room.

The last caretaker took a series of photos of the outside of the house. When they were developed, he showed Polly*, a volunteer guide, the photo which he had taken of the turreted corner of the house that houses Ella's room. In the window was an unmistakable human figure.

"I locked up the house," he told Polly quietly "and I was outside. So who was that?"

Newly married, he brought his bride home to his caretaker's apartment which had been carved out of the attic. She spent two nights there and refused to stay another night, terrified by "something about the house."

Six-year old Stephanie* visited Brownella Cottage with her mother. While her mother chatted with the guides, Stephanie studied the pictures on the wall until her attention was caught by a movement on the stairs next to the big clock on the landing. She didn't say anything until they were on their way home and her mother was talking about the house's haunted reputation. Then she said, "I think I saw something on the stairs."

Stephanie described a woman in a white dress with her hair in a bun, standing just beyond the landing with her hands on the stair rail. "I looked at her for a little bit and—poof!—she disappeared. It might have just been my imagination," she added apologetically.

"Couldn't it have been the guide who had showed us around the upstairs?" asked her mother.

But Stephanie was sure it was not. She pointed out that the upstairs guide had worn a maroon dress and her hair was loose. In no way did she resemble whatever it was Stephanie saw on the stairs. Stephanie's mother was worried by the incident and even asked Stephanie's teacher if she thought Stephanie was a fanciful child or one given to making up stories. "Absolutely not, she's very truthful," was the teacher's reply.

Some say that the Bishop still haunts the house. Nick* lived just around the corner from the Cottage, which had a strange reputation after Brown's death. Most people wouldn't go near the place after dark. When Nick was fifteen, his visiting cousin dared him to peek into the windows of Bishop Brown's study. The two boys tiptoed across the lawn to the bushes surrounding the small building. Nick stood up, his hands trembling on the sill, and looked in at the tall window.

He came face to face with a man standing in the darkness, his white face pressed to the glass, peering out at them. Nick and his cousin raced across the lawn, taking the tall iron fence in one bound. Just the caretaker trying to give two trespassers a scare? Or the Bishop pondering Eternity in his study?

There are those who say they have seen the figure of the Bishop taking his constitutional in the long glass walkway. He walks slowly, absorbed in some improving book while the rain patters on the roof. He casts no shadow on the glass.

The day I visited it was raining. As I walked to the Bishop's little brick study, I studied the delicate patterns of leaves and fern that had been pressed into the walkway's cement floor so long ago. Standing in the study at the end of the glass tunnel, time shifted. I could almost see the Bishop still sitting in a pool of lamplight at his desk, pen in hand. I looked back towards the main house with a strong sense that the air would darken and I would see a tall shadowy figure stride by the rain-streaked glass. But nothing happened.

The guides at Brownella Cottage do not believe that Bishop Brown returns to the house. The Bishop, they say, was a scientific-minded man of anti-superstitious bent. In one of his pamphlets he stated, "What is the greatest of all known facts? The fact that man is a part of nature, evolved out of the image and likeness of a beast, not made in the image and likeness of the God, Jehovah; and, therefore, death as surely ends all for humans as for animals." As a man who did not believe in the supernatural, did not believe in an afterlife, Bishop Brown would not have believed in the ghost of himself.

The Ghost of a Prayer

In the Convent of St. Thomas in Zanesville the nuns were assembled for general recreation. Sr. Helen* had forgotten her sewing basket so she asked permission to be excused to fetch it. Passing the chapel on her way back from her cell, she opened the door as was the custom of the community, just to say "hello" to Jesus.

When she opened the door, she saw a nun kneeling at the altar rail adoring the tabernacle. Not wishing to disturb her sister, Sr. Helen quietly closed the door and went along to recreation.

At recreation, the nuns are allowed to talk freely and Sr. Helen speculated aloud on the identity of the nun at the altar. There was an embarrassed silence. Sr. Helen looked about, puzzled that no one seemed to be missing.

"Nobody else beside you left the room," said one sister, her eyes fixed on the stocking she was darning. "And I've seen her too."

At that several other nuns confessed that they had seen the figure in front of the altar.

"No use going back to see if she's still there, she won't be if you go looking for her," said Sr. Margaret crustily. "I know," she added "I've tried it."

In a flurry of excited chatter, it was found that no one knew who the ghostly nun was. No living sister had ever seen her face. And none knew whether she exists in purgatory, doing penance for an unknown sin, or whether she has found Paradise, praising God for Eternity before the altar of the Lord.

The Old Serpent

Chester Bedell of North Benton was a real hell-raiser. He was a self-proclaimed atheist—an infidel, his neighbors muttered, scandalized. After his wife's family tried to force Presbyterian doctrine on this stiff-necked pioneer, he revolted and began his crusade against the church. He made trips to the Holy Land and studied the scriptures, religiously, to gather ammunition to use against Christianity. He wrote a book called *Twenty-one Battles fought by Chester Bedell with Relations and Presbyterian Intolerance with a short sketch of his life.*

He even went so far as to have a bronze statue of himself made to be placed on his grave. He was depicted holding his anti-Christian creed, trampling a scroll labeled "Superstition," or some said, stamping on a stack of Bibles. Bedell went to his death in 1908, mutely unrepentant, and seemingly unaware of the flames licking like serpents' tongues at his heels.[5]

Just after his burial people began to whisper that he had challenged God on his deathbed: "If there is a God," he was reputed to have said, "let snakes infest my grave!"

God is not mocked. The rumor spread that if you approached the grave, the ground seemed to writhe and churn with hundreds of snakes—common garter snakes, sinister black snakes, poisonous copperheads. The faithful came from all over the United States to see the snakes proclaiming the truth of the Gospel. No doubt one or two of the pious smiled as they thought of stinging asps tormenting Bedell for Eternity.

In 1943 the statue of Bedell was taken down and hidden away by his family, tired of the old scandal. They still don't like to talk about it. As for the snakes, were they an optical illusion? A practical joke? A genuine plague of serpents? Or did they truly proclaim the doom of the great heretic in the jaws of the Old Serpent Himself? Some visitors still claim to see snakes; others scoff at what appears to be an ordinary grave. Yet if I were visiting, I think I would tread lightly.

A Pillar of Fire by Night

Earley Church, a small country church in Wheeling Township, Guernsey County, was founded by the Rev. John Earley who went to his rest in 1853. That rest was to be disturbed only ten years later by an appalling church desecration.

A gang of outlaws had terrorized the neighborhood for some time, uprooting crops, destroying farm machinery, killing horses and, in one instance, it was whispered, a schoolmaster. These sons of Belial, no doubt thrilled by the thought of sacrilege, stole a lamb, the pet of a crippled boy, and carried it to Earley's Church where they broke open the door. One placed the open Bible on the altar, another cut the lamb's throat. The blood gushed forth, soaking the pages of the Bible and flowing down the altar to stand in an obscene pool at its base. The stench in the church was unspeakable.

Another young man climbed into the speaking platform.

"John Earley!" he roared, thumping his fist on the pulpit, "come forth from your grave!"

At this, the door of the church burst open and all the house was filled with smoke. Through the chaos came a pillar of fire that swayed with horrible slowness down the aisle. A beam of light shot out of the smoke and struck the man in the pulpit blind. He could not stand or speak and the other desecrators dragged him as they fled, stumbling and incoherent with terror. Behind them on the altar, the dying lamb twitched.

When worshipers arrived on the next Lord's Day, they found the doors broken open. Inside, the sanctuary reeked with the stench of the rotting lamb which was carried from the church "on two sticks." No church services were held that day or for two weeks, so foul was the odor.

Many of the congregation wanted to track down the desecrators, but a descendent of John Earley spoke, saying, "Let them alone; this is God's House that has been desecrated and God will take care of it!"

God did. One by one, tortured by their consciences, the men came forward. They pleaded to be arrested and punished so they could clear themselves. But "Vengeance is mine," saith the Lord, so no one in the congregation would swear out a complaint.

Later the desecrators went mad. The pulpit-pounder died stone-blind. His father, a drunkard, died so awful a death that "he kicked the bed down." Two were imprisoned for murder. All died in various horrid ways. If there were mourners, it is not recorded. Writes the chronicler: "News came of the death of all of them. They all died without hope."[6]

Angels over Bellbrook?

From an 1890s edition of the *Bellbrook Moon* comes this curious story of Heavenly visitants:

> I will mention one more strange phenomena that I witnessed in Bellbrook, August 19, 1841. We were viewing what, to us, was an unusual sight in the shape of an unusual band, when we noticed excited families of the neighborhood in the streets viewing the south-eastern sky. A glance in that direction showed a phenomenon which consisted of angel forms in solemn procession, marching with stately tread, through the realms of space in full view. In the heavens, marching by twos, was a parade of what appeared to be human forms clad in flowing robes. As fast as one company consisting of from 10 to 15 couples would disappear from view, another would take its place. And the vision lasted ten minutes. The forms were so lifelike that seemingly the movements of the limbs could be distinguished. The people at that time were greatly excited at the angelic visitation, and in several instances, families carried invalids out of doors that they might view the scene. The occurrence took place between 9 and 10 o'clock in the evening. The forms of the spirit visitors were to all appearances covered by a gauzy substance and their existence in companies was visible to the eye through a space of probably 30 degrees in a northwest direction....
>
> No music of any kind was heard yet the angels moved in beautiful harmony. Scenes such as this stir up impulses of the soul, calling us to higher planes of inspiration and glory, giving us, as it were, a foretaste of bliss that is in heaven for all the brotherhood of man.[7]

The Ghostly Penitent

Our Lady's Dorm, as it was known then, was found on the third floor of the Old Motherhouse at St. Mary's of the Springs, Columbus. The large room was divided into neat cubicles by muslin curtains that surrounded each bed. Since silence was observed at night, it was a rule that all were to walk as quietly as possible. It was also a rule that no one was supposed to be out of bed at night.

So it was a shock to the nuns tucked up in their beds to hear footsteps that definitely should not have been there. They were light footsteps, like a woman's, and they pattered through the main door and up the center aisle of the dorm itself. They were heard going into a closet at the end of the room and there they ceased.

Our Lady's Dorm had been the Motherhouse chapel, before the new chapel had been built. The closet had originally been a confessional in the old chapel. Perhaps the footsteps belong to a nun who tried, but failed to confess some sin when she was living. Unable to rest, every night she visits the confessional, hoping—each night more hopelessly—to hear a ghostly voice behind the screen pronounce the absolution so she can go to the Light.

THE OLD SCHOOL SPIRIT
The ghosts of higher education

And in the School of Darkness learn
What mean
"The things unseen."
-John Banister Tabb-

College students and ghost stories have always gone together. Student pranks, fraternity hazing stunts, and urban legends account for most ghostly doings on campus. But not all...

The Vanishing Student

Perhaps the most notorious Ohio school spirit is that of Ronald Tammen, a student who disappeared from his room in Fisher Hall on the Miami University Campus. On April 19th, 1953, Tammen's roommate returned from a weekend visit home to find the lights on in their second-story room. The radio was playing, an open textbook lay on the desk, along with a wallet and some other items he recognized as Tammen's. It seemed as though Tammen had merely stepped out to stretch his legs, but after an hour, Tammen's roommate began to get a little uneasy. Tammen might have gone to his fraternity, but his coat was still in its place and it was a cold snowy night. His roommate slept fitfully, thinking that every creak of the window in the wind, every footstep in the hall signaled Tammen's return. He called in the police the next morning.

Tammen was a 20-year old sophomore and a Dean's List student. He wrestled with the varsity squad and played bass with a local dance band, "The Campus Owls." His car was found in its usual place, locked. The bass was in the back seat. His fraternity brothers searched the area, joined by 400 ROTC cadets. They searched the Tallawanda woods, drained a cistern behind Fisher Hall, even looked as far as Acton Lake at Hueston Woods, five miles away. The Butler County sheriff's department was called in, then the State Highway Patrol and, finally, the FBI. Airports, bus and railroad stations were checked. Tammen's photograph was placed in the papers.

Finally a lead came: a woman near Hamilton reported that the night of Tammen's disappearance a knock had come on the door. A dark-haired, polite youth asked her where he could get a bus. He seemed a little confused, she said and police theorized that Tammen had suffered from amnesia. That was the last time anyone ever claimed to see the youth.

The following fall students in Fisher Hall were startled by a voice singing—first in a bass voice, then in falsetto—in the formal gardens and from the woods. For the next two nights the voice tantalized the students, apparently approaching Fisher from the direction of the gardens, then fading back into the woods. The second night, two students claimed to see a long-haired figure striding into the dark. The third night a group of counselors heard the voice and gave chase across the golf course. On the fifth night a tall figure in a long black coat was chased and lost in a wooded ravine. The rest of the week was filled with rumor and counter-rumor as students blundered about the campus in the dark trying to capture the phantom.

In 1957 Fisher Hall was condemned as unsafe for residential use. The upstairs was sealed off and Fisher's lower floor was remodeled into facilities for the drama department including a small theatre. Theatre students saw mysterious shadows, heard muffled sounds from the supposedly uninhabited rooms overhead. In 1967 a medium was brought in with the hopes of solving the mystery once and for all. But no spirits came; no manifestations occurred. The next day the noises from upstairs began again.[1]

Some said the ghost was the acquisitive Judge Elam Fisher (see THE PHANTOMS OF THE OPERA) who roamed the hall collecting oddments like a theatre winch and a portrait bust of himself. One can't help wondering: Did he collect Tammen as well?

Shades of Purple: The Ghosts of Kenyon College

The Gates of Hell

According to some students, the Gates of Hell are located on the campus of Kenyon College. Survivors of "Hell Week" at other colleges might dispute this, but Kenyon does seem to have an unusually active collection of school spirits. Kenyon's Gates of Hell are two columns that flank the Middle Path to the center of campus. Supposedly the Church of the Holy Spirit sits atop the pit of Hell although some think that the trapdoor leading to eternal damnation actually lies in the basement of Mather Hall.

High Student Spirits

A ghostly insomniac who committed suicide still paces the halls of Norton. A frustrated student who died before she could attend classes rearranges the furniture in Manning Hall. A freshman who hanged himself in the attic of Lewis turns the light on and off, knocks on doors, turns radios on and off abruptly, and flushes all the toilets at once—sophomoric pranks, of course.

Psychical Fitness

At Wertheimer Hall in 1975 a solitary student was putting away the football projector in the fieldhouse. Suddenly he heard music which he assumed came from the record player in the "cage." When he investigated, the music stopped. Frightened, he ran into the locked door to the coach's office. The door swung open by itself. When he stepped through, he tripped over "someone," fell flat, and was almost overwhelmed by the feeling of a "presence." Security guards at Wertheimer often hear a ghostly runner on the track. The idea of a ghost keeping in shape is an odd one. Psychical fitness?

Let There Be Light

At least one security guard believes that Hill Theater is haunted. Supposedly Hill stands on the site of a drunk-driving accident where the driver and his passenger were killed. A light is always left on on the stage, but on his rounds the guard repeatedly found the light bulb unscrewed. He would screw it back in and go about his business, only to find it unscrewed a few hours later. He also would find the curtains open on his first round and then closed when he came by again.

The Haunted Swimming Pool

The most famous spirit at Kenyon is the Ghost of Shaffer Hall. Now Shaffer Dance Studio, it formerly housed an indoor swimming pool which is the focal point of the haunting. Supposedly a diver on a high bounce hit the glass ceiling, broke his neck and drowned. No accident of this kind has been recorded, but this hasn't detered the ghost—or whatever it is.

One evening while two swimmers were at the pool, one heard a voice calling him from the locker room, which proved to be empty. Another evening, as one swimmer was on the phone, a voice behind him said "Hi!" loud enough so that the person on the other end could hear it. The caller instantly whirled around, but there was no one there.

In 1979, a lifeguard turned out the lights, locked the doors and headed home. He looked back over his shoulder; the lights were blazing and there were splashing sounds coming from the pool. He raced back to the pool. The lights remained on, but the splashing stopped and, of course, the building was empty.

In 1984, after Shaffer Pool became the dance studio, a young woman was practicing alone one night when she heard a noise like a diving board rebounding. Startled, she went to the dressing rooms to check it out. On the floor leading into the empty locker room was a line of wet footprints.

This aquatic ghost is said to bring good luck to the Kenyon Swim Team and still manifests itself today. Wet footprints walk up to walls and then apparently walk *through* them, showers turn on and off by themselves, the sounds of splashing still resound late at night, and sometimes a wet face, hair slicked back with water, peers from a small window in Shaffer Hall.

Kenyon's Tragic Ghosts

Many of the ghosts of Kenyon have their origins in the numerous campus tragedies like the Old Kenyon Fire, the D.K.E. pledge death, and a student who fell to his death in an elevator shaft at Caples Hall.

The ghost of Caples is believed to be the spirit of a young man who accidentally? fell down an elevator shaft. One version says that after spending the night in his girlfriend's room, the student pushed the elevator button, the doors opened, and he stepped or (some say) was pushed into Eternity. Either he was too tired or too drunk to notice, but the elevator had jammed at another floor.

The official version of the story was less romantic and more mysterious. In 1979 police believe a student deliberately stopped the elevator car and climbed into the shaft, only to fall to his death. Apparently no one else was involved. Possibly he was fulfilling part of a fraternity ritual. Riding the tops of elevators was, and still is, a challenge to thrill-seeking students.

Whatever the true story, a ghost arose out of the tragedy. The student's girlfriend began having horrible nightmares, including the sensation of icy cold hands on her face in the middle of the night. Terrified, she moved out. She was standing at the elevator when she realized that she'd left something behind. The friend who was helping her move went back to the room, but found the door completely blocked by the chest of drawers.

The ghost seems to bear some resentment towards female students. The dead student has been seen leaning transparently against a woman student's bookcase. He flits through doors and once he tried to suffocate a student with her own pillow.

The Delta Kappa Epsilon initiation tragedy in 1905 created one of Kenyon's most durable ghosts. Stuart Pierson, a freshman pledge, was struck by a train and killed as he waited on the railroad bridge over the Kokosing River. Every year on October 28, Pierson returns to his old haunts, staring out of a bulls-eye window in D.K.E. Division as the fatal train passes. The ghost is apparently confined to the fourth floor of Old Kenyon. Windows open and shut—or are slammed—in dead calm weather. Fourth floor residents hear footsteps above them, where there is no floor.

The tragic Old Kenyon Fire in 1949 killed nine male students. The dorm burned to the ground, but was later rebuilt. Students have reported seeing legless torsos gliding down the first floor halls. Lights flicker on and off and toilets flush on the fourth floor by themselves. One resident who unknowingly occupied a room where one victim had been trapped heard cries of "get me out!" and pounding noises. Another student saw a locked closet door tremble violently as if someone were inside. When the door was unlocked there was nothing but a layer of dust on the floor.

These ghosts demand to know what modern students are doing in "their" rooms, shake people awake at night, shouting "Ed, wake up, FIRE!", and leave candles smoldering by 1949 yearbooks, opened to the page with the names of the nine students killed in the blaze. Nine fiery deaths created nine ghosts who go on hoping that they are alive.[2]

Sorority Spirit at Bowling Green

Bowling Green State University, like many colleges, has a sorority ghost: Amanda of Chi Omega. Two tales account for her existence. In one, a little girl who strayed from a park behind the Student Union where the Chi Omega house now stands, was killed by a train. Not knowing she is dead, she continues to play in a park that no longer exists.

The second story alleges that Amanda rushed Chi Omega a long time ago. She was killed by a train the very night she was to "receive a bid." So desperate was Amanda to be a Chi O, she returned to the sorority as a spirit.

Amanda is very much a part of Chi O life. One room is dubbed "Amanda's Room," where weird things—like falling mirrors, locked doors and turned-off stereos—regularly occur. Items also mysteriously vanish, only to reappear in the house utility closet, called "Amanda's Closet," which sometimes locks itself. In every house composite photo, a blank spot is left, labeled "Amanda." Amanda was inadvertently left out of the 1986-87 composite; *that* photo routinely falls off the wall.

A few years ago psychic investigators "saw" a woman with brown hair, wearing a skirt. She was most evident in the kitchen, they said. In the kitchen, the clock refuses to stay on the wall and noises like plastic cups falling are heard, although no mess is ever found.

It is by such pranks that Amanda, the darling of Chi O, manifests herself. Just don't mention her name during Rush Week.[3]

The Student Who Saw Through Time

On the campus of Dayton's University of Dayton, Ted Peters and his friends were ready to party one Sunday night in April, 1991. In fact, Ted had already gotten a start on the evening's festivities by drinking a fifth of Southern Comfort. He was able to walk—barely—but he felt ready to take on the world: seen or unseen. Ted was used to premonitions and the seeing of "entities," and he had warned friends Greg and Kelly that somehow it was going to be an "odd night."

Crossing a courtyard by the Chapel of the Immaculate Conception, Ted kept looking back over his shoulder. Then he began to walk backwards. Finally he stopped. It seemed logical at the time, he explained, "When I looked back over my shoulder, 'they' were appearing and disappearing. When I stopped moving, they stayed.

"Greg and Kelly walked back to me. Kelly said, 'What is it, Ted?'"

Barely able to talk, Ted described a courtyard filled with children playing around the black-clad figure of a priest. He caught the year: 1856 and the priest's name: Father M.

"I was having a hard time vocalizing, I was stuttering, 'I see children. And I see a priest, Father M—Michael, Marcus, I don't know. Two dates stand out in my mind: 1928, 1856 or 1854." Then he covered his eyes, "I see flames and then they're gone."

"Is that all?" questioned Kelly.

"Yes."

With that Ted staggered on towards an off-campus bar. Later, at home he passed out and didn't give his vision another thought. But Kelly did.

Ted says, "When I went back to college the following Tuesday, I heard from Kelly. 'You're not going to believe what I just found out,' she said. Kelly had read a paper her neighbor had written on the history of the University of Dayton.

In 1850, St. Mary's School for Boys was founded by Father Leo Myer, one of the first Marianist missionaries to the United States. Brother Maximin Zehler was the first teacher. In 1854 Stuart Mansion, the original school building of St. Mary's, burned to the ground. In 1856 St. Mary's Convent was built on the site where today's St. Joseph Hall stands, which also burned in 1987. The significance of 1928 was not found.[4]

"The vision was all in black and white," said Ted a month later, puzzled. "And I said children, but they were not young children, more like fourth to eight graders. I hadn't ever been to UD before that. I had never seen any of the buildings. I didn't even think anybody was paying any attention to what I was saying." Ted believes that the alcohol somehow lowered his inhibitions so he could see back through time, but he has not repeated the experiment.

Ghosts at Sinclair

The buildings of Sinclair Community College in Dayton are sleek and modern, the last place you'd expect to see ghosts. But, says Patrick R.*, a former employee of the college, "Sinclair is full of 'em. The [old Dayton] hanging field was right under the cafeteria. They hung thieves and cattle rustlers there." Apparently some of them are still hanging around.

"In Blair Hall, you'd feel people tugging on you. They'd come right up to you and yank on your coat. Or they'd smother you, press down on your chest. I'd hear people laughing when I knew darn well nobody was in there. When I first started working at Sinclair I thought the noises were a lot of outside noise sucked in through the air vents, but then I realized, 'Nah, this place is haunted!' Elevators would move by themselves and open up. You'd hear people talking. You'd hear *cats*, cats meowing in the walls, just as plain as you and I talking. Sometimes I could hear two people dancing back and forth on the stage. It was bizarre!

"In Building Seven on the third floor, I'd know there was nobody there, but I'd check it out and there'd be doors slamming and people talking. At first I thought it was the public relations guy in his office, but there was nobody in the building."

Sometimes Patrick would get "just a passing glimpse" of the spirits. More often he would hear "talking, laughing, music, little babies crying.... Especially at Blair Hall, it was full of them! You'd hear the big heavy fire doors in the cafeteria shut. Nobody was ever there.

"Actually," he says, "it was kind of neat. You'd think 'here comes an elevator!' It would pop open and you'd expect to see somebody—and it was empty!"

Patrick laughs. "It was a real learning experience working at the college."

13

THE HAPPY HAUNTING
GROUNDS
The haunted skull and
other Native American hauntings

A hunter of shadows, himself a shade.
-Homer-

The Hundredth Tongue

"The ugliest man who ever lived" is said to roam Mohican
State Park searching for a gruesome trophy. This Indian
warrior, called Tom Lyons by settlers, wore a necklace of 99
dried human tongues strung on a strand of human sinew. He
vowed that he would kill his 100th white man and add his
tongue to the string. Before he could fulfill his vow, Lyons
was killed on the stage coach road and his body thrown into
Killbuck Swamp. Now he stalks the picturesque paths of
Mohican State Park with his ghostly ax at the ready for his
100th victim.[1]

Native Americans and the Life Beyond

Native Americans have always been supposed to live closer to nature and to phenomena that the early settlers found inexplicable. The Indian could track game almost by scent, he could see in the dark, and detect the invisible signs of a prey's passage. He seemed to possess some unique psychic faculty that had decayed in his more "civilized" brethren.

Native American shamans originated phenomena later imitated by 19th century rapping mediums. The Great Spirit manifested his power in a "shaking sweatlodge"—the origin of the shaking "spirit cabinet" of Athens County medium Jonathan Koons. Within a short time, Indian spirit guides like "Blue Bird" and "Red Eagle" (and one who claimed the unlikely name of "Chlorine") were materializing in seance rooms across the country.[2]

Among the Shawnee, one of the largest tribes in Ohio, the dead were referred to as *ahsanwah*, "vanished" or "disappeared," and were believed to return to prey on the living if "ghost feasts" were not held to honor them.[3]

At a ghost feast, the spirits were invited to partake of food and drink. If a ghost had been seen recently, the makers of the feast might respectfully ask it to not bother the living. Then all fires and lights were put out and the food was left for the spirits, who took only the "essence" or "spirit" of the food, although sometimes a drinking cup would be found mysteriously emptied after the feast.[4]

The Ravenous Dead

The Chippewa also believed that the dead needed to be propitiated by offerings of food, as illustrated by this tale from southeastern Ohio, of "The Two Jeebi-ug."

There was a hunter who lived with his wife in an isolated lodge near the Pennsylvania border. One winter's evening he did not return at his usual time and his wife feared that he had had an accident. When at last she heard the sound of footsteps, she opened the door, thinking to see her husband. Instead, two stranger women stood outside.

Politely she invited them in although their looks made her uneasy. They were stick-thin and pale as maggots. Their eyes were sunken deep in their skulls—starved birds looking out of holes. The women refused to sit in the visitor's seat by the fire, but huddled far away in a chilly corner of the lodge. They hid their faces in their robes and did not speak.

The fire flickered eerily as a gust of wind swept through the lodge. "Great Spirit, have pity!" moaned a voice "The Dead walk, clothed like the living."

At this the woman trembled and would have fled, but as she opened the lodge door, her husband stood there, laden with a large deer.

Instantly the two strangers cried, "What a fine fat animal!" and running to it, they pulled off the choicest pieces and gulped them down greedily. The hunter and his wife were amazed, but being polite hosts, they said nothing, for the women looked as though they were starving.

The next day the hunter returned with another fine deer. This the strangers also tore to pieces and ate ravenously. On the third day, the hunter, wishing to be a good host, bundled up all the fattest parts, and placed them before the women. They bolted the choice morsels, then, still unsatisfied, they attacked the wife's portion and polished it off. Husband and wife were astonished at such manners, but again said nothing.

For many months the strange women stayed at the lodge, sitting silently in their corner during the day, creeping out at night to gather firewood. If they needed a tool or an eating utensil, they always returned it precisely to the spot where they found it. They never spoke again and they never laughed.

The winter was nearly over when one evening the hunter returned with another fine deer. He laid it before his wife, but the two women plunged in front of her and tore off the fat so voraciously that the wife grew angry. She restrained herself however and only quietly remarked that her guests seemed hungry.

At this the two women looked stunned and withdrew to their corner. The hunter tried to question them as to what was wrong, but they would not speak. That night the hunter was awakened by the sobs that came from the two women. Deeply upset he said, "Tell me what has caused your sorrow? Has my wife been inhospitable or rude?"

Weeping, they shook their heads and at last spoke: "You have treated us with every kindness, but now we must depart. We came from the land of the dead to test the living. Often we heard the bereaved say, 'Ah, if only my loved one would come back to me, I would give my life to making them happy!' The Master of Life and Death sent us to see if mankind really meant this. If the living proved sincere in their desire to please the dead, then He who has the power over death would restore the departed ones to life. We were sent to try your tempers with our outrageous behavior. But now the dead will never return."

The two women sobbed bitterly and the lodge was plunged into a darkness like the grave. The hunter and his wife heard the door open and shut. When light returned, the two women were gone forever, to the land from whence no one returns.[5]

The Death Lights of New Philadelphia

In Tuscarawas County, in the 1770s, a Mingo chief married a white woman settler. They were both Christians and decided to attend a mission at Schoenbrunn led by missionary David Zeisberger. At this meeting, the chief met a much younger Indian woman who threw herself at him. Flattered, the chief responded favorably and eloped with the young woman. But the chief's wife was maddened by jealousy and she followed the lovers to New Philadelphia where she pursued them up a high ridge by the Tuscarawas River.

With a howl of fury she flung herself at her husband, who was taken by surprise and tumbled backwards off the cliff. The younger woman screamed as the wife attacked her. Desperately she grappled with the woman but the wife was too strong for her and pushed her to the cliff's edge. She clawed and bit, then feeling herself falling, clutched at her attacker. Together they went over the edge into the river below.

The broken bodies were carried back to Schoenbrunn, but Rev. Zeisberger, appalled by the scandal, refused them Christian burial. Ever since that day, three lights—two red and one white—swirl at the edge of the steep cliffs at Stone Quarry until they fall and are extinguished in the river.[6]

The Haunted Indian Skull

Many Native American tribes object very strongly to the desecration of their ancestors' remains. In Xenia a long-dead Indian took matters into his own head.

Steve Hale, forensic sculptor, is a man with a thousand faces, all of them built on the faceless remains of the anonymous dead. He tries, using clay and paint, wigs and glass eyes, to bring the dead back to life, to give each of them a name and a past so they may go to their graves in peace.

His story began in the fall of 1987 when a cow rubbed up against a sandy bank in an old quarry near Spring Valley. A skull popped out of the hillside, rolled down the bank, and was found by farmer Ed Gordon* who called the sheriff. The sheriff called the Coroner's office. Steve Hale took the call.

Hale was instantly interested; bones are his business. As a forensic sculptor and criminal investigator for the Prosecutor's office, he handles thousands of human remains every year. Grinning skulls hold no terror for him. Instead, they fascinate him with the stories they have to tell: the muscle twisted—just so—across the cheek, a large nose, heavy browbones, they make the naked skull as individual as the person who once inhabited it.

Calling in Dr. Anna Bellisari, of Wright State University's Sociology/Anthropology Department, Hale went to the scene with camera and excavating equipment.

"I wanted to treat it like a homicide, which is what you do until you know what you have."

With Dr. Bellisari's help he excavated a nearly complete skeleton of a male.

"He was buried in a ceremonial fashion, arms down at his sides, face up, legs straight. He was also buried under a very large tree, on top of a hill, which was a favorite site for Native American burials." It was also a good site from Hale's point of view. The sandy soil had preserved the bones beautifully.

After examining the teeth of the skull, they both agreed that the skeleton was probably that of a Native American of an unknown date. Bellisari advised him to put the remains back in the ground since the Native American tribes in the area have had concerns about the reburial of their ancestors' remains.

"I had nightmares of this getting in the newspapers," she says. 'Just leave them.' I told him." And she left the scene.

Hale had a different idea: "I wanted the bones myself—to study them." I asked him about his feelings about studying other people's relatives' remains. He laughed, "I'd dig up my own grandfather if I thought I could learn something from it. I don't have any problem with that."

So, getting Gordon's permission, he personally collected all the bones and put them in a box.

"The bones were in perfect condition, absolutely pristine. They were very strong, which is unusual in bones of this age." But because of his investigative background and his inquisitive nature, Hale wanted to know more about them.

"The bones were from a man in his 30s. There was no trauma; no known cause of death. I wanted something more definitive."

He got something definitive—but definitely more than he had bargained for.

Within two weeks of the excavation, Hale had moved out of his home and began divorce proceedings against his wife. Within a month, he had been forced from his job at the Coroner's office under very unpleasant circumstances. Unhappy as the time was, he didn't associate any of it with the boxed skeleton in the storage area of his apartment, or with the skull he kept on his apartment worktable. He was fascinated by the perfectly preserved skull. He wanted to learn everything he could about the skull—and the man.

The face held some surprises: "It was a softer face than I would have expected. I guess I expected some big, bony kind of face. The guy had a real ski-slope nose, like Bob Hope. He had a typical bite like a Mongolian. He was missing his first four upper incisors; I made him some."

He was in his final days at the Coroner's office when a woman artist asked if she could borrow the skull for a research project she was doing for a museum on facial characteristics of ancient Indians. Within a week she brought the skull back, abruptly abandoning it in a box on his desk with a terse note: "I'm returning this to you. Call me."

Hale called and she spilled out all the fears and accidents of the past weeks.

"She started telling me about all this bad luck she'd had. The chain on her bicycle came off and it flew up and cut her eye. Then her back went out of place and two or three other horrendous things. That was the beginning of the story of the curse of the skull. She believed her misfortunes began when she picked up this skull and she decided she'd better bring it back. Fast."

Intrigued, Hale had his friend, Pennsylvania psychic Karyol Kirkpatrick, look at the skull.

"She held it. She told me about who he was. She said he was a half-Native American who had been friendly to the settlers. He died in 1790 from a brain inflammation. She described what he looked like, including an amulet he wore around his neck. She said he didn't mind being studied by me, but he was becoming restless that his remains were still disinterred."

Not only did Kirkpatrick tell Hale that the skull's owner was unhappy; she herself became a target of the skull's wrath. The fall after she talked with Hale, he sent her a sketch of a photo he'd taken of her holding the skull. She proudly displayed the drawing in her living room. The result?

"There was turmoil in the house!" declares Kirkpatrick. "The whole household was on edge." The picture was kept in the room where she gives her psychic readings. "If the picture was in sight when I was doing a reading, everything would be upset. There was a lot of confusion; *everything* bothered everybody. It was like the energy was scraping everybody's nerves. My husband even threatened to divorce me!"

Kirkpatrick feels strongly that the Native American was upset that he was on display. "He didn't mind being studied, but now he wanted to be in private." She slid the picture out of sight behind another picture in a frame and there was peace again. But whenever she tried to display the picture, the same emotional reactions occurred. Now she keeps the sketch permanently covered.

Anthropologist Bellisari disagrees with Kirkpatrick's dating of the skull. "The bones were definitely prehistoric—

possibly 5,000 years old. The farmer who owned the property had found other prehistoric objects."

No matter what the date of the skull, Hale still didn't make the connection.

"I just didn't give the whole idea much thought. It took a long time to realize that there was something to it. Something beyond the normal."

Criminal investigators are trained to be skeptical, but from childhood, Hale believed in things that go bump in the night. His home in West Liberty was supposedly haunted by the former owner's ghost.

"It was a lavish house, built by this millionaire—three-car garage, swimming pool, and everything. The millionaire died in the kitchen in the 1920s, so the story went. We'd hear things at night, and it wasn't just the old steam heat system—it was doors slamming and footsteps walking upstairs. I'd be in the house and think one of my brothers had come in and then find out they were all waiting for me outside in the car. Even the dog was spooked by that house. So I believed in ghosts.

"It wasn't that I *disbelieved* in the skull, but until I started thinking about what was happening to *me*, I didn't think there was anything to it. And I didn't want to believe because I wanted to keep the skull. But then I went through these dramatic changes—I got divorced and lost my job under bad circumstances. It was the first time in my adult life I had no job and I was kind of lost. Shortly after I decided that we needed to get this guy back in the ground."

Hale boxed up the skull with the skeleton and called Ed Gordon.

"I asked him to rebury the skeleton in an undisclosed location. 'Bury him. Don't tell me where,' I told him. 'Just bury him facing east because the psychic said he wants to be buried that way.' Gordon and his wife came down to the office and got the box of bones. And they just kind of walked off into the sunset with them."

And has his luck changed since then?

Hale thought back. "I had the skull about a year. Much of the year I was either out of work or working a really awful job with a detective agency. It was right after I made the decision to rebury him that the Prosecuting Attorney picked me up in the fall of 1988. I was even at the Prosecutor's office when Gordon picked up the bones. And since then I've done some real interesting things: I teach at Northwestern University, I've developed a unique kid's ID program for missing children. I'd say things are definitely better."

Hale tried to explain his ambivalence about the skull: "I always had [felt] the presence of a real person because I had reconstructed his face and seen what he looked like. Much as I loved the skull and wanted to keep it, it was still quite eerie to look at." He struggled for the right word to describe his feelings. "Not morbidity in the normal sense, like people are afraid of skulls—it looked quite, I don't want to say 'evil,' but 'ominous.'"

Has he felt any ending to the story of the haunted skull?

"Hopefully he's now at rest. On the day he was buried I saw the biggest hawk I'd ever seen on a tree by Route 35 just east of Valley Road. I stopped and watched him. He was huge; big as an eagle. He was watching another hawk in the road who had been killed. Suddenly he took off and flew majestically away. I've never seen one that big since."[7]

GHOST WRITERS
Ohio's haunted authors

After so many deaths I live and write...
-George Herbert-

The Days After "The Night the Ghost Got In"

James Thurber always said that his view of reality was
skewed by his defective eyesight. Certainly poor eyesight can
turn harmless objects like chairs with robes draped over them
into crouching fiends. Thurber, however, was extremely
clearsighted when it came to the supernatural. Hilariously
improbably as it sounds, his story, "The Night the Ghost Got
In," an account of the misadventures arising out of some
phantom footsteps, is based on fact. Thurber tells the factual
story:

> My own experience in this mysterious area came
> one night, about 1912, in a house my family lived in at
> 77 Jefferson Avenue in Columbus....It consists of the
> heavy steps of a man walking for nearly a minute
> around our dining room table, while I was in the
> bathroom upstairs drying my face with a towel before

going to bed. At the time I was a junior at college, studying journalism, and a non-believer in ghosts. In fact, the word ghost never crossed my mind that night. I thought a burglar or a crazy man had got into the house. My father and younger brother were in Indianapolis and I knew that neither of them would walk silently around that table. I roused my older brother from sleep and brought him to the head of the back stairs that went down into the dining room. As soon as he reached my side, the steps ceased. Finally, in something like terror, he asked me "What's the matter with you?"

I said, in a loud voice, "There's someone down there," and up the stairs, right at us, two at a time, came the heavy steps of a running man. Without a word, my brother ran into his bedroom and locked the door. I stood there until one more step would have taken the invisible thing into me and then, by a reflex, I slammed the door at the head of the steps. The next day I asked the corner druggist, who had been in business there for thirty years, if he had ever heard of any strange stories about 77 Jefferson Avenue. He said, in surprise, "Didn't you know about the steps that go around the dining room table and run up the stairs?" I then began a long research on the business, even slept downstairs several nights alone, at the proper hour on the proper night of the week, but never heard the steps again. It turned out that several families had previously moved out of the house because of the steps. I turned this into a comic story called "The Night The Ghost Got In" nearly thirty years ago, but now I am telling it factually...

My careful researches, more than forty-five years ago, revealed the story of a man who had lived in that house, had walked around the dining room table, then ran up the steps and shot himself in one of the second floor rooms. He left a note describing his final behavior, but it was destroyed by the family. I found out, and the police have never heard of it, and I promised I would not tell about the note.... A strange

voice, anonymous, had telephoned him at his office
one morning and told him that if he went home around
ten A.M., entered the kitchen door, and stood quietly
in the dining room, he would hear his wife making her
daily assignation with her lover and this is precisely
what happened.[1]

Thurber planned a long essay on ghosts, which he apparently never wrote. As he told Edmund Wilson in a letter of
May 24, 1959, in a discussion of other writers' approaches to
the supernatural:

> I figure that only a tiny percentage deals with the
> subject gravely or even seriously, for one admits he
> experienced a ghost with as much reluctance as he
> might admit having once been homosexual. Then, too,
> there are the vast numbers of crackpots who are taken
> about as seriously as Conan Doyle and his photo-
> graphs of ectoplasm....As a result, the ghost has
> become either a figure of comedy or a dramatic
> device, or a symbol in poetry, and the result of *that* has
> been a remarkable indifference to sound exploration of
> death and after death....My running ghost was heard by
> my older brother, too, and he ran to beat hell and
> locked himself in his room, not having said a word
> after my, 'there's somebody down there' was followed
> by the steps coming up the stairs two at a time. I
> should add that a man who had lived in that house in
> Columbus shot himself in an upstairs bedroom, having
> last been figured to be alive as he paced the dining
> room floor. We never heard it again, although I tried
> the words at the same hour, slept downstairs, or stayed
> awake, and so on....I can only believe that the old
> specter hasn't walked or run for years.[2]

There Thurber was wrong. The "old specter" continued to
walk, or rather run, long after the Thurbers moved away. In
1936, Margaret*, a woman from Springfield, rented rooms in
the Jefferson St. house. Her landlady had one small peculiarity: she asked that one of her tenants stay home with her each

weekend evening. Margaret often heard the sound of steps running briskly up the back staircase. At the time she assumed the noises came from the tenants next door. It wasn't until several years later that she met Thurber's brother William who mentioned that the house was haunted. Recalling the sounds, Margaret realized that not only were the walls of the house a foot thick, and soundproof, but also that the tenants next door were an elderly couple who were unlikely to be running up stairs.

On a return visit to the house, Margaret slept in what used to be the dining room. She was awakened—by what she wasn't sure. She sat up in bed and saw a figure hunched over with his elbow on his knee sitting in the rocking chair in the corner of her room. It wasn't necessarily a ghost, Margaret insists—although she does believe in ghosts—but it was certainly an image of someone in despair. She lay back down in bed, sat up again, and the figure was gone.

Yet another tenant who lived in the attic described noises like footsteps that began in the second-floor hallway. Most of the time they merely creaked up and down, up and down the stairs. But sometimes they came up to the top of the stairs and stopped dead at his door. He would lie there quietly, just listening. "I would swear someone was coming up to see me," he recalls. But no one would knock. This went on night after night. He was curious to know who was there, but he never opened the door.

The "old specter" continues his activities even today. The Thurber House has been restored and now houses a library and an annual Writer-in-Residence.

One of these writers actually saw the ghost:

> In my second or third week at the house, as I
> stepped out of a car in the back parking lot, I happened
> to look up to the apartment and the ghost—a hefty,
> somewhat stooped, black torso shadow, apparently
> dressed in a raincoat with the collar turned up, moving
> at a silhouette's pace—made a single pass through the
> hallway lights just as my eyes traveled up the building
> wall, as if waiting there, set in motion by my glance.

I took the sighting seriously. I even made Donn
Vickers walk me upstairs, but when we got to the spot,
only the spot was there.

Later in my stay, I heard unaccountable clattering
of the lower kitchen cupboards, light gentle fast
frustrated slamming, as if a mouse were inside trying
to push out with its nose, but there was no mouse
when I looked.

Another writer was awakened at 2 A.M. by the security
service who said that the burglar alarm had gone off. In the
confusion, the police were sent, only to find all the doors and
windows locked on the inside "tight as a tick" as the cop says
in "The Night the Ghost Got In." A mysterious short circuit
was one theory, but one police officer had another: "It must've
been a ghost."[3]

The Poets' Family Ghost

Poets Alice (1820-1870) and Phoebe Cary (1824-1871)
were sisters from Cincinnati. Their appeal has faded, but
Phoebe was once acclaimed "the wittiest woman in America,"
while Alice's poem "Pictures of Memory" was hailed by Edgar
Allan Poe as "one of the most melodious lyrics in the English
language." Today Alice is best remembered for her hymn,
"One Sweetly Solemn Thought."

Late in the autumn of 1869, on her deathbed, Alice spoke
of the Cary family ghost story:

"...Almost every family *has* a ghost story, you
know? Ours has more than one, but *the* one foreshad-
owed all the others."

"Do tell it to me," said the friend sitting by her
bed.

"Well, the new house was just finished, but we
had not moved into it. There had been a violent
shower; father had come home from the field, and
everybody had come in out of the rain. I think it was
about four in the afternoon, when the storm ceased and
the sun shone out. The new house stood on the edge

of a ravine and the sun was shining full upon it, when some one in the family called out and asked how Rhoda and Lucy came to be over in the new house, and the door open. Upon this all the rest of the family rushed to the front door, and there, across the ravine, in the open door of the new house, stood Rhoda with Lucy in her arms. Some one said, 'She must have come from the sugar camp, and has taken shelter there with Lucy from the rain.' Upon this another called out, 'Rhoda!' but she did not answer. While we were gazing and talking and calling, Rhoda herself came down-stairs, where she had left Lucy fast asleep, and stood with us while we all saw, in the full blaze of the sun, the woman with the child in her arms slowly sink, sink, sink into the ground until she disappeared from sight. Then a great silence fell upon us all. In our hearts we all believed it to be a warning of sorrow—of what, we knew not. When Rhoda and Lucy both died, then we knew. Rhoda died the next autumn, November 11; Lucy a month later, December 10, 1833. Father went directly over to the house and out into the road, but no human being, and not even a track, could be seen. Lucy has been seen many times since by different members of the family, in the same house, always in a red frock, like one she was very fond of wearing; the last time by my brother Warren's little boy, who had never heard the story. He came running in, saying that he had seen 'a little girl up-stairs, in a red dress.' He is dead now, and such a bright boy. Since the apparition in the door, never for one year has our family been free from the shadow of death. Ever since, some one of us has been dying."[4]

Spirit Poetry

Some spirits have a literary bent, as this account from Guernsey County suggests:

In Quaker City, the Bay family—brothers William and Andy and sister Susan lived with the mysterious "Dr. French."

Dr. French had sandy hair streaked with grey, always wore heavy glasses and carried a cane, and possessed a vicious wooly black dog. The doctor didn't work, as far as anyone could tell, but he could heal by the laying on of hands.

A traveler who had a spiritualist adventure with the foursome wrote an account of it to *The Jeffersonian*, November 8, 1883:

> There was a doctor there, whose name I forget. All the talk was about Spiritualism and spirits until I thought I had got into a veritable bedlam. So it went on until late before we went to bed, they trying to illustrate their beliefs by argument and experiment, by so-called spirit writing, spiritual (trick) mirrors, etc., until I was heartily wearied....

The traveler went to bed, but was suddenly awakened.

> A cold, clammy hand had touched me and moved upon me, so it seemed. Again I thought I had been dreaming, but sleep came slowly, and before I was asleep again I felt distinctly, not one cold hand but two of them moving over my arms and body; yet there was nobody there. I felt about, got up and made a light. The doors were closed as I had left them; but the distinct impression was left with me and is with me yet, that hands did touch....The folks coolly told me in the morning that I had been visited in the night by their brother William, who was dead, and that they had been visited by him, too.
> Of course, ready explanation may be suggested for this, but on the table, under my watch, was found a poem, said to be in a handwriting much like that of William Bay....

The poem begins in a macabre vein:

> Your planet is legions of leagues away,
> And seems like a blood-shot eye--
> Like the eyes of a demon here, they say

As they sigh,
As they turn with a sorrowful sigh.
They have heard of your horrible curse up here,
Your beasts and your blood, and your ghouls and all,

It goes on to list literary notables to be found in Hell:

For Dante has taken a flight up here
And told all,
Told all the terrible tale of your fall.
And Poe is here drinking a fiery draught,
Distilled from the lavas of hell,
And swears that tonight like a shaft
from the archer, he'll back to the dell
Of death dews, and death damps, and death mould
To the tomb of Lenore, dark, silent, and cold
Dark, silent and cold.... [5]

The Haunted Stowes

Harriet Beecher Stowe was born in Connecticut, but lived in Cincinnati longer than any other place except Hartford. In Cincinnati she met and married the haunted Calvin Stowe, bore her children (and buried one), and began her career as a writer, so Ohio can rightly claim her as an author who was deeply interested in spiritualistic questions.

Harriet had many psychic experiences and said that *Uncle Tom's Cabin* was "given" to her, inspired by a vision:

Mrs. Stowe was seated in her pew in the college
church at Brunswick during the communion
service...Suddenly, like the unrolling of a picture
scroll, the scene of the death of Uncle Tom seemed to
pass before her. At the same time the words of Jesus
were sounding in her ears: "Inasmuch as ye have done
it unto the least of these my brethren, ye have done it
unto me!" It seemed as if the crucified, but now risen
and glorified, Christ were speaking to her through the
poor black man, cut and bleeding under the blows of

the slave whip. She was affected so strongly that she could scarcely keep from weeping aloud.

That Sunday afternoon she went to her room, locked the door, and wrote out—substantially as it appears in the published edition—the chapter called "The Death of Uncle Tom"....It seemed to her as though what she wrote was blown through her mind as with the rushing of a mighty wind.[6]

Harriet called her husband, the plump, balding, immensely learned Calvin Stowe, "my old rabbi." Born and reared in a small Massachusetts village by his deeply religious mother after his father's death, Calvin was fascinated by the more occult incidents in the Bible—The Witch of Endor; Ezekiel and John of Patmos with their weird visions. Innocently supposing that everyone saw the same things he did, Calvin also began to have weird visions of all things visible and invisible.

"The facts," he wrote soberly in a paper read to his fellow-members of Cincinnati's Semi-Colon Club, "appear to me to be curious and well worth the attention of the psychologist. I regard the occurrences in question as the more remarkable because I cannot discover that I possess either taste or talent for fiction or poetry...I can remember observing a multitude of animated and active objects, which I could see with perfect distinctness...passing through the floor, and the ceilings and the walls of the house...

Calvin spoke of his easily excited nervous system, then went on:

[When I was four] I occupied a bedroom that opened into the kitchen. Within this bedroom...was the staircase which led to the garret...some of the boards which enclosed the staircase were too short and left a considerable space between them and the ceiling. One of these open spaces was directly in front of my bed, so that when I lay upon my pillow my face was opposite to it.

Every night, after I had gone to bed and the candle was removed, a very pleasant-looking human face would peer at me over the top of that board, and gradually press forward his head, neck, shoulders, and finally his whole body as far as the waist, through the opening, and then, smiling upon me with great good-nature, would withdraw in the same manner in which he had entered. He was a great favorite of mine; for, though we neither of us spoke, we perfectly understood, and were entirely devoted to, each other. It is a singular fact that the features of this phantom bore a very close resemblance to those of a boy older than myself whom I feared and hated: still, the resemblance was so strong that I called him by the same name, "Harvey."

Harvey's visits were pleasant ones, but those of other visitants were not:

I saw at an immense distance below me the regions of the damned....From this awful world of horror the tunnel-shaped clouds were ascending, and I perceived that they were the principal instruments of torture in these gloomy abodes...but a little distance from my bed, I saw four or five sturdy, resolute devils endeavoring to carry off an unprincipled and dissipated man of the neighborhood...of whom I had stood in terror for years. These devils...had neither red faces, nor horns, nor hoofs, nor tails. They were in all respects stoutly built and well-dressed gentlemen. The only peculiarity that I noted...[was that their heads] were perfectly bare, without hair or flesh, and of a uniform sky-blue color, like the ashes of burnt paper before it falls to pieces....

Calvin also saw fairies on the window-sill, "in white robes, gamboling and dancing with incessant merriment" and, once, a ghastly luminous ashy-blue skeleton lying beside him in bed. How much of this had to do with his extremely bad eyesight, we do not know. He sometimes mistook his own wife for a vision.[7]

In 1857, the Stowe's first-born son, Henry, was accidentally drowned. In her intense grief, Harriet tried to contact him through mediums. Although she could have been rendered vulnerable by her bereavement, with her usual good sense she was wary of fraudulent spiritualist claims.

As Harriet wrote in an article in *The Independent*, if it was possible to roll away the stone from the grave, she wanted it done by "an unquestionable angel, who executes no doubtful juggle by pale moonlight or starlight....If the raps and squeaks and tricks with tables and chairs constituted 'communion with the dead,' sadly and soberly we say we had rather be without it."

As for the communications of spirits claiming to describe things in the spirit world, Harriet said, "we can conceive of no more appalling prospect than to have them true...If the future life is so weary, stale, flat, and unprofitable as we might infer from these readings, one would have reason to deplore an immortality from which no suicide could give an outlet. To be condemned to such eternal prosing would be worse than annihilation."[8]

Haunted Hearn

Lafcadio Hearn is best known for his books on Japan, including several volumes of ghost stories. Less well-known are a series of articles on spiritualism that Hearn wrote as a reporter for the *Cincinnati Enquirer:* "Modern Spiritualism," on January 4, 1874, "Occult Science" on January 11, and "Among the Spirits" on January 24th.

Hearn was a complete sceptic, a muck-raker, hired to expose the city's mediums in a sensational manner that would sell papers. Unexpectedly, in the last of the series, he found his own vulnerabilities exposed.

"Among the Spirits" opens with a description of a seedy room and the medium's phony patter. Hearn was contemptuous, but suddenly, through an obvious charlatan, he found himself speaking with the spirit of his dead father:

> "I am your father, P---,"
> "Have you any word for me?"
> "Yes."
> "What is it?"

"Forgive me"—in a long whisper.

"I have nothing to forgive."

"You have, indeed"—very faintly

"What is it?"

"You know well"—distinctly....

"I wronged you: forgive me"—a loud, distinct whisper.

"I do not consider that you have."

"It would be better not to contradict the spirit," interrupted the medium, "until it has explained matters."

"I do not wish to contradict the spirit in the sense you imply," answered the reporter. "I thoroughly understand the circumstances alluded to; but I wish to explain that I have long ceased to consider it as a wrong done me."

What the sensation-seeking public did not know was that Hearn and his mother had been abandoned by his father when Hearn was a child. Hearn was laying the ghost of his father in more ways than the obvious one.[9]

The Horrors of Ambrose Bierce

Ambrose Bierce, dubbed "Bitter Bierce" by his British colleagues, was noted for his horror and ghost stories like "A Jug of Sirup," "An Occurrence at Owl Creek Bridge," "The Boarded Window," and "The Damned Thing." Born in a log cabin in Meigs County into a family of eccentrics whose behavior bordered on madness, his works revel in the violent, the shocking, and the perverse.

In *The Devil's Dictionary* Bierce defined ghost as "The outward and visible sign of an inward fear." Ambiguity, fear, horror, and the loss of love are the hallmarks of stories that torment the reader with psychic insecurity. He once said, "To know that a man is dead should be enough." But for Bierce, it wasn't enough. Obsessive as a necrophiliac, he delved into the deepest graves of man's subconscious fears.[10]

Here is one of "Bitter" Bierce's ghost stories, based on a true tale from Ohio.

A Fruitless Assignment

Henry Saylor, who was killed in Covington, in a quarrel with Antonio Finch, was a reporter on the Cincinnati *Commercial.* In the year 1859 a vacant dwelling in Vine street, in Cincinnati, became the center of a local excitement because of the strange sights and sounds said to be observed in it nightly. According to the testimony of many reputable residents of the vicinity these were inconsistent with any other hypothesis than that the house was haunted. Figures with something singularly unfamiliar about them were seen by crowds on the sidewalks to pass in and out. No one could say just where they appeared upon the open lawn on their way to the front door by which they entered, nor at exactly what point they vanished as they came out; or, rather, while each spectator was positive enough about these matters, no two agreed. They were all similarly at variance in their descriptions of the figures themselves. Some of the bolder of the curious throng ventured on several evenings to stand upon the doorsteps to intercept them, or failing in this, get a nearer look at them. These courageous men, it was said, were unable to force the door by their united strength, and always were hurled from the steps by some invisible agency and severely injured; the door immediately afterward opening, apparently of its own volition, to admit or free some ghostly guest. The dwelling was known as the Roscoe house, a family of that name having lived there for some years, and then, one by one, disappeared, the last to leave being an old woman. Stories of foul play and successive murders had always been rife, but never were authenticated.

One day during the prevalence of the excitement Saylor presented himself at the office of the *Commercial* for orders. He received a note from the city editor which read as follows: "Go and pass the night alone in the haunted house in Vine street and if anything occurs worth while make two columns." Saylor obeyed his superior; he could not afford to lose his position on the paper.

Apprising the police of his intention, he effected an entrance through a rear window before dark, walked through the deserted rooms, bare of furniture, dusty and desolate, and seating himself at last in the parlor on an old sofa which he had dragged in from another room watched the deepening of the gloom as night came on. Before it was altogether dark the curious crowd had collected in the street, silent, as a rule and expectant, with here and there a scoffer uttering his incredulity and courage with scornful remarks or ribald cries. None knew of the anxious watcher inside. He feared to make a light; the uncurtained windows would have betrayed his presence, subjecting him to insult, possibly to injury. Moreover, he was too conscientious to do anything to enfeeble his impressions and unwilling to alter any of the customary conditions under which the manifestations were said to occur.

It was now dark outside, but light from the street faintly illuminated the part of the room that he was in. He had set open every door in the whole interior, above and below, but all the outer ones were locked and bolted. Sudden exclamations from the crowd caused him to spring to the window and look out. He saw the figure of a man moving rapidly across the lawn toward the building—saw it ascend the steps; then a projection of the wall concealed it. There was a noise as of the opening and closing of the hall door; he heard quick, heavy footsteps along the passage—heard them ascend the stairs— heard them on the uncarpeted floor of the chamber immediately overhead.

Saylor promptly drew his pistol, and groping his way up the stairs entered the chamber, dimly lighted from the street. No one was there. He heard footsteps in an adjoining room and entered that. It was dark and silent. He struck his foot against some object on the floor, knelt by it, passed his hand over it. It was a human head—that of a woman. Lifting it by the hair this iron-nerved man returned to the half-lighted room below, carried it near the window and attentively examined it. While so engaged he was half conscious of the rapid opening and closing of the outer door, of footfalls sounding all about him. He raised his eyes from the ghastly object of his attention and saw himself the center of a crowd of men and women dimly seen; the room was thronged with them. He thought the people had broken in.

"Ladies and gentlemen," he said, coolly, "you see me under suspicious circumstances, but—" his voice was drowned in peals of laughter—such laughter as is heard in asylums for the insane. The persons about him pointed at the object in his hand and their merriment increased as he dropped it and it went rolling among their feet. They danced about it with gestures grotesque and attitudes obscene and indescribable. They struck it with their feet, urging it about the room from wall to wall; pushed and overthrew one another in their struggles to kick it; cursed and screamed and sang snatches of ribald songs as the battered head bounded about the room as if in terror and trying to escape. At last it shot out of the door into the hall, followed by all, with tumultuous haste. That moment the door closed with a sharp concussion. Saylor was alone, in dead silence.

Carefully putting away his pistol, which all the time he had held in his hand, he went to a window and looked out. The street was deserted and silent; the lamps were extinguished; the roofs and chimneys of the houses were sharply outlined against the dawn-light in the east. He left the house, the door yielding easily to his hand, and walked to the *Commercial* office. The city editor was still in his office—asleep. Saylor waked him and said: "I have been at the haunted house."

The editor stared blankly as if not wholly awake. "Good God!" he cried, "are you Saylor?"

"Yes—why not?"

The editor made no answer, but continued staring.

"I passed the night there—it seems," said Saylor.

"They say that things were uncommonly quiet out there," the editor said, trifling with a paper-weight upon which he had dropped his eyes. "Did anything occur?"

"Nothing whatever."

In the end, Ambrose Bierce left the world with a true mystery of his own. In 1914, he went to Mexico to follow Pancho Villa's army and vanished.

THE HEADLESS MOTORCYCLIST
And other haunted conveyances

The dead travel fast.
-Bram Stoker-

The last journey.... The Egyptians buried ships to carry their dead to the afterlife. The Greeks placed a coin in their corpses' mouthes to pay Charon to ferry them across the River Styx. The Vikings, who called death "the journey elsewhere," placed their dead warriors on a boatload of treasure, then set the sails to the West and torched the ship into a floating pyre.

We have not come so far from these traditions. Our dead, in their boat-like coffins, travel in glossy black hearses. A motorcycle gang leader is buried with his Harley. A woman asks to ride to eternity in her favorite pink Cadillac. Death is a journey we will all make one day; a journey that some souls are still making.

Doggy Cross's Ghost

With the colorful history of steam transport on the Ohio
River, it is strange that there are no spectral steamboats plying
the Ohio, full of ghost-gamblers dicing for their souls. One of
the few river ghosts is that of the steamer *Kanawha*. In January
of 1916, the *Kanawha* wrecked at Lock No. 19 on the Ohio
River. No lives were lost, but shortly after the wreck, strange
lights began to be seen at the foot of the rock bluff along the
Ohio shoreline just west of Mustapha Island. The lights were
seen in good weather and bad for many years and were
witnessed by hundreds of people, including experienced river
craft personnel. First noticed by pilot Monroe "Doggy" Cross,
the lights were known as "Doggy Cross's Ghost" or the
"Mustapha Island Ghost."[1]

The Spectral Sailors

In the 1880s two sailors fell to their deaths from the
topmast of a Lake Erie sailing vessel. The rumor got about that
the ship was unlucky—a "Jonah" and many of the crew were
reluctant to rejoin her. One of them wrote an account of the
ghosts to the *Chicago Times* in March, 1885:

> On its arrival at Buffalo, the men went on shore as
> soon as they were paid off. They said the ship had lost
> her luck. While we were discharging at the elevator,
> the story got round and some of the grain-trimmers
> refused to work on her. Even the mate was affected by
> it. At last we got ready to sail for Cleveland, where
> we were to load coal.
> The captain managed to get a crew by going to a
> crimp, [press-gang operator] who ran them in, fresh
> from salt water. They came on board two-thirds
> drunk, and the mate was steering them into the
> forecastle when one of them stopped and said,
> pointing aloft: "What have you got a figurehead on
> the mast for?" The mate looked up and then turned
> pale, "It's Bill!" he said, and with that the whole lot

jumped onto the dock. I didn't see anything, but the mate told the captain to look for another officer. The captain was so much affected that he put me on another schooner, and then shipped a new crew and sailed for Cleveland. They never got there. They were sunk by a steamer off Dunkirk.[2]

Gretchen's Ghost

A network of canals built in the early 1800s opened up the Ohio Territory to commerce and statehood. At Beaver Creek State Park in Columbiana County there survives part of a lock and canal system from 1836. One of the locks is named "Gretchen Lock." A charming tribute to a family member, one might think, but the place has a macabre history.

Gill Hans, the engineer who built the lock, brought his family over from Holland. His young daughter Gretchen pined for the Low Country until, weakened, she contracted malaria and died August 12, 1838, raving about going home. Distraught, Hans had Gretchen's coffin temporarily entombed in a vault within the lock's stonework until the family could return to Holland together. He made arrangements to sail; Gretchen's coffin was loaded onto the ship and the entire family sailed into oblivion. The ship went down in an Atlantic storm with all hands.

Yet even death could not take Gretchen home. On the anniversary of her death, the young Dutch girl can be seen walking along the lock that bears her name.[3]

The Camera-Shy Ghost

Another lock at Beaver Creek State Park is named "Jake's Lock" after a former lock keeper. He always carried a lantern when he went about his duties at night. But one night he was struck by lightning and fell into the water, a blackened, smoking corpse.

Now Jake seems to come and go as he did when he was alive, taking the day shift, then the night. Some nights you can still see his lantern shining brightly underneath the water.

Oddly, when Jake's spirit is present at the lock, no camera will function. Perhaps the flash reminds him of the lightning that caused his death.[4]

The Vanishing Hitchhiker

The stories are always the same: a driver picks up a young woman hitchhiker. Often she is not dressed for the weather and he gallantly gives her his coat. When he arrives at the address she has given him, the woman has mysteriously vanished from the locked car. Inquiring at the house, he is told that she has been dead for some time, killed in an auto accident. When he visits the young woman's grave, he finds his jacket draped on her tombstone.

Why do these girls wander along the highways, waiting for the one driver who will stop? They are wet, lonely, and unhappy; they only want to go home to their mothers, to warmth and life. They never quite make it; their last stop is always the grave. But they try again and again, standing by the road with the patience of the dead, waiting for the driver who will give them a lift home.

Folklorist Richard Gill heard the following tale in his high school folklore class in Fostoria:

> My father was driving down the road between Arcadia and Fostoria and saw a woman in a long white evening gown. She was not hitchhiking, but walking down the side of the road. He stopped and offered her a ride. When he offered her the front seat she ignored him. He got out and opened the back door. She got in. He then went around the car and got in the front seat. When he got in, she had disappeared.

The student said that this happened to her father. Then an odd thing occurred: two other students in the class responded that the same thing had happened to their fathers. Gill questioned them and determined from their comments that the events occurred between November 1971 and February 1972 on a stretch of road between Arcadia and Fostoria. All three tales were alike in details: the white evening gown, the woman's indifferent silence, the even deeper silence of the empty car.[5]

A Traveling Spirit

On the edge of Quaker City, on S.R. 513 North stands a small bridge haunted by a ghost who enjoyed buggy rides. Travelers by night first saw him walking by the side of their buggies. Next thing they knew, he'd be sitting companionably next to them in the seat. The ghost also had a horribly friendly habit of coming up behind a traveler and tapping him on the shoulder. Fortunately, the ghost, like so many supernatural creatures, couldn't cross running water, so he waved goodbye to terrified travelers at the bridge.[6]

The Ghost of Flight 191

From Cincinnati comes the story of a man who saw the ghost of a doomed airliner ten days before her fiery death.

David Booth woke up in a cold sweat. The dream had been too vivid: an American Airlines jet cartwheeling in a ball of flames. It was a three-engine plane coming in for a landing, only the engines didn't sound right. Then the plane rolled over and slammed into the ground, flames fountaining into the air. Booth closed his eyes, but the picture replayed itself over and over.

"It was like I was standing there watching the whole thing," Booth said "like watching television."

The next night he dreamed the same dream, more vividly than ever.

"I did everything to stop sleeping from then on. I'd watch TV until 2 A.M. One night I got drunk." But for seven more nights the dream recurred. Finally Tuesday, 22 May, Booth decided he had to do something.

He called American Airlines. He called the Federal Aviation Administration. He called Cincinnati's Airport Control. There he was finally taken seriously.

"It didn't sound like a prank," said Cincinnati Airport official, Ray Pinkerton. Thursday, 24 May, Pinkerton's colleague, Paul Williams, got Booth's story.

"What he described to me, I thought might be a 727, because I knew that American Airlines flew Boeing 727s. Another possibility was a DC10. He specifically identified it as an American Airlines aircraft with an engine on the tail. He described his vantage point as beside a gravel road running up towards a flat-roofed building. He described the plane at rather a low altitude which I took to be two to four hundred feet. It suddenly turned sharply and dived into the ground. He described in great detail the explosion. He became quite distraught, almost as if he was seeing death occurring." Williams was convinced, but, maddeningly, no one could think of anything to do.

On Friday, May 25th, American Airlines Flight 191, a three-engined DC10 crashed on take-off at O'Hare. One of the engines broke away; the plane turned over on its back and crashed in flames.

Says Paul Williams, "I heard about the crash on Friday afternoon on my way home from work about 5 P.M. As I was listening to the description of the crash on the radio, it sounded like a replay of what I'd heard the day before from David."

"It was uncanny," said FAA official, Jack Barker. "[Booth] named the airline, he called the right type of plane— three-engined—he said the plane came in inverted, which it did, and of course he reported it to officials just...before it happened."

Paul Williams reflects, "Perhaps the most remarkable coincidence of the whole thing was the similarity of the maneuver the plane made. It's a very unusual maneuver for plane to make before crashing. Most of them crash with wings horizontal. They run into some obstruction or there is a mid-air collision. But the maneuver David described was very unusual. As a matter of fact, it's the only one I've heard of in a plane that size."

The Chicago DC10 crash of 1979 was the worst air accident in the United States, with 173 people killed. Chilling pictures of the falling plane caught by an amateur photographer etched the tragedy on the minds of all who saw them. But for David Booth, the nightmare pictures of a doomed plane were finally ended.[7]

The Headless Motorcyclist

An anonymous wag has said, "Death is Nature's way of telling you to slow down." But death has not slowed the pace of a motorcyclist doomed to spend eternity repeating his fatal ride in the Great Black Swamp.

> *The legend goes that a serviceman, returning from the Great War rode his motorcycle to visit his girlfriend, only to find that she had married another. Enraged he rode off, took a curve too fast and went into a bridge railing. When they found his body, it was headless. Ever since then, if you blink your headlights and honk your horn on the anniversary of the accident, the motorcyclist will repeat his fatal ride. In 1968 folklorist Richard Gill investigated this story.[8]*

The moon is up. I am riding.

It seems like I've ridden this road a thousand times before, always on a cold March night, with the stars shivering above the flatness of the northern Ohio plains. I am going to see the girl who will soon be my wife.

The farmhouse looks the same. A little smaller than I had remembered, but then, everything looks small compared to a war. I cut the engine at the road, unfasten my helmet, and wheel the bike up to the house, the way I used to. I hope she doesn't hear the crunching of the wheels on the drive. I want to surprise her.

> *On March 21 of that year Gill went to the site near Elmore with a friend, a tape recorder, and two cameras: one movie camera and a still camera set to take a series of time exposures. They parked the car, then blinked the lights three times and honked the horn three times. A light appeared at the farmhouse, moved down its driveway, down the road and then disappeared around the middle of the bridge.*

She smelled of lilacs. No other girl, not even the street women in France had smelled like that. We were to be married, she understood, when I returned from the war. If I didn't come back—well, we never discussed it. Sometimes in the muck of the trenches I thought of her sitting in the rocker in the kitchen, grown old and unmarried in her father's house, lifting her head at an unexpected sound, thinking it might be me come back to claim her. I thought of her pining for me, struggling on her deathbed to rise and embrace my ghost.

Her father didn't approve of me. Said I spent too much time roaming around on that machine of mine—it's an Indian—a real beauty from her V-twin engine to her gleaming red paint. I keep her in good trim. She's like a woman, needs to be fed and cosseted and complimented. I sometimes dream about riding her at speeds that only happen in dreams, taking curves heeled over at incredible angles, defying gravity, laughing at death.

But her father hated me because I want to take her away from the farm. I wanted to take her to town, get a job in a factory, buy her a house with a picket fence and indoor plumbing and electric lights. Her father thought I was full of crazy schemes. Sometimes, returning from the chores, foul to the knees, he'd see us sitting on the porch swing and do an about-face to the barn, until I said goodnight and left her sulking on the swing.

Like most girls she could be moony, always wanting flowers and whispered sweet talk, but it would have been all right once we were married. There was a song we sang in the trenches, "Whose Little Heart Are You Breaking Now?" Sometimes I wondered if she was sitting on the porch swing with anyone else. Those days I wished we could go over the top with bayonets fixed instead of sitting in the mud, taking bored potshots at helmets stuck up on sticks and Hun washing hung out to dry.

She's beautiful, I guess. It has been a long time since I last saw her face. The night I left she wore a white dress, with finicky little ruffles that made her push me away when I tried to kiss her. The air was full of lilacs or maybe that was something I thought up later. I marched in mud up to my eyebrows, past dead men bloated and rotting in the trenches. And I thought of her, so fragrant, so pure in that white dress.

"Things may not be the same," my folks warned me. But what could have changed? A promise is a promise.

> *Gill's friend tied a string across the road in the middle of the bridge. He returned to the car, blinked the lights three times, and honked the horn three times. The light appeared again, moved down the road and disappeared in the center of the bridge. They got out of the car to examine the string and found that it was intact.*

It was dark when I got there, and cold in the late spring dark. I looked through the window, hoping to catch her unawares, before she saw me. She was standing at the table, peeling potatoes. The light in the kitchen made her look golden, like a Christmas angel. Her hair stood around her face in little wisps like a halo. Then *he*, came up behind her and put his arms around her. She leaned back into his arms like he owned her.

I tore open the door. She screamed as if she'd seen a ghost. I stared at her white face while words buzzed in my ears—words I couldn't understand, couldn't hear. She raised her hand to show me a ring. It sparkled in the lamplight. He took her hand, shelteringly, protectively. I lifted a hand to stop the words that buzzed like insects around my head. Then I turned and went out into the dark. The insects followed me. If she watched me go, I never saw.

> *Gill's friend then decided to stand in the middle of the road. Gill went back to the car to blink the lights and honk the horn. Once again the light appeared, moved down the road and disappeared in the center of the bridge. Gill waited. And waited some more. When his friend did not return Gill went looking for him. The man had disappeared from his place in the center of the road. When Gill finally found him in a ditch, he was unconscious, apparently badly beaten. Gill brought him around, but he had no idea what had*

*happened. At first Gill thought his friend was faking it
or playing a joke, but he knew his friend's character
and it didn't seem very likely.*

The muddy gravel drive sank under my wheels as I turned
the bike around. I stopped at the road, mechanically pulling on
my gloves, my goggles. In the ditches, the water stood, sky-
deep. The moon stared up at me like the reflection of a long-
dead friend, floating face up in the trenches.

I turned the throttle. The wind cut my face. My scarf
whipped over my eyes and I struck it away. The wind brought
tears, running down my cheeks, blurring the goggles. I tore
them off and let them go, tumbling into the darkness. I urged
the motorcycle on, rocking and heaving as if I were forcing
myself into her. Love had nothing to do with it, any more than
love had anything to do with this road or the wind screaming in
my ears. I twisted the throttle open, leaving behind everything
weak and weary and sad.

*For the team's fourth experiment, they moved the
car into the road on the near side of the bridge, facing
away from the farmhouse. They blinked the lights
three times and honked the horn three times. As the
light appeared, they accelerated slowly. The light
came up from behind, passed through the car and went
on in front of the car, only to disappear in the center
of the bridge. It was at that time, says Gill, that he
began to believe in ghosts. His friend wanted to stay
and perform other experiments, but since it was Gill's
car they just kept going.*

*The movie film showed nothing. The still camera
showed a light source of some kind. And the tape
recorder picked up a humming sound.*

The headlamp wavered with each rut and rock. Icy tears
blinded me. My gauntlets were slick with wiping them away.
We hit the curve at the bridge. The wheels tore at the gravel
then broke free. We plunged over the bridge, then off the road,
the exhaust snarling.

I saw the fence, its barbed wire stars glittering with frost, in the light of the headlamp. Then my head spun and I saw sky as I fell like a hedgeapple into the frosted weeds. Far away I saw my body, lying half beneath the bike, which struggled in the grass like a wounded animal. Then suddenly everything was still.

I don't know how long I lay there. The night was cold. I saw the moon smiling, unconcerned, closer than my own headlight. I heard a horn honk three times. And I rose again from the frozen grass and screamed to the stars: Where is myheadmyheadmyhead

The moon is up. I am riding...

APPENDIX 1
HAUNTING PEOPLE
Ghost-hunters, tale-tellers, and tours.

Gespenster sind fur solche Leute nur/Die sie seh'n wollen
Ghosts only come to those who look for them.
-German saying-

Ghost-hunter Anne Oscard is one of the most talented tarot card readers I've ever met. She also does hypnosis and past-life regressions. She's one person I'd like to have along when confronting a ghost.
> 672 H Residenz Parkway
> Kettering, OH 45429
> (513) 293-4612

Teresa F. Barnes gives a talk on ghosts called "Ghosts—Not Just 'Things That Go Bump in the Night'"
> 7180 Gomer Road
> Gomer, OH 45809

The Columbus Landmarks Foundation Ghost Tour is held (naturally) every October. They visit landmarks like Thurber House (site of James Thurber's story, "The Night the Ghost Got In") and Kelton House where the late Miss Kelton rearranges the furniture.
> (614) 221-0227

Psychic Kathleen Cook can help to send earthbound spirits on to their rest. Readings by referral.

2307 Regency Ct.
Fairborn, OH 45424
(513) 878-1924

Let Waynesville Town Crier and Historian Dennis Dalton
show you the invisible sights of "Ohio's Most Haunted Town"
with his "Not So Dearly Departed" Tour. By appointment.
Waynesville Chamber of Commerce, (513) 897-8855
or
Historically Speaking
PO Box 419
Waynesville, OH 45068

Pennsylvania psychic Karyol Kirkpatrick can help unwanted
spirits move along. She works with the police and does psychic
readings by phone.
(717) 393-8827.

Rich Strong, Psychic Investigator and President of Psychic
Science International, can tell you if the things going bump in the
night in your house are ghosts or merely escaped gerbils.
"People *do* imagine things," says Strong, wryly. His profes-
sional work is in safety and mishap prevention and he uses many
of the same techniques in investigating paranormal phenomena.
"It's a combination of engineering analysis and spiritual
sensitivity," says Strong. "You look at clues and use accident
investigation methods to verify occurences. It's a very methodical
procedure."
Psychic Science International, a MENSA special-interest
group, also holds rescue circles.
7514 Belleplaine Dr.
Huber Hts., OH 45424-3229
(513) 236-0361

This very gifted psychic and psychometrist Robert A.
Thompson can identify and send on earthbound spirits. He also
demonstrates spirit energy before audiences and gives readings.
(513) 882-6350

Robert Van Der Velde is a delightful ghost hunter who has
traveled all around the United States in his quest for the Unknown.

You can book his slide shows on Cleveland-area ghosts, American ghosts, or Dr. Samuel Mudd and other Civil War topics.

7733 Dahlia Dr.

Mentor-on-the-Lake, OH 44060

The Warren Ghost Walk is a unique look at the ghosts of Millionaire's Row and of Trumbull County. As participants walk from site to haunted site, actors portray ghostly doings.

For example: "Bish Perkins" and his Aunt Lizzie lived in the house which is now Warren City Hall. Perkins committed suicide several months after the mysterious death of a servant girl. Aunt Lizzie now wanders the grounds of City Hall with a lantern, searching for her lost nephew—or, it is rumored, unable to rest because of her involvement in these deaths.

Warren's "Happy Ghost" haunts the first home in the Warren area to have electricity.

The Ghost Walk is held the third and fourth weekends of October. Tickets are available in advance and you can call for a free brochure.

216-399-1212

Chris Woodyard is available for the following lectures at libraries and educational institutions. Call for rates and availability.

Ohio: The Haunt of It All How does a person who is terrified of ghosts become a real-life ghostbuster? Hauntings around the state.

Ghosts of the Dead and Famous A survey of some famous and infamous Ohio people who had encounters with the unseen world, including our haunted presidents. Ghosts and Ohio history.

Buckeye Bigfoots and Other Spectral Animals Bigfoot in Greene County? Black Panthers in Ottawa? Sea serpents in Lake Erie? From giant frogs to ghostly kangaroos, weird and ghostly animals around the state.

What is a Ghost? Six theories and some tentative answers to that age-old question, Also, how to rid yourself of unwanted visitors.

Miami Valley Ghosts Includes the ghosts of the US Air Force Museum, Patterson Homestead, Victoria Theatre, Miami Valley Hospital, Sinclair Community College, Woodland Cemetery, University of Dayton and much more.

(513) 426-5110

APPENDIX 2
HAUNTED PLACES
Sites open to the public

BUTLER CO.
> *Miami University*, Oxford, OH 45403. Fisher Hall has been torn down.

CRAWFORD CO.
> *Brownella Cottage*, contact the Galion Historical Society, PO Box 125, Galion, OH, 44833

ERIE CO.
> *Thomas Edison Birthplace*, Thomas Edison Birthplace Museum, Milan, OH off Rt. 250 near junction of 113 (419) 499-2135

FRANKLIN CO.
> *Camp Chase Confederate Cemetery*, contact Hilltop Historical Society, 2456 W. Broad St., Columbus, OH 43204 (614) 276-0060
> *Kelton House*, 586 E. Town St., Columbus, OH 43215 (614) 464-2022
> *Thurber House*, 77 Jefferson Ave., Columbus, OH (614) 464-1032

KNOX CO.
> *Kenyon College,* Gambier, OH, 43022-9623 1-800-848-2468 or (614) 427-5776

MONTGOMERY CO.
> *Memorial Hall,* 125 E. First St., Dayton, OH 45402 (513) 224-9000

Patterson Homestead, 1815 Brown St., Dayton, OH 45409 (513) 222-9724

Sinclair Community College, 444 W. Third St., Dayton, OH 45402 (513) 226-2500

Sorg Opera House, 63 S. Main St., Middletown, OH (513) 425-0180

United States Air Force Museum, Springfield Street, Gate 28-B, Wright-Patterson Air Force Base, Dayton, OH accessible from 675 S or 75 S, (513) 255-3284

University of Dayton, 300 College Park Ave., Dayton, OH, 45409 (513) 229-1000

Victoria Theatre, 138 N. Main St., Dayton, OH 45402 (513) 228-3630

Woodland Cemetery, 118 Woodland Ave, Dayton, OH 45409 (513) 222-1431

MORGAN CO.

McConnelsville Opera House Theatre, 15 W. Main St., McConnelsville, OH 43756 (614) 962-3030

RICHLAND CO.

Malabar Farm, Malabar Farm State Park, off Rt. 95 near the junction of 95 and and 603 in Richland County (419) 892-2784

Mohican State Park, Rt. 3 just north of Rt. 97, Loudonville 1-800-472-6700 or (419) 994-4290

WOOD COUNTY

Bowling Green State University, Theatre Department, BGSU, Bowling Green, OH 45403 (419) 372-2222

REFERENCES

Chapter Two - Dearly Departed

1 *Mansfield Daily News*, 8 July 1899
2 *Ibid.*
3 *Ibid.*
4 *Ibid.*
5 *Ibid.*
6 *The Wapakoneta Daily News*, 19 Aug. 1987, 6
Personal interviews with Kathy Cook and Rich Strong

Chapter Three - It Is Very Beautiful Over There

1 B.C. Forbes, "Edison Working on How to Communicate
  With the Next World," *The American Magazine*, Oct. 1920
2 Matthew Josephson, *Edison A Biography*, (New York:
  McGraw-Hill Book Company, Inc., 1959), 438-9
3 Ronald W. Clark, *Edison the Man who made the Future*,
  (New York: G.P. Putnam's Sons, 1977)
4 Hamlin Garland, *Forty Years of Psychic Research, A Plain
  Narrative of Fact*, (New York: The Macmillan Company,
  1936) 134
5 B.C. Forbes, *Op. cit.*, 10-11
6 *Ibid.*, 10
7 *Scientific American*, Oct. 30 1920, 446
8 *Ibid.*

9 B.C. Forbes, *Op. cit*. 83

10 Norman Vincent Peale, *The True Joy of Positive Living, An Autobiography*, (New York: Morrow, 1984), 288

11 Daniel Cohen, *America's Very Own Ghosts*, (New York: Dodd, Mead & Company, 1985), 17-20

12 Letter from Larry Russell, Curator, Edison Birthplace Museum, Milan, Feb. 20, 1991

13 *Proceedings* of the American Society for Psychical Research, Vol. 2, 1908, quoted in Rogo and Bayless, *Phone Calls from the Dead*, 130-31

14 See Konstantin Raudive, *Breakthrough*, (New York: Taplinger, 1971) and Suzy Smith, *Voices of the Dead?*, (New York: New American Library, 1977)

15 John G. Fuller, *The Ghost of 29 Megacycles*, (New York: New American Library, 1981)

16 D. Scott Rogo and Raymond Bayless, *Phone Calls from the Dead*, (Englewood Cliffs, NJ: Prentice-Hall Inc., 1979), 24

Chapter Four - The Ghostly Grandpa

1 Trevor Hall, *The Spiritualists*, (London: Gerald Duckworth & Co. Ltd, 1962), 77-8

2 Editors of *Fate Magazine*, *Strange Twist of Fate*, (New York: Paperback Library, Inc., 1967), 107-110

3 Lonzo S. Green, *Tales of the Buckeye Land*, (n.p., 1963), 160

4 Emma Hardinge [Britten], *Modern American Spiritualism: A Twenty Years' Record of the Communication Between Earth and the World of Spirits*, (1869) , 205

5 Louisa E. Rhine, *Hidden Channels of the Mind*, (New York: William Morrow and Company, 1961), 231

Chapter Five - Old Soldiers Never Die

1 Helen Meredith, *Ghosts!*, (Coschocton: Helen Meredith, 1967)

2 Carol A. Guyer, "Simon Girty: A Local Legend", *Ohio Folklore Society Journal*, (Summer 68): 103-7

3 Elizabeth B. Custer, *"Boots & Saddles" or Life in Dakota with General Custer*, (New York: Harper & Brothers, 1885), 263-5

4 Samuel Bowles, *Interviews with Spirits*, (Springfield, Mass.: Star Publishing, 1885), 122-27

5 Richard O. Boyer, *The Legend of John Brown, A Biography and a History*, (New York: Alfred A. Knopf, 1973), 450, 452

6 Benet, Stephen Vincent, *John Brown's Body*, (New York: J. Rinehart & Co., 1954)

7 Hardinge [Britten], *Op. cit.*, 504-05

8 John Switzer, "Flowers add to ghost story," *Columbus Dispatch*, 29 Oct. 1989

9 Danton Walker, *Spooks Deluxe*, (New York: Franklin Watts Inc., 1956), 128

10 David Beaty, *Strange Encounters: Mysteries of the Air*, (New York: Atheneum, 1984), 44

11 Bergen Evans, *The Natural History of Nonsense*, (New York: A.A. Knopf, 1946)

Chapter Six - The Phantoms of the Opera

1 Emily Vosburg, "Dark Legends of BG," *The Insider*, Bowling Green State University, Friday, 15 March, 1991

Chapter Seven - Grave Matters

1 *University of Dayton Flyer News*, 30 Oct. 1989, Vol. 37, No. 15, 6

2 "Murder and the Supernatural," *Ohio Folklore Society Journal*, (Fall 1968): 187-88

3 Ruth Ensworth, Helen Vaughn, *Early Sharon Township*, (n.p., 1984), 165

"Spooky tales pepper locale's history", *Columbus Citizen-Journal*, 29 Oct. 1980, 12

4 Frank Edwards, *Strange World*, (New York: Ace Books, 1964), 82

5 Robert Price, *Johnny Appleseed, Man and Myth*, (Gloucester, Mass.: Peter Smith, 1967)

6 "Johnny Appleseed Is Seen Again", *Columbus Citizen-Journal*, 26 Sept. 1943, 8-D

Chapter Eight - A Ghost Around the House

1 "Local spooks leave some haunting tales," *Columbus Citizen-Journal*, 31 Oct. 1980, 17

Chapter Nine - Resting in Pieces

1 Mary Sherman, *Ghosts and Legends of Bellbrook*, (n.p.), 4-5
2 *Columbus Citizen-Journal*, 3 April 1970
3 Letter from Jan Fields, Ohio Dept. of Natural Resources.
4 F. A. Morgan, *Hants and Hangings: Stories of the Odd, the Bizarre, the Sensational in Area Early History and Folklore*, (Quaker City: Home Towner Printing, 1976)
5 William G. Wolfe, *Stories of Guernsey County*, (Cambridge, OH: Wm. G. Wolfe, 1943)
6 Letter from Betty Plank, Ashland County Historical Society
7 Charles M. Skinner, *Myths and Legends of Our Native Land*, (Philadelphia, J.B. Lippincott, 1896)
8 George E. Condon, "Ghastly Labor and Ghostly," *The Cleveland Plain Dealer*, 3 Sept. 1963, 15
  George E. Condon, "Ghost Hunt Yields Bodies," *The Cleveland Plain Dealer*, 16 Sept. 1963, 39
9 Skinner, *Op. cit.*
10 *Western Star*, 27 August 1891

Chapter Ten - Our Haunted Presidents

1 *Cincinnati Commercial*, 31 May 1878
2 Frederick Drimmer, *Body Snatchers, Stiffs and Other Ghoulish Delights*, (New York: Fawcett, 1981)
3 *Cincinnati Commercial*, 1 June 1878
4 Rita Stevens, *Benjamin Harrison, 23rd President of the United States*, (Ada, OK: Garrett Educational Corporation, 1989)
5 Peter Underwood, *The Ghost Hunter's Guide*, (Poole, Dorset: Blandford Press, 1986), 170
6 Anne Canadeo, *The Fact or Fiction Files, Ghosts*, (New York: Walker & Co., 1990), Fact, 31
7 Hardinge [Britten], *Op. cit.*, 302

8 Elizabeth Keckley, *Behind the Scenes*, (New York: G. W. Carleton and Company, 1868)

9 Jean H. Baker, *Mary Todd Lincoln: A Biography*, (New York: W.W. Norton & Co., 1987), 230

10 Justin G. Turner, Linda Levitt Turner, *Mary Todd Lincoln Her Life and Letters*, (New York: Alfred A. Knopf, 1972), 220

11 Jeff Rovin, *The Spirits of America* (New York: Pocket Books, 1990), 54-57

12 Lloyd Lewis, *Myths After Lincoln* (New York: Harcourt Brace and Company, [1929], 125-26

13 William F. Smith, *History of Western Ohio*, (New York: Lewis Historical Publishing Co., 1964), 526

14 Lewis, *Op. cit.*, 344-45

15 Marion Meade, *Free Woman, The Life and Times of Victoria Woodhull*, (New York: Alfred A. Knopf, 1976); Johanna Johnston, *Mrs. Satan: The Incredible Saga of Victoria C. Woodhull*, (New York, G.P. Putnam's Sons, 1967)

16 Julia Dent Grant, *The Personal Memoirs of Julia Dent Grant*, (New York: G.P. Putnam's Sons, 1975), 93

17 Ida Clyde Clark, *Men who Wouldn't Stay Dead*, (New York: Bernard Ackerman, Inc., 1945) 257

18 Grant, *Op. cit.,* 157

19 Richard Winer and Nancy Osborn, *Haunted Houses*, (New York: Bantam Books, 1979), 125

20 Lucy Elliot Keeler, *Diary*, March 31, 1915. Used by special permission from the Rutherford B. Hayes Presidential Center Collection, Spiegel Grove

21 Margaret Leech and Harry J. Brown, *The Garfield Orbit*, (New York: Harper & Row, Publishers, 1978), 15

22 Raymond Lemont Brown, *The Phantom Soldiers*, (New York: Drake Publishers Inc., 1975), 136

23 James A. Garfield, *The Diary of James A. Garfield*. Harry James Brown, Ed. and Frederick B. Williams, (East Lansing, MI: Michigan State University, 1967), I, 4 June, 1851

24 *Ibid.*, I, 18 July, 1852

25 Barbara Seuling, *The Last Cow on the White House Lawn and other little-known facts about the Presidency*, (New York: Doubleday, 1978) 38

26 Communication from former curator.

27 Clark, *Op. cit.*, 257

28 A. Wesley Johns, *The Man Who Shot McKinley*, (South Brunswick and New York: A. S. Barnes and Company, 1970), 19

29 *Ibid.*, 269-70

30 *Medina County Historical Society Newsletter*, (Summer Issue), June, 1979

Debbie Palmer, "Spirited house?", *Sun Times Sentinel*, 5 Sept. 1985

31 Francis Russell, *The Shadow of Blooming Grove, Warren G. Harding in His Times*, (New York: McGraw-Hill), 1968

32 *Ibid.*, 353

33 *Ibid.*, 354

34 *Ibid.*, 371

35 Gaston B. Means, *The Strange Death of President Harding, from the diaries of Gaston B. Means*, (Guild Publishing Corporation, 1930)

36 Nan Britton, *The President's Daughter*, (The Elizabeth Ann Guild, 1927), 240-1

Chapter Eleven - Eternal Rest Grant Unto Them, O Lord

1 Morella Raleigh and J.J. Thompson, "Dark Legends of BG", *The Insider*, Bowling Green State University, Friday, 15 March 1991

2 "Infamous infidel, Chester Bedell troubles from beyond the grave", *Ravenna-Kent Record-Courier*, 28 Oct. 1990, C-2

3 "Blood-Smeared Bible Recalls 'Pillar of Fire' That Blinded Its Desecrators 80 years ago." *Columbus Dispatch*, 31 August 1941, A-7

4 Peale, *Op. cit.*, 296

5 *Ibid.*, 297

6 *Ibid.*, 298

7 Sherman, *Op. cit.*, 12-13

Chapter Twelve - The Old School Spirit

1 Walter Havighurst, *The Miami Years*, (New York: G.P.
    Putnam and Sons, [1969]), 282-84
2 Heather S. Frost, "Shades of Purple", (unpublished ms.,
    Kenyon College, 1990), By permission of The Greenslade
    Special Collections of Olin and Chalmers Libraries at
    Kenyon College.
3 Tim Funk, "Dark Legends of BG", *The Insider*, Bowling
    Green State University, Friday, 15 March 1991
4 *Hallowed Memories and Miscellanea, Compiled by Edward
    H. Knust, S.M. A chronological history of the University of
    Dayton.* 1950-63. n.d. n.p.
William O. Wehrl, S.M., *A History of the University of Dayton*,
    n.p. Jan. 1937.

Chapter Thirteen - The Happy Haunting Grounds

1 Letter from Jan Fields, Ohio Dept. of Natural Resources
John Switzer, "Beware Haunted Parks," *Columbus Dispatch*,
    30 Oct. 1986, 1-D
2 Robert Galbreath, "Explaining Modern Occultism", *The
    Occult in America*, (Urbana, IL: University of Illinois
    Press, 1983)
3 William Albert Galloway, *Old Chillicothe, Shawnee and
    Pioneer History, Conflicts and Romances in the Northwest
    Territory*, (Xenia: Greene Co. Historical Society, 1979),
    118
4 Joab Spencer, *The Shawnee Indians*, 391, quoted in James H.
    Howard, *Shawnee! The Ceremonialism of a Native Indian
    Tribe and Its Cultural Background*, (Athens: Ohio Univer-
    sity Press, 1981), 154, 286-7
5 John Bierhorst, ed., *The Red Swan, Myths and Tales of the
    American Indian*, (New York: Farrer, Strauss & Giroux,
    1976), 229-233
6 Lonzo S. Green, *Op. cit.*, 163-64
7 "'Spring Valley Man' at rest again", *Dayton Daily News*, 26
    Nov. 1988, 3-A
Interviews with Steve Hale and Karyol Kirkpatrick

Chapter Fourteen - Ghost Writers

1 For the factual version of "The Night the Ghost Got In"
    Copyright © Rosemary A. Thurber. Reprinted in *The
    Thurber House Organ*, The Thurber House, Columbus, OH
2 For the May 24, 1959, letter to Edmund Wilson Copyright ©
    1959 James Thurber. Copyright © 1975 Helen Thurber and
    Rosemary A. Thurber. Used by special permission.
3 *The Thurber House Organ*, (Autumn 1988) Vol. 6, No. 2.
    (Columbus: The Thurber House, 1988)
4 Mary Clemmer Amers, *A Memorial of Alice and Phoebe Cary*,
    (New York: Hurd & Houghton, 1873), 17-18
5 Morgan,*Op. cit.*
6 Lyman Beecher Stowe, *Saints, Sinners and Beechers*,
    (Freeport, NY: Books for Libraries Press, 1934), 181-82
7 Forrest Wilson, *Crusader in Crinoline*, (Philadelphia: J. B.
    Lippincott Company, 1941), 107
Milton Rugoff, *The Beechers*, (New York: Harper & Row,
    1981), 222-23
8 Wilson, *Ibid.*, 256
9 Elizabeth Stevenson, *Lafcadio Hearn*, (New York: The
    Macmillan Company, 1961), 40
10 Robert A. Wiggins, *Ambrose Bierce*, Univ. of Minnesota
    Pamphlets on American Writers, #37, (Minneapolis: Univ.
    of Minnesota, 1964)

Chapter Fifteen - The Headless Motorcyclist

1 *S & D Reflector*, June, 1966, 22
2 *Chicago Times*, March 1885, quoted in Dennis Bardens,
    Ghosts and Hauntings, (New York: Ace Books, 1973), 226
3 Letter from Jan Fields, Ohio Dept. of Natural Resources
4 *Ibid.*
5 *Ohio Folklore Society Journal*, (Dec. 1972): 49-50
6 Wolfe, *Op. cit.*
7 John Fairley and Simon Welfare, *Arthur C. Clarke's World of
    Strange Powers*, (New York: G.P. Putnam's Sons, 1984) 65-
    66
8 Richard Gill, "The Headless Motorcyclist," *Ohio Folklore
    Society Journal*, (Dec. 1972): 46-48

OTHER TERRIFYING TALES

Any book by Suzy Smith

Anderson, Jean *The Haunting of America, Ghost Stories from Our Past* (Boston: Houghton-Mifflin Co., 1973)
Designed for kids, but adults will enjoy it too. Storytellers would also find it useful.

Britten, Emma Hardinge, *Modern American Spiritualism: A Twenty Years' Record of the Communication Between Earth and the World of Spirits,* 1869
It was "modern" for 1869. Lots of interesting stories about spiritualists, but all taken so seriously. It's fascinating to note the celebrated mediums who have since been unmasked as frauds.

Caidin, Martin, *Ghosts of the Air,* (New York: Bantam, 1991)
A spellbinder! It gave me a couple of very scary nights. Caidin goes to great lengths to establish the credibility of his witnesses. He also knows how to spin a creepy yarn.

Canadeo, Anne *The Fact or Fiction Files, Ghosts,* (New York: Walker & Co., 1990)
A relatively balanced look at some famous hauntings, although it comes down slightly harder on the side of debunking. For hard-core debunking see any book by James Randi. Also *Fads & Fallacies in the Name of Science* and *The New Age: Notes of a Fringe-Watcher* by Martin Gardner.

Fuller, John G., *The Ghost of 29 Megacycles,* (New York: New American Library, 1981)
This may be a complete hoax, for all I know, but it's one heck of a story.

Gerrick, David J., *Ohio's Ghostly Greats,* (Lorain: Dayton Press, 1982)
Lots of good raw material for storytellers, although a few too many personalized versions of old chestnuts like "The Vanishing Hitchhiker" for my taste.

Keene, M. Lamar, *The Psychic Mafia*, (New York: St. Martins, 1976)
A spirited and mind-boggling expose of spiritualist fraud by a former spiritualist minister.

Meredith, Helen, *Ghosts!*, (Coschocton: Helen Meredith, 1967)
An interesting pamphlet collection of unusual local ghost stories.

Morgan, F.A. *Hants and Hangings: Stories of the Odd, the Bizarre, the Sensational in Area Early History and Folklore*, (Quaker City: Home Towner Printing, 1976)
They are indeed odd, bizarre, and sensational. Many taken from Wolfe's *History of Guernsey County*.

Musick, Ruth Ann, *The Telltale Lilac Bush and Other West Virginia Ghost Tales*, (Lexington: University of Kentucky Press, 1965)
These are tales from West Virginia, but many of them are set in coal mines and could also be applicable to southeastern Ohio. Scared my socks off!

Myers, Arthur, *The Ghostly Gazetteer: America's Most Fascinating Haunted Landmarks*, (Chicago: Contemporary Books, 1990)
_____*The Ghostly Register: Haunted Dwellings, Active Spirits. A Journey to America's Strangest Landmarks* (Chicago: Contemporary Books, 1986)
_____ *The Ghosts of the Rich and Famous* (Chicago: Contemporary Books, 1988)
A good diversity of stories, but I find them dry as grave dust.

Ohio Folklore Society Journal
If you like your ghost stories as straight folklore instead of tabloid journalism.

Rhine, Louisa E., *Hidden Channels of the Mind*, (New York: William Morrow and Company, 1961)
Dry, but occasionally startling tales of ESP and precognition.

Rogo, D. Scott, and Raymond Bayless, *Phone Calls from the Dead*, (Englewood Cliffs, NJ: Prentice-Hall Inc., 1979)
    Leans heavily on a few cases, but those cases *are* remarkable.

Rovin, Jeff, *The Spirits of America* (New York: Pocket Books, 1990)
    One of my favorites. A haunted computer, a phantom dinosaur, and many more unusual tales.

Scott, Beth and Michael Norman, *Haunted Heartland*, (New York: Warner Books, 1985)
    Covers Illinois, Indiana, Iowa, Kansas, Michigan, Minnesota, Missouri, Nebraska, Ohio, and Wisconsin. The most extensive collection of Midwestern ghost stories to date. Don't miss it.

Sherman, Mary, *Ghosts and Legends of Bellbrook*, (n.p.)
Local tales from "Ohio's Sleepy Hollow."

Skinner, Charles M., *Myths and Legends of Our Native Land*, (Philadelphia, J.B. Lippincott, 1896)
    A florid style, but a great resource for story-tellers.

Underwood, Peter, *The Ghost Hunter's Guide*, (Poole, Dorset: Blandford Press, 1986)
    A real ghost-buster comments on the tools and tricks of the trade as well as some of his cases.

Winer, Richard and Nancy Osborn, *Haunted Houses*, (New York: Bantam Books, 1979)
    _____ *More Haunted Houses*, (New York: Bantam Books, 1982)
    Diverse tales, but somehow lifeless. Osborn is a medium and parapsychologist so she does her own research first hand.

PERMISSIONS

For entry in Lucy Elliot Keeler's *Diary*, March 31, 1915. Used by special permission from the Rutherford B. Hayes Presidential Center Collection, Spiegel Grove

For Heather S. Frost, "Shades of Purple," (unpublished ms., Kenyon College, 1990) By permission of The Greenslade Special Collections of Olin and Chalmers Libraries at Kenyon College.

For the factual version of "The Night the Ghost Got In" Copyright © Rosemary A. Thurber. Reprinted in *The Thurber House Organ*, The Thurber House, Columbus, OH

For the May 24, 1959, letter to Edmund Wilson Copyright © 1959 James Thurber. Copyright © 1975 Helen Thurber and Rosemary A. Thurber. Used by special permission.

INDEX

INDEX OF STORIES BY LOCATION

THEY'LL BE BAAACK!

HAUNTED OHIO III is in the works. We invite readers to send us their stories of apparitions and haunted houses. We are especially interested in spirit photography, haunted art and antiques, haunted highways, ghosts in libraries, hospitals, schools, theatres, and the workplace. Also stories of lake monsters like South Bay Besse.

We also would like to collect ghost stories of any sort from the following counties: Allen, Belmont, Carroll, Clinton, Defiance, Harrison, Highland, Hocking, Holmes, Jackson, Jefferson, Lawrence, Logan, Lucas, Mahoning, Marion, Meigs, Mercer, Miami, Monroe, Noble, Paulding, Pickaway, Pike, Portage, Putnam, Scioto, Shelby, Stark, Trumbull, Union, Van Wert, Warren, Washington, Wood, and Wyandot.

SOME FUTURE CHAPTERS
Code Blue: Haunted hospitals
The Exorcists: Spirit rescues
The Men in Black: Ghostly gentlemen
Tales from the Crypt: More cemetery spirits
Ghosts at Work: Ghosts in the workplace
The Ghost in the Machine: Spirit photography
The Dead Zones: Haunt-spots of Ohio

Some places and creatures we'd like to hear more about: Piatt Castles, Franklin Castle, Loveland Castle, Schwartz Castle (Columbus), The United States Air Force Museum (Dayton), Our House Museum (Gallipolis), Sun Watch (Dayton), The Crosswick Monster and the Loveland Frog

Send your stories to Kestrel Publications, 1811 Stonewood Dr., Beavercreek, OH 45432. Please include an address and phone number. Anonymity will be guaranteed.

HOW TO ORDER YOUR OWN
AUTOGRAPHED COPIES OF *SPOOKY OHIO*
AND THE *HAUNTED OHIO* SERIES
(also T-Shirts, etc.)

Call **1-800-31-GHOST (314-4678)** with your VISA or MasterCard order or send this order form to: **Kestrel Publications, 1811 Stonewood Dr., Beavercreek, OH 45432 • (513) 426-5110**

☐ FREE CATALOG! "INVISIBLE INK: Books on Ghosts and Hauntings" - Over 500 books of ghost stories from around the world!

_____ copies of *SPOOKY OHIO* @ $8.95 each		$_____
_____ copies of *HAUNTED OHIO* @ $10.95 each		$_____
_____ copies of *HAUNTED OHIO II* @ $10.95 each		$_____
_____ copies of *HAUNTED OHIO III* @ $10.95 each		$_____
_____ copies of *HAUNTED OHIO IV* @ $10.95 each		$_____
_____ *Spooky Ohio* T-shirt @ $12.00 each		$_____
Size ____M ____L ____XL ____XXL		
_____ *Haunted Ohio* T-shirt @ $12.00 each		$_____
Size ____M ____L ____XL ____XXL		

+ $2.50 Book Rate shipping, handling and tax for the first item, $1.00 postage for each additional item. Call (513) 426-5110 for speedier mail options. $_____

TOTAL $_____

NOTE: We usually ship the same or next day. Please allow three weeks before you panic. If a book *has* to be somewhere by a certain date, let us know so we can try to get it there on time.

MAIL TO (Please print clearly and include your phone number)

_____
_____
_____
_____

FREE AUTOGRAPH!

If you would like your copies autographed, please print the name or names to be inscribed. _____

_____

PAYMENT MADE BY:

☐ Check   ☐ MasterCard   ☐ VISA
($15 min. order on credit cards)

Card No. _____   Expiration Date:

Signature _____   Mo_____ Yr_____